CRIME WAVE

CRIME WAVE

A novel
by
John Wynne

JOHN CALDER · LONDON
RIVERRUN PRESS · NEW YORK

First published 1982 in the U.S.A. by
Riverrun Press Inc.,
175 Fifth Avenue,
New York,
NY 10010

and in Great Britain 1982 by
John Calder (Publishers) Ltd.,
18 Brewer Street,
London W1R 4AS

British Library Cataloguing in Publication Data

Wynne, John
    Crime wave.
    I. Title
    813'.54(F)   PS3573.Y62

    ISBN 0 86676 000 8 casebound

First Edition

Typeset in 11/11½ point Baskerville by Ged Lennox Design
Printed and bound in Canada by The Hunter Rose Co. Ltd.

For Harold Schmidt

This world was once a fluid haze of light,
Till toward the centre set the starry tides,
And eddied into suns, that wheeling cast
The planets; then the monster, then the man.

Tennyson
The Princess

Chapter One

It was a hazy afternoon. Flies filled the air around the West Side docks, their phosphorescent blue tails richer and creamier than the close sky itself. Jake Adams headed north, his Nikon camera hung around his neck.

West Street was deserted. He daydreamed a moment about capturing one of the thousands of flies in a photograph — a detailed study, close-up of the hair, legs and wings. The picture buzzed. It was alive, an enlargement on the wall of a darkroom. Jake shook himself. The water danced from his head. It wasn't particularly hot. Still, he was in a cold sweat from a moment ago.

He had strolled to the end of Christopher Street where the state of New Jersey could be seen across the Hudson if anyone wanted to look. Today Jake was interested as he could make out coal black vapors rising high into the haze. He stationed himself at the very edge of the pier and took a peek through his camera's strong zoom lens. There was no structure in Jersey City that was recognizable. Any landmark was obscured by a raging hot fire that was laced with piles of smoldering rubble. He reasoned that the fire had been contained within a fairly small area yet the flames and the smoke obliterated the landscape behind it so that it was simple to imagine that the entire city had been consumed.

Jake flinched at the wail of a siren close by. The police car pulled right to the embankment, two cops got out and scanned the water. Jake approached a bench filled with down and out men, drunks whose rags clung to them by threads.

"What's it all about?" Jake asked.

"The shit's comin' down, that's what," a wino spat, then rolled his red eyes up toward Jake and pulled a sorrowful face, mumbling, "I tried to hold my belt out to him."

A polished ambulance stopped at the curb next to Jake. A crowd of indolent teen-agers — their portable radios blaring — and screaming younger children gathered, while two men emerged from the vehicle, in full diving gear. No one had to ask. One voice rose above the others anyway, "They're looking for a body."

The crowd pursued the divers to the edge of the river, pushing the men until the police glared throwing a few choice words at them. They backed away much like scavengers scared off from their prey. The divers consulted the cops for a minute, then slipped over the side and under the water. "Goddamit, I told you to stay back." One of the cops shoved a teen-age boy toward the benches. "And shut that music off— now!"

Jake knelt beside the wino and in his suavest investigative manner coaxed, "Look here. You seem to be the only one who knows what's happened. You've seen something important. . . "

He smirked to his pals beside him, "Sure, I seen it all — but I ain't sayin' it's important." They bellowed with laughter. The wino itched his crotch, "I've gotta do something about them critters. They're close on drivin' me crazy."

"Do us a dance like you did last night," one of the men laughed. "Thought you'd shake 'em off that way, didn't you?"

The wino again rolled his eyes at Jake and appeared penitent. "I got crabs, son," he explained. "But you tell them cops I tried to give him the belt. I did! I did! He said it was so hot . . . that it was a damn hot day —"

"Who did?" Jake demanded.

"That young feller with the black hair — lived in the room above me at the hotel— " he indicated the rambling waterfront tenement behind him. "He was high on *something* everyday, he sure was. And today . . . ain't he so high and mighty as to say he wanted a swim!" From his buddies came piteous sighs. He waited for silence, then went on, "He peeled off his shirt, in he goes, but a minute later he calls out that he's tired and needs help. Well, I mean goddam, we wasn't goin' in *there*, the water's filthy, stinkin' fish can't catch a breath around here. Look for yourself. All kinds of shit's floatin' in it."

"Go on," Jake prodded.

He continued almost absent-mindedly. "Anyway . . . the

steps up the pier was only a few feet away."

"But you knew he was too tired to get there," somebody said.

Tears filled the man's eyes, he seemed past a hundred-years-old at that moment. "I tried to hold out my belt, see? Dangled it over the side of the wall. He'd just grab at it like a baby'll bat at a rattle and try to catch it. He touched it once but couldn't get a grip."

"So he went under," Jake finished the story. "Why didn't you jump in and save him?"

A sharp fierceness appeared in the wino's face. "I don't know what you're gettin' at," he replied slowly, "but I don't like it. We called the police, mister."

A bone thin old vagrant at the end of the bench shook his finger accusingly at his pal, "Yeah, we called the cops . . . called 'em a half hour after he went under."

"So what?" The wino balanced on the wave of hysteria. "You can't bring a drowned man back to life!" He was suddenly quiet again as if under some spell. The red in his eyes seemed glossed over by black. "He grabbed onto my belt . . . then he just slipped under . . . real gentle like . . . there was a little bubble like a fart, then he must of sunk so far down, way down to China, way down there, the other side of this earth, we'll never see him no more, never —"

"Stand back!" The cops edged the crowd away to make room for the divers as they hoisted their underwater catch onto the dock. Jake had prepared himself in advance for this inevitable moment and thought surely he was jaded enough that the sight would give his heart a moment's bristle and little else. Yet he found he was the only one in the crowd to turn his head away. He crossed himself.

The divers maneuvered the man onto his stomach and pumped out the water. The white froth came forth in torrents. Jake hadn't noticed that among the teen-agers who were shoving each other in a pretense of horror were about a dozen mongoloid boys watched over by a stern, matronly woman. One of the mongoloids followed the trail of froth with curiosity and thrust his finger into the liquid, then smelled it while one of his friends pointed to the sky and said, "Birds . . ."

The dead man was flipped onto his back. Jake saw that he was about twenty-five. His chest was white and supple, his stomach hard until the end, refusing to bloat with the water that had killed him. A line of pink roses tattooed on his arm seemed to point to his developed muscles, his lips were open, full and sensual, his eyes shut tight. Piercing ha-ha-ha's. Acting as if overcome by potent laughing gas, the wino was oblivious to the drowning victim and busy sharing a titillating anecdote with one of his buddies. A cop slapped him across the cheek to shut him up. The divers forced the rigid body into a dark leather container that looked remarkably like the case Jake had used as a boy to transport his prized violin to the house of his maestro professor, a white-haired scholar from Romania. For a second he heard the old man tapping in rhythm against the case.

This man was young. His death had been untimely, and his reward for a lazy, boastful summer swim was a journey to the morgue. This new journey would be short, swift, direct. Jake tightened the strap of his camera and headed up West Street in the opposite direction of the divers who drove off with the lifeless body beside them.

Stewart Reggino leaned out of his window which overlooked West Street and shouted to Jake who was passing by. Jake saluted in return to let Stewart know he was coming up.

Stewart lived in a red brick townhouse at the very end of Charles Street. The building, nearly two hundred-years old, was famous for having housed at the turn of the century a group of rebellious, eccentric young actors whose modern ideas and methods had set playgoers on their ears. But then Stewart never cared much about this little slice of history since he wasn't interested in acting or the theater. He was a welder and a gun enthusiast and he thanked God that this was his passion and calling. Hearing Jake's footsteps down below, he flung open the door and thrust his chest over the railing. "Hurry up! I've got something to show you!"

When Jake walked in Stewart commanded softly, "Close the door." Jake pushed it shut. Before taking in the room he slid his camera from around his neck and laid it gently on the cushion of a beat up orange sofa.

Stewart beckoned Jake to a long table in the middle of the room. "Well, what do you think? A regular little arsenal. . ." The table served as a showcase for about a dozen weapons, including a .357 Police Magnum, a couple of Colt .45 automatics, their barrels open, newly lubricated, sparkling clean with no traces of rust or leading, an Italian automatic .22 calibre tear gas gun and a couple of "Paralyzer" tear gas weapons, a sawed-off shotgun, two six-inch daggers, and a submachine gun.

"Reggino, I think you're nuts," Jake answered calmly and sat on the window ledge.

Stewart laughed. "Just you, me and the moon know about this little set up."

Jake looked doubtful. Stewart added, "And — hey — don't worry, I'm not the trigger-happy kind."

"It's not so much that," Jake lit a cigarette. "It's just that if you're caught with this stuff, they'll haul your ass to jail on some pretty stiff charges."

Stewart took a couple of glasses from a shelf and poured a shot of whiskey in each. "That's my man, Jake. Always so sensible in the face of adversity." He handed one to Jake. "Whiskey — from the glass I used to keep my false teeth in."

"Bullshit."

Stewart laughed again and downed his drink. "What are you worried for, anyway? I mean, I've got connections, you know. I didn't spend a year in the N.Y.P.D. for nothing."

"Yeah, but you aren't a cop now."

"It doesn't matter. I have the same friends who aren't going to let anything happen to me. Where do you think I got most of this from, anyway? From cops. Everybody helped everybody else — all illegal, of course." He swung the SMG off the table and struck a military stance. "What do you think of this Mother, huh? Huh? . . . I don't think you're very impressed."

"Educate me on its finer points."

"This little fucker is a Czeck Skorpion. Got it two years ago off the black market. Came in on a Swedish trawler about midnight on the coldest damn night of the year. New Year's Eve, in fact. See, this Swede I know is best friends with an MP in Stockholm who is interested in U.S. Army paraphernalia, so I trade with him. Anyhow, he unwraps it real slow and I'm excited as hell — I could hear the shouting and singing on Times Square but I was higher in the clouds than any of those merrymakers when I held this little baby against my chest. Look. It's pistol size. It fires from a closed bolt just like a pistol. This sub's only about three pounds and I'm making a silencer for it. It's almost finished."

Jake couldn't help feeling a ripple of disgust at Stewart's relentless enthusiasm. While growing up together in the seashore town of Sayville on Long Island's south shore, Jake had known Stewart to be a hyper kid. He always had more energy than the others and probably more guts and that's why all the boys in their middle class community accepted Stewart as their leader. But during high school Stewart drifted, never showing interest in any field. They had remained friends though, even after separate moves to New York, and Jake had seen Stewart through a hectic year on the police force before he quit, dis-illusioned by its routineness. Jake watched him run a fragile indigo blue handkerchief along the butt of his rifle and he felt butterflies in his stomach. It was eerie to watch Reggino act out all the combat fantasies he'd had for years — right here — alone in his apartment. Everything was perfect — his talk, the way he carried himself, the way the Army fatigues and spotless white T shirt clung to him, not haphazardly but carefully. Yet Jake felt it was unreal. For Reggino, for all his good looks and strong, athletic build, his wavy sandy hair brushed lovingly back from a forehead with just the right amount of manly creases, reminded him most of a slight boy with a fake pistol in his hand.

"That scheme I told you about . . . have you made a decision yet?" The question came dryly from Stewart who now was busy polishing his shoes.

Jake shrugged and glanced at the cloudy pink sun dipping behind the riverfront warehouses. "I don't know. It's a funny day. Maybe something in the air is telling me to investigate."

"Look. There's a prostitution-theft ring at the Dove Hotel on 42nd Street which is in itself not so unusual, right?"

"Right."

"There's a catch," he nodded to Jake. "Some pretty weird people are involved, and some city cops are in on it." He whipped the cloth across the black leather until it gleamed. "You know," he continued, "you're a writer just starting out and I've given you a terrific lead. I mean, how can you be choosy? You need a good story, don't you?"

The flies had followed Jake from the dock and had fastened themselves to the windowpanes. But now one grazed Jake's eyelid and tickled the strands of his damp hair while another attacked his ear, spinning in angry circles. "Goddamit," he flung himself off the window ledge. "You can't even lose the frigging flies."

The Hotel Dove stood unobtrusively on the south side of 42nd Street between 8th and 9th Avenues. A weak neon sign with the hotel's name was suspended by an iron bar over the entrance. The building was tall and narrow and vacant lots filled with garbage and thrown-out clothes bordered its side walls.

About a week after he had visited Stewart, Jake happened to be passing by on his way to the Garment District where he was finishing a story about escalating crime in the area. It was the noontime rush hour but he was oblivious to the noisy crowd. He paused with a cup of Italian ice in his hand, savoring a quiet moment on a lovely day where the sun seemed as intimate and welcome as a close friend . . . he was lifting up his head to get the benefit of its rays when he made direct eye contact with the hotel. The sun seemed to lie comfortably on its roof like a crown and gave the hotel a brilliant shine. "So that's it," Jake wondered aloud. Forms, black phantoms, moved with agility behind the drawn, transparent blinds. In one of the lots the wind blew the branches of a lone beech tree and the leaves touched against the side wall and rubbed the stone lightly.

That evening as Jake was ready to draw the curtains in his apartment he happened to look out across the small park to the limestone church and there, superimposed over the facade, was the Hotel Dove, the sun again its crown, casting that impressive luster. Jake laughed at himself; he hadn't thought of the hotel all afternoon. It was ridiculous for him to have this vision now. He watched the children in the park as they tried to launch box kites, then he hunted the red building cattycorner to see if old Mrs. Block was at her window as was her evening habit; seeing that she was cozily hunched in her armchair enjoying the view of the square, he decided that Mrs. Block could take over as the summer evening voyeur and he could get some work done. He pulled the curtains tight and turned on the lamps.

Jake Adams lived by careful design on the tranquil square known as Gramercy Park. Having spent the last three years on freelance journalism and photography assignments, working many long unorthodox hours, he had finally decided to create a retreat for himself. He had found his large room overlooking the park and had painted it a bluish white so that his photographs seemed to move along the wall as if they were floating down a river of chalk. The lighting was soft and familiar and he had wired some of the lamps himself; some had bases of shell, some of redwood, some of rock. His big desk slanted down in the corner, more like a drawing board or a child's antique desk

where the stool is high, the floor far away. There was a small
bathroom and a large closet which he had converted to a
darkroom. His loft bed was above the compact kitchen.

Jake was particularly tired this evening. He poured a glass of
dry white wine, climbed to his bed and stretched his muscles.
He smoked several cigarettes and let his mind wander but
stopped it short of lighting on anything specific. He surveyed
his photographs on the walls. He liked most of them, never
displaying false modesty when he was discussing them with
friends. His eye rested on a photograph of the church across the
square, a straight shot, conservative, yet with perfect lighting,
the detail of the figures on the stained glass windows remarkable, and the bold bronze doors seeming to say, *Enter only if
you're prepared to worship*. Or so he thought as he gave himself to
sleep.

Jake woke at nine. His nap had not been refreshing, and deep
inside he was cross with himself for sleeping since that meant he
wouldn't feel tired until early morning. He sat straight up in his
bed and said aloud, "I'm bored as hell."

Jake was a photo-journalist for a new magazine, simply
called *City*, which explored, in somewhat titillating stories,
contemporary urban living, the problems, the fresh solutions,
the ways in which innovative or eccentric people were orches-
trating their lives to blend with their busy environments. He
was due in about an hour to meet his regular group from the
office for a late supper in Chinatown. But he didn't feel like a
long session with the keen young editors, writers and reporters
he practically breathed with everyday. He called one of them,
"Look. Give everybody my regards. I know it looks bad to skip
this since I've only been with the magazine two months, but I
feel tonight I might break an important story." Then he called
Stewart Reggino.

Jake didn't recognize himself in the mirror. Tonight Stewart
had outdone any past efforts in camouflage by fitting Jake in his
old police uniform. The men were roughly the same size,
though Jake was maybe an inch taller: he stood over six feet in
his stockings. His hair was lighter than Stewart's, true blond
and straight, the strands like even rows of cut wheat on his
forehead. His eyes were a washed out lavender-blue and his
general complexion was very light. Though he was considered

handsome, Jake thought he looked anemic and older than his twenty-seven years.

"Beautiful," was Reggino's slow appraisal.

"I might have expected you to use just that word." Jake was relieved to hear his own words which made the mirrored image him again without question. He turned to Stewart. "The gun's not loaded I take it."

"Of course it is," Stewart shot back. "Are you crazy?" Jake poured himself more white wine. Stewart said, "If you follow my directions and act confident, there'll be no problem. The cops are from all over the city, from Jersey too. So it's not as if they all know each other. . ."

Jake shrugged, "But I don't walk like a cop."

"Jake Adams, you walk just like a cop."

"All right, you drive me there."

"I'll let you out at the entrance. But you have to be in before 12:15, because it's then they shut the doors. And they shut them quick."

The cop with the heavy moustache leaned over to Jake and whispered, "It's like when you're at a shooting gallery. You take aim at whatever hits your fancy."

"What do you mean?" Jake asked.

"The whores all line up in a neat little row. Like tin ducks. You'll see. And the fantastic part is they've all been inspected, you know, for clap and crabs and all that."

Jake had headed through the hotel entrance at the same time as this officer, Kevin Price, and since Price was talkative and inquisitive, Jake, not wanting to slip up, thought it best to declare that this was his first visit. The officer was eager to fill him in. They stood now in the lobby mulling with other cops, about ten altogether. Their low drones drifted to the huge art deco ceiling and reverberated.

The room was filled with furniture from the '20s and '30s. The worn chairs were collapsing in front of his very eyes, yet Jake thought they looked snug and, in a way, beautiful. A heavy chandelier made of thick glass, expertly crafted, cast its glow on the men below and on the Oriental rugs which didn't seem too threadbare in its easy light.

Jake couldn't help wondering why he had come. He was tired of Kevin Price's drivel and couldn't hear the other conversations. He had almost made up his mind to leave when, without warning, a skinny teen-age boy in an ill-fitting T shirt stepped out from behind the hotel desk. The boy nodded to the cops who waved in greeting, then he took a last puff on a Havana cigar, extinguished it on a tin plate and crossed to the front door which he locked tight then bolted with a giant wooden pole. After that he pressed a button and a steel sheet came down, sealing them in as effectively as the unbearable stones Egyptian priests used to secure a Pharoah's tomb for all eternity.

Then came the whirring noise, sounding like muted traffic on 42nd Street, but Jake studied the steel sheet and realized that particular sound couldn't penetrate it. And there were no windows, just long velvet curtains which were pulled open to frame painted murals of the Grand Canyon and Niagara Falls.

The elevator glided to the lobby. Jake whistled under his breath. It was all glass with fresh green ivy climbing up each corner and ten women inside crowded against each other, trying to jostle for better positions so they could see the men in the lobby.

The cops, and Jake made certain he was among them, gathered together in a cluster and the teen-age desk clerk pulled back the elevator door. The women, in spiked heels and blonde wigs, strapped into multi-colored lingerie, immediately struck whorish poses. Kevin Price's fingers absent-mindedly caressed his billy club and one of the whores saw this and laughed. Price blushed, but he cursed too. "They're dressed for bed," Jake muttered under his breath but loud enough so that the cop next to him heard and whispered back, "Dressed to spread."

The women lined up, just as Kevin Price had predicted. They stood a moment with their big tits pushed out and half exposed, then turned around to stick out their asses. As they did this, they laughed and chatted with each other, and the cops, in the business of choosing partners, discussed pros and cons.

Jake did a double take at the fifth girl in the line. She had a wiry little body and her face was gaunt, reddish black hair stuck out in every direction — it hadn't been combed for weeks, yet unlike the other women her hair was real. And dark. Jake was riveted to her in this sea of blondeness. She had a bored expression which bordered on contempt and she was too busy biting her fingernails to talk with the girl next to her. She turned around again but she didn't stick her ass in the air. Her backside was straight as a board and her purple nightgown clung unflatteringly, almost impertinently, to her bony rib cage. She turned frontwards again, her face was lovely in a way, her lips wide in a pout, her eyes large and dark blue, a little thoughtless as if they had vacated her body and were resting alone in an agreeable void. She somehow reminded Jake of his aunt during the summer they had taken a cruise up Cape Cod. The weather had been very rough and she had become seasick though she tried valiantly to deny it. This girl seemed to be suffering that same spirited seasickness, or was it a weariness of the sea itself? Now this girl spoke, she broke into a laugh and said to the woman on her right, "Funny to have Pandora up in her room and not down here."

The heavy blonde nodded understandingly. "For God's sake, they should do something about her."

A couple of cops had made their decisions and approached the whores. To Jake's surprise, a burly, if not fat, cop of about twenty, with golden hair cropped close in curls and a sandy beard, tapped the dark girl on the shoulder. She nodded. He put his finger in the small of her back and pushed her toward the elevator. Two other women had been picked and they too were being escorted to the elevator. Jake didn't want to lose sight of that girl, for what reason he didn't know and refused to even consider, and he thought quickly and kissed a tall blonde on the lips. One cop holding the elevator called out, "Hurry up. There's just room enough." They stepped inside and the cop shut the door but they were so pressed together that Jake didn't have time to get his foot out of the way and the door slammed on the bone. He yelled in pain.

"Sorry," the cop mumbled.

Jake moved his foot back and the door successfully closed. The elevator moved upwards. Jake craned his neck around to see if the girl with the flaming dark hair had reacted to his outcry but he couldn't see her face. His back was pushed against the young cop who had picked her up and he was completely blocking Jake's view. The cop's ass moved against Jake and thrust him up against the glass.

"For Christ's sake," he said angrily.

"Oh, dear, listen to him," came a high voice from the heavy blonde. She wiggled her finger at him. "He doesn't know how lucky he is that he ain't down the shaft like some other poor creature I know. Right?"

"Bee, shut up. You talk too much," Jake's trick said,

"It's no secret," whined the other.

"What's it all about?" asked one of the cops.

"My God, you didn't know Pandora!" Bee exclaimed. "She was a sweet girl but she takes these drugs to calm her nerves. I mean, I do too. Who doesn't?" The elevator hardly seemed to move and Jake had the sensation that it was slowly turning on its side in a pool of dim light and that it would never open again and he would be trapped with all of them sideways in a curious optical illusion. "Pandora," she continued, "lives on the third floor, thank God she wasn't higher, because at four in the morning she decided to go to the lobby for cigarettes, pressed for the elevator, the door opened and, well, she stepped inside but nothing was there and she fell down the shaft and was impaled on an iron spike for twelve hours. When they found her she was out of her mind and, of course, they had to amputate her leg up to her waist. But she's better now. . ."

The door finally opened onto a dark hall and the group disembarked.

"That's a terrible story," a cop said. "Why didn't we read about it in the papers?"

"Probably wasn't gruesome enough for them." There. It was her voice, a kind of low chuckle. He could barely make out her face but could see her unmistakable figure outlined against the window at the end of the corridor. She and the cop had walked the opposite way than the trick who was leading Jake by his belt. The dark girl and the cop turned into the room at the very end while Jake found himself in a cubicle only a few steps from the elevator.

"I'm Fern," the girl said, switching on a light. "But you can call me any name — or names — you want, officer." For a moment Jake had forgotten about his uniform, about any mystery behind the hotel operation, about his story. He remembered quite clearly now but didn't care. He only thought of the girl at the other end of the hall.

Fern said, "Anything special or shall I just undress?"

"Oh," Jake said. "Just undress."

Fern made quite a show of dropping her negligee and unstrapping her tight bra. Her breasts were huge and firm and Jake found himself with a hard-on almost against his will. She dropped her pants and lay on the bed, her legs spread. Jake didn't really want this woman yet he felt stupid to turn her down since he was aroused by her. He calmly stripped, folding his uniform and paraphernalia in the nearby chair.

"Lights on or off?" Fern asked.

"Off," Jake replied.

"Then can you get the switch, cutie?"

Jake woke at dawn. He lay there, sleep in his eyes, listening for something. At last he heard a door open and some footsteps. He heard the blinds being raised at the window at the end of the hall. He quietly left the bed and dressed himself in the dimness. He opened the door.

There she was, kneeling by the elevator, prisms of orange light floating through the window and playing at her feet. She looked up at him, no, she was looking past him, at something else. A ragged kitten skittered under Jake's legs to the elevator where the girl put down a saucer of milk. She waited on her knees, watching as the kitten contentedly began to drink. The noise it made with its tongue as it lapped up the liquid was the only sound to be heard. Both Jake and the girl waited several minutes in silence until finally the little cat was finished and had set about licking its paws and washing its face.

Jake shut the bedroom door behind him and stood against the elevator, looking down at the girl.

"What's your name?" he said.

The girl stared at him oddly. A slight smile played at her lips. She picked up the empty saucer and stood up. "Renee Cloverman."

"How long have you worked here?" Jake smiled.

"I don't work here," she answered. "I just live here." Jake was confused and showed it but his heart was beating fast as he stared into her large eyes and he was certain his interest in her was showing as well.

"I'm not a whore," she added. "I have my own money and I never take anybody else's for sex."

"Well, what are you then?"

"I'm a masochist."

"Oh," Jake said. "Though I still don't understand."

"I like to degrade myself sexually. Does that make it any clearer?"

"I guess so."

"Good." Jake felt as if she had hit him in the face. He looked away. She continued, "I'm really a sado-masochist. I do have sadistic tendencies, especially toward children."

"But not animals," Jake laughed, hoping she was joking.

Renee paused. "Most animals. Not this particular one though." She bent down and patted it. It rubbed against her knees. She softened a little, "Not toward most cats, anyhow. Scientists say they're only dumb beasts, much inferior to dogs, but they don't realize that cats have their own intelligence . . . a different kind of intelligence . . . that we don't understand."

A door across the hall burst open and the girl called Bee stumbled out, scaring the cat who ran down some narrow stairs. "I feel like I got cholera this morning!" she screamed to Renee.

Renee crossed over to Bee and felt her head. "Take a pill and get some sleep. That always does the trick."

Bee was not to be placated. "You couldn't lend me some money, could you, Renee? I'm flat broke and I want to get some medicine."

"Come by my room later, I might help you." Renee started back down the hall.

Bee shouted after her, "Renee, I really feel like I got cholera!"

Renee turned. "You do, Bee, you do." She slammed her door. Bee swore under her breath and stormed back into her own room, leaving Jake alone by the elevator. Now the hall was filled with strong light and Jake imagined the sun was close above his head in the same place as he had seen it from the sidewalk yesterday, gradually sliding over the roof of the Hotel Dove.

Chapter Two

Renee Cloverman emptied the contents of her bag onto the counter and frantically continued the search for her American Express card. "It's here somewhere, after all," she explained to the uncomplaining young salesgirl, but she couldn't locate it among the vials of watered down jasmine spray, lipsticks, scraps of paper, at least ten loose keys of contrasting sizes and moulds, several pairs of silk gloves and spools of grey and black thread which the hotel cat sometimes toyed with. The clatter attracted the girl's supervisor who regarded Renee somewhat less benignly. Renee caught her stare and knew that the woman, exceedingly conservative and sedate, despised her tight leather skirt, red T shirt and uncombed hair.

With one swift move Renee swept the contents back into her bag as if it were so much dust that had gathered on the glass top. "Goddamit," she muttered, "I can't find it. It's been stolen."

The salesgirl carefully returned the gold necklace to its original position. "You'd better report a stolen card then," she said with little conviction. Renee paused, thinking, lost in a daydream, then from the vacuum came the disagreeable voice of the supervisor, "My girl is very busy, miss. She doesn't have time for conversations. Better move along."

When Renee realized the remark was addressed to her she turned a blazing red yet bit her lip to control her temper. She felt that nothing was worth an argument, at least not today. But as she walked away she said cheerfully, "I suppose you wouldn't believe me if I told you that necklace was for my mother."

It had seemed like a lie, but she actually had been selecting a piece of jewelry for her mother. There was no special occasion. Renee just liked to buy things for her, to spoil her if possible, now that she had money coming in.

She rode the escalator to the furniture department on the fifth floor. Her mother's birthday was in a couple of months and she wanted to find a nice sofa and have it shipped to her. She hated this store. The crowds were unbearable. It would be impossible to find a couch that hadn't been picked over — one on which the material round the edges wasn't irreparably soiled or worn, the contour of the springs showing through the slender cloth.

She strolled by the model dining rooms; she counted ten altogether in a neat row. Some were filled with English oak furniture, some had a Spanish contemporary slant, others featured rattan specials from the Philippines. A young bearded designer was wiring up a neon tube which stretched under a chic, ultra-modern table of heavy glass. The silver neon light beat on and off the table top and reminded Renee of the flashing lights down 42nd Street which she sometimes stared at for hours on end. The designer smiled at her. "I like your clothes!" he yelled encouragingly.

"Thanks," said Renee. She wandered to the very recesses of the department to where stacks of lawn furniture lay dimly in folds of dust. Heavy tables of black cast iron encircled chairs covered with polished strips of yellow and green plastic. Imposing iron lamps stood nearby. They were lamps which gave off a special kind of light or odor, Renee wasn't sure which, that was supposed to kill summer bugs.

She returned to the sofas. The only one she half-liked was being used as a trampoline by a boy and a girl and she somehow knew that there would be no others in stock. "This isn't a gym," she snapped at the children. "That's a piece of furniture some person might like to buy and put in his home."

"We can do what we want!" the girl whined. She now bounced with all her strength, trying to tax Renee.

"This is not my day," Renee said sarcastically to a saleslady who replied in sympathy, "I know what you mean, my dear."

"I think you should take those children off that sofa."

The woman laughed a high, queer laugh. She agreed that the children were bad mannered but there was little that could be done. "Their mother's in another department. Glassware, I think. We'd have to wait for her."

"I see," Renee nodded gravely. She turned to the children

and kneeled in front of their bouncing bodies and said in a low voice, "You both should be very thankful that I don't work here." The children stopped moving quicker than the speed of light. They stared into Renee's face. Then they looked at each other. Then the little girl started bouncing again and her brother, though hesitant at first, soon followed her example. Renee left the store.

The streets were hot, dust and grime rising from the curbs. The girl in front of Renee thought she was stepping over a puddle of melting chocolate yogurt but the end of her heel came down on a portion of it and a little jet sprayed onto her hose, but she didn't seem to notice, only hurried to make the green light. Renee cursed. She shook her head in little rapid movements in an effort to shed a feeling of bewilderment that had come upon her. Funny. It was easy to be mesmerized by objects as ordinary as people's shoes floating through the traffic, or by rows of sofas, beds, chairs, inanimate, usually quite uninteresting. Renee often found herself drifting during the last few months, hypnotized by the commonplace. *It will be wonderful to leave town for the week-end, even if I spend my time with Mother.*

Mother lived in a four-room house on the outskirts of the town of Toms River, New Jersey. The house was only a few blocks from the Atlantic Ocean and sometimes the wind and the rain rushing from the sea were so fierce that they blew the shingles from the roof and carried them far away where no one could find them. One of Renee's earliest memories was of a young carpenter who lived down the block, who came after each storm and glued new shingles over the skeletons of the old; after five years the roof seemed like a pointed spear. Her mother had then lovingly named the house "Our Gingerbread Cottage" because of the jagged roof. Renee and her sister had loved it when it stormed because the carpenter offered to pay the girls a dollar for each shingle they could return to him. But search as they may, it was always in vain. It wasn't until Renee was around thirteen that she learned the reason why. One winter morning, after a short but severe blizzard, she was awakened by the sound of a prowler outside her window. She lifted the blind less than an inch and held her breath fast. Even though the sky was still a lonesome dark color she could make out the face of the prowler — it was the carpenter and he was collecting the shingles that were sticking through the snow.

And he was still a slave to his devious nature, Renee realized.

He had been sent to prison a year ago for the armed robbery of the threadbare gas station a mile north of town. And rumor had it that he was being driven mad there and causing unnameable, violent scenes which usually led to his confinement in a strait-jacket and a few weeks in the black hole. Henry Wess . . . Renee thought of him now because she had been watching his younger sister, Anna, sitting in the front of the bus, ever since they had left New York. As the bus rolled slowly through the small villages, Renee had studied Anna, had fantasized about why the girl had been to New York, what was in the six or seven packages that hemmed her in her seat, and why she had such a sad face. Anna hadn't acknowledged Renee, although there really was no reason why she should since she hadn't seen her in years and hadn't known her very well in the first place.

The bus passed a crumbling drive-in movie theater, the screen little more than a monstrous dirty cloth, the weeds pushing up around the speakers. It was there that she and Anna had double-dated, years ago. Everyone in the car had seemed tedious to Renee so she pretended to be a prude and kept her eyes fixed on the actresses flying through the amusing, romantic world of high-fashion, their exotic dresses blooming fireworks against the sky. Now the sun was beginning to set over the torn screen. The red eye of the Cyclops that had watched her as a child watched her now as well, sending his crimson glory spinning through the bus windows, lending her cheeks his strength, his solidity. And at the depot his sound light still hovered.

Renee passed Anna who was struggling with her parcels. "Hello, Anna," Renee whispered. The girl looked up, nodded curtly, then pretended to check her belongings. Renee wondered why she was avoiding her. Perhaps she was embarrassed about what had happened to her brother, ashamed to have a criminal in the family, and a lunatic at that. Suddenly, Renee laughed. She continued to giggle effortlessly and for no apparent reason during her entire walk home.

It was not a long distance to the house, but there was a steep hill to climb that always seemed to knock her out of breath. This evening proved to be no exception. She paused, winded, at the very top and stared down into the little valley. There was her mother, swinging on the front porch, a heavy black Bible in her lap. Renee sighed, then called to her mother and waved.

Milly Cloverman insisted on carrying her daughter's bag to her old bedroom even though Renee protested that it was much too heavy. "Don't be a fool, Mother!" she grabbed for the bag but her mother was too quick and Renee was left holding an edge of her cotton dress which slipped through her fingers.

Milly snapped open the yellow blinds. "Just like always," Milly sighed. "Bed made and your portable radio there on the bureau where you left it."

"Mother, my last visit here was only a few months ago. You act as if I haven't been back since I was a little girl."

"Well," Milly patted her slyly on the cheek. "You still are a little girl in many ways." Renee sank slowly to the bed. Milly continued, "There's the latest picture of your sister. I put it by your bed."

Renee, without looking at the photograph, reached out and turned it face down.

"All right, if that's the way you feel. I should have known it."

"Yes, Mother, you should have."

Milly made a clucking sound with her tongue that echoed through the empty house and sounded like an old hen in a well, fidgeting and fussing and wondering how she ended up in that dark pit.

"All right," Renee put her hands over her ears. "Stop making that sound. You'd go on with that forever if I didn't say to quit it."

Milly ceased at once and stood, hands quietly in her apron pockets, looking fearfully at her daughter, then her eyes began to roam the room and her expression became more relaxed. Renee knew that countenance well: it meant that their conversation from now on was to consist of nothing but trivia, matters totally without importance to either of them and she supposed that was a good thing. If her mother would ask her a question it would be in the tone of a disinterested visitor just being polite and her own responses would be equally cold, transparent.

"Why don't you change out of that hot skirt, darling, and then come sit on the porch with me," Milly drifted from the bedroom.

Renee slipped out of her leather skirt, took off her T shirt and searched the closet for something at least moderately cool to wear. She finally found at the very back an orange chiffon dress that was years old. The dress had an unusual pattern: a row of prancing bears came up over each shoulder and spilled down a thin strip to the waist. The bears wore downy dresses or crisp black suits and held spoons and bowler hats and the baby bears held precious bouquets of lilies of the valley and forget-me-nots. She was able to squeeze into the dress with some effort. It was little wonder, really, that it pinched her and that she couldn't quite pull the material over her skinny knees — she hadn't worn the dress since her eighth grade graduation. She washed her face and rubbed some cleansing cream over her cheeks and colored her lips with some magenta lip gloss. The whole time she stared resentfully at the overturned photograph of her sister.

She and Sue weren't in contact any longer. Renee had always been her mother's pet and Sue, a few years younger, had resented it and was determined to show her sister up. She had gone to Buffalo to a nursing school and after the training had secured a job in the city's largest hospital. There she had set out to marry a doctor, it didn't matter who the man was, as long as he could provide a high standard of living for her. She had married a monster twice her age and was proud as a queen of this lifetime catch. Milly was proud too. And Sue had sent a new picture. Probably in a wedding gown.

Renee couldn't suppress her curiosity any longer and turned the picture up. It was an old photo of Sue in a nurse's outfit with the white cap on top of protruding ears and a phony smile that meant she hadn't a care in the world. "Shit," said Renee.

She paused at the screen door. Milly sat on the swing, staring across at the neighbor's weedy front lawn. Renee knew that her mother was aware of her silent presence at the door, yet Milly would pretend to be oblivious to everything, everything but the weeds across the street. Renee felt her face grow hot and her heart pounded a little harder. The Bible sat on the table next to Milly. Milly would never preach to Renee about religion or God because she knew her daughter wouldn't stand for it; Sue, in fact, was not fond of Milly's religious zeal either. So instead of aggressively trying to convert her daughters to Christianity she would leave the Bible around the house where the girls couldn't help coming face to face with it. *Subtle*, Renee thought. *But at least it's a step up from the back of the toilet where she kept it last visit.*

Milly had had a hard life and Renee knew it, but Renee also knew that her mother was not the kind of woman who minded it or even realized that her life of trials was anything out of the ordinary. Her husband had died from a painful lung cancer and she had raised the girls herself on little means. Her own mother had been a victim of tuberculosis. Her brother had been killed in the Second World War. And she suffered from rheumatism and arthritis. Still, Milly's face was young and girlish for her fifty years and her hair was free even from a suggestion of grey; in fact, it was a baby's fine blonde.

Renee eased into a wicker chair and took a sip of sugary lemonade that her mother had prepared.

"They've been trying to sell that house across the way for a year," Milly indicated the deserted four-story dwelling. "They moved away at Christmas, but still haven't been able to find any takers. Mrs. Montgomery and her mother. Remember them?"

"Sure I do."

"Rumor has it that they're asking too much. Of course anything seems too high these days."

"Remember, Mother, Fay Montgomery used to make hats and sell them on nice spring afternoons, right in the front yard."

"I bought one for your grandma and she never got over it. Was tickled to death. Fay used to fix them up so pretty with ribbons and shady big brims. She spared no expense."

"Where did they move?"

"Who knows."

A couple of boys shot down the hill on skateboards, weaving dangerously close to one another. The cement shrieked.

"Isn't that a damn fool thing to do?" Milly scoffed. A police car cruised by and the cops looked disparagingly at the boys but didn't say anything.

Renee closed her eyes. The whole neighborhood seemed close and wet, adhesive. Her neck felt like a flooded staircase; she couldn't help inhaling the dampness.

"Still have those awful nightmares, Renee?"

The question came softly, unheralded, and Renee gasped. She moistened her lips with her tongue. "No, not much," she answered defensively. "I have a hard time sleeping sometimes, though."

"You mean you have insomnia?" Milly tried to make her daughter be specific.

Renee peered closely at her mother but without much emotion. "Yes, it's the getting to sleep that's hard."

"Are you sure you're living right, Renee?"

"In what way?"

"Well," Milly hesitated, searching for the appropriate

words. "Well, I mean, residing in a hotel and all, where you say the girls come and go so freely. . ."

"Meaning what?" An exasperation was coming into Renee's voice.

"I think you belong in a house, Renee, not a hotel. You belong in a house back here in the country."

"With a white wooden fence, flowers in the yard, a postman for a husband and five brats down my throat. Thank you very much, Mother, but that will never be." She crossed her legs swiftly and her fingers made absent-minded circles around the figures of the bears.

"Then what is it you want out of life?" came the question from Milly. She seemed totally confused.

"What is it you want out of life?" Renee fired back. "You can't answer such a crazy question any more than I can." She stood up and paced back and forth, her hands flying in the air for emphasis. "Is this what you've wanted all your life? Here? This place? Have you lived your dreams? Have you ever *had* any?"

"I've had you and your sister."

"A bitter harvest," Renee replied and went inside, leaving Milly alone. She had decided to watch television but she remembered that at this hour there was nothing on but news or game shows and neither appealed to her. Besides, the reception on her mother's set was terrible. As she passed it she reached out and pulled off the foil wrapped around the antenna. It was rusted and torn and she would replace it tomorrow. She shut herself in her room, let the blinds back down and fell onto her bed with the weight and frigidity of a plaster statue and slept. She had bad dreams but when she woke around midnight all she could remember was being choked by one of the ribbons that Mrs. Montgomery decorated her hats with; as the unknown strangler put more pressure around her neck and the pain became more intense, she saw the ribbon turn slowly all colors of the rainbow and become from time to time alive with insects that cried with little voices which dissolved into music of harpsichords; or the ribbon would become a leaf or finally a heavy strand of spinach as hot as coals.

Mother must be asleep. Renee tossed on the mattress. She felt her nipples tighten, hard and firm, and she reached down her dress and twisted them. She played with them for a few moments as she left her dreamy state behind and became wide awake. She pushed her hand up her dress and began masturbating, slowly at first, then more quickly and rhythmically. Her eyes searched the bedroom for an object that would feel better, bigger than her fingers; but she could see nothing but the dim sphere of the cheap alarm clock on the mantle and she saw that it was quite late. She pulled herself out of bed. She crept to the door and listened for sounds from her mother's room but everything was still. She felt flushed all over. She longed for sex; for the feel of a man breaking into her and never coming out again. She slipped from the house and walked feverishly toward the center of the little town.

A gust of wind tore down the street and pushed at her back; she almost stumbled, caught off guard by its savageness. Main Street was empty, locked shut. *Void, vacant, blank.* The market window was protected by a comic orange cat whose whiskers stood on end. She tapped her fingers on the glass and it jumped at them. At the end of the street was a lighted bar and at the curb outside an empty police car. Silhouettes at the door. Her heartbeat quickened when she saw two cops move into the light of the street lamps. One finished a swallow of beer and, after a quick look around, tossed his bottle in a trash container. She heard glass shatter. The other, slowly sipping coffee, seemed lost in thought. The men started up a conversation, their words drifted to her though she couldn't make them out. They got into the car. *A chance, at least a chance.* Her feet seemed to carry her without effort and she reached the car in less than seconds. The cops were startled by her shadow thrown against the hood. She stopped next to the window. Her hand slid from her shoulder and started massaging her tits.

The men traded amazed looks. "Drunk?" the driver shrugged his shoulders to his partner. The driver was middle-aged, greying, tending to fat, while his partner was lanky, flat-faced, little more than a youth, with inky black hair and a long square chin. His eyes slid toward his cup of steaming coffee and he stirred the black liquid. The driver started the engine.

"What's the matter?" came Renee's voice, strong, clear, as if from a hollow honey jar. "Never seen a bitch in heat before?"

The motor idled. The younger cop threw his coffee onto the street. They both stared at Renee, quietly. "I'm looking for action," she continued. "I'm trying to find a guy or two who's horny enough to give it to me."

The men exchanged glances, then the driver said to her, "Go on. Get in the back."

They had gone less than a block when the young cop with the

jet black hair turned around to see Renee's head leaning back, her eyes closed, her dress pulled up to her waist, her pussy shining against the black seat. His hand involuntarily went towards her, but smashed against the mesh, the wires that separated them. "Shit, look at that," he edged his partner who, with the aid of his rear view mirror, had missed nothing. The cop began driving erratically, his chest began heaving and his breath came out in frantic little gusts. "Where can we go?" he murmured. "We've both got wives at home."

"How about that corn field west of town?" his partner suggested.

"No, I know a place," Renee's voice cracked. "An empty house. The Montgomery place down the street."

"But they've locked it up," the driver complained.

"Break and enter it," Renee said.

"Yeah," the young cop added. "We can take out a window in the back."

They pulled up to the Montgomery home. Renee saw her own dark house across the street. "We've got to be real quiet, no use raising a stir so the neighbors will wake up," the driver warned. The three of them fought the weeds all the way to the rear. There the cops jimmied the lock on the kitchen window. They raised it and climbed inside, then helped Renee through. The moonlight showed the dusty squares and circles where the appliances and tables had once stood.

Renee went up to the older cop and ran her fingers over his badge. Then she felt the heavy material on his arms and let her hand wander over his gun and belt. "Nice," she sighed. "Very nice." He reached inside her dress and squeezed her tits. She felt the tall cop push up behind her and reach under her dress. He shoved first one finger then another up her ass and pushed further and further forward. "Wait," she said as she extricated herself from them both. "Put some handcuffs on me."

The young cop said, "Let me use yours, Mel." Mel handed his cuffs to his partner who fastened them around Renee's wrists. She could hardly rub her hands together, the cuffs were so tight. But they felt marvelous to her; she felt trapped. She dropped to her knees in front of the young cop who thrust out his stomach and started to undo his belt.

"No," she stopped him. "Don't help me." She set to work with her teeth, loosening and pulling the belt from the pants, the hard, metallic teeth of the buckle grinding against her own.

Then she fastened her mouth to the woolly fleshy material of the pants and pulled them down around his knees. She took them further, to the floor, and her nose almost rubbed the boards; she was aware of dust and the ghosts of refrigerators and stoves. She worked on the underwear next and finally the cop's cock was ready, at her eye level.

He grinned down at her, understanding. "It's all yours, baby."

Chapter Three

The Scotchsmith house was on the right side of town; that is, it was perched on a sloping hill which flowed into Ocean Vista Road which, in turn, ran along the sparkling sea on the correct, the impressive side of town. The house itself was a wide, white-framed New England style cottage, the twelve rooms spacious, full of sun and sea air, and furnished by Ella Scotchsmith with a certain delicacy and sensible refinement. The children found their Connecticut home both comfortable and secretly grand; for Mr. Scotchsmith it was a silent retreat from New York City, the "monstrous megalopolis" as he nicknamed it for the children, only two boring hours away by commuter train. The trip was worth the bother, Peter Scotchsmith told himself one glorious June morning as he sat on the terrace, drinking a cup of strong coffee and glancing at the news about Africa before reading the financial report from the Common Market. It was certainly worth it if he could enjoy this peace, all this beauty manifested by the cool, soft lawn that met the towering bushes of hydrangeas and rhododendrons, these flowers forming an effective shield against the noise and curiosity of the summer tourists who drove their cars along the scenic ridge of the bay. He must commend Ella for her brilliance in planting the budding bushes in such a clever spot.

Martha was the eldest child, twelve-years-old, quiet yet interested in a variety of subjects; for instance, in school she was very good in math and quite proficient in French. She had a knack for mimicking languages—the Scotchsmiths had opened their home to two foreign high school students who had stayed for one year each, and Martha had had no trouble conversing fluently first with the Danish boy and then with the girl from Ceylon. Martha was good with her hands; she loved macrame and knitting and needlepoint. She was already preparing Christmas gifts for her family: sweaters for her brothers and sister and an elaborate needlepoint, whose design was a golden bowl of fruit, to be hung Christmas Eve upon her parents' bedroom wall. She was a girl who was always full of surprises and secrets and everyone expected Martha to bring them something unusual at very inconspicuous moments, much as a magician will bring the rabbit from the hat just as the audience is rubbing its eyes. Martha loved to help her mother cook and would often nibble before meals. As a result she was gaining weight and being told to watch her figure.

Her brother, Perry, was less than a year younger. He was a very bright, energetic boy, terribly handsome, with an infectious grin, the kind that the makers of television commercials love to find and photograph over a bowl of soggy cereal. Perry had their favorite look, or rather, attitude, and as a result was invited to make several commericals which he found fun but silly. His mother, Ella, was very proud of this as the other mothers on the block found it a continuing excuse to heap praise on the boy and his family and Ella enjoyed that, although she had a stock line that she used on each neighbor after they had commended Perry for being such a smart child and irresistible little actor. "Perry will stop this when he's twelve. Then he's going into sports." And if Perry was along he would look as if he were nonchalantly kicking pebbles across a driveway, but he would really be cursing his luck as he booted the rough stones, not caring much for either acting or sports. He was unhappy that his young life was mapped for him so carefully. He would have preferred to spend his free time with his telescope or books about the stars, as he wanted to become an astronomer and felt that there was so much to learn that he should get started at once. So he waited in dread for next year to arrive when he would be firmly ensconced in baseball, or football, and put out on the field where he didn't want to be, with a group of boys whom he liked but didn't want to play with.

Patricia was eight, blonder than her sandy-haired older brother and sister and more spoiled. She had an annoying habit of whining whether she did or didn't get her way and spent far too much time in front of the television set where she would watch family situation comedies where children lived in houses much like hers and whose mothers and fathers looked and acted like her own. But sometimes she would fantasize that the television girls and boys were her own brothers and sisters and after a few weeks of steady viewing she would prance around the dining room table asking Perry and Martha and Ron why they couldn't be more like the children on television who were always winning contests at school, who were always so popular and meeting rock stars or falling into delicious adventures. She even renamed Sleepy, their dog, after the dog in one of the shows who was called Dutch. Even after a stern conversation with her father she refused to call the dog by its correct name. Her marks at school were fairly low, but everybody sort of ignored them and never said much to her about her scholastic progress.

Patricia's perfect foil was her younger brother, Ron, who would be eight-years-old next month. He was a wild little boy, sometimes provoking everyone in such a way that he became mean rather than just undisciplined. He was never still; he always had to be crashing into everyone else's business; if other children were playing a game and he wasn't allowed to join, he would literally overturn the board and toss the pieces down the toilet; if his brother received a compliment he would leave his chair at the dinner table and hit him hard on the back; he would spend entire afternoons tormenting the house pets, fastening tight clothespins to the dog's tail or shutting the cat in the refrigerator until the maid opened the door and shrieked with terror. Then he would deny he had put the cat there. After the maid had complained to Ella about it, Mrs. Scotchsmith had a serious talk with her husband. But he said, "All boys do that sort of thing. My God, have you seen his friends at school? They all are up to these pranks and worse. It's all part of being a boy. It won't last that long either." So Ella dutifully forgot any misgivings about the boy and the next time the maid complained about the cat in the refrigerator, Ella simply said, "Ron didn't shut it in there, he told me so himself. The door is sometimes left open when the kids get into the fruit punch and the cat wanders in by itself." So, while they ignored Patricia, everyone tried to see Ron as spirited and rambunctious and his very worst behavior they sanctioned with a weak smile.

Peter Scotchsmith sold insurance and had recently been made vice-president of one of the largest and most successful companies in Manhattan. His children were ecstatic about the promotion mainly because he moved from a very pleasant, ample office to an imposing suite on the thirty-fourth floor. From every window the children found incredible views of the city and watching the thousands of buildings growing fast like weeds held their attention longer than anything else. Of course, the spell was soon broken, and then Ron was off to push every button and confront every gadget in the room while Patricia gave orders to the frail secretary and Martha made her father some stout coffee and Perry leafed through his father's business affairs, turning paper after paper and badgering him with questions. It was these rare afternoons when the children visited that were among the most rewarding aspects of fatherhood for him. He felt proud of them, but more importantly he felt noble, gratified at being able to appear a convincing, stimulating figurehead.

Another time he had a sense of satisfaction was around Christmas when he sat them down by the holiday fire and read aloud from Dickens' *Christmas Tales,* keeping a strict eye on the lookout for misbehavior. He would read in a boisterous voice which echoed through the hallway and had power far beyond its need. Afterwards he would praise Dickens and call him as great as Edison, Lincoln or Franklin, then return the book to the shelf and forget about it, or any other book, until next Christmas. All the while, his wife, Ella, would be sitting by the fire, stirring ashes in the grate with the iron tongs, listening to her husband and feeling the flush from a glass of dark burgundy which she drank only on such special occasions. She would be thinking good thoughts about her husband whom she rarely considered much during the other days of the year as she was too concerned with the children and keeping the house in order. But she always fell in love with him again at Christmas and remembered the moment they first met at a party on Cape Cod on a sunny, windy afternoon, and how they were both tall and blond and glad to find each other. They were still tall and blond, she thought, although a softness had seeped into their bodies, in fact, into their very bones, and she turned to tend the flames.

Perry parked his bicycle in the garage and hurried into the kitchen where he found his mother and Fanny, the maid, arguing about how to prepare the beef for dinner. He interrupted them, "Mom, you know that house down the street

— the one where the little Portuguese girl stands outside and says hello to everybody who goes by?"

"Of course I know it," Ella answered, sticking her finger into the cream she was whipping and tasting a tiny bit.

"Well, I was riding past on my bike and there was a big CONDEMNED BY THE BOARD OF HEALTH sign on the front saying, UNFIT FOR HUMAN HABITATION."

"Oh, dear," Ella shook her head.

"But, I mean, isn't that terrible?" Perry continued as he tasted some of the cream from a wooden spoon that his mother held for him. "Yes, it's real good," he replied and she laughed. "I mean," he tossed his cap into the living room and lifted himself onto the counter, "I feel sorry for that little girl. She was always so nice, the nicest person on the whole street, really. The friendliest."

"I know, honey, but nobody's hurting her. She'll be O.K."

"But I mean, it's embarrassing, isn't it, to have that sign put up on your house?"

"It is embarrassing, yes," Ella replied. "But, Perry, there have to be some kind of housing standards for the community, otherwise some people would live in shacks and never clean them. Of course, I don't know what was wrong with this particular house —"

"Nothin' was wrong with it," Fanny, a fat old woman with white hair and horn-rimmed glasses nodded from the table where she sat shelling peas. "That's all politics, don't you know that, Mrs. Scotchsmith?"

Ella sighed. She was not in the mood to hear Fanny's words of wisdom this afternoon. "Fanny," she said. "It seems no matter what I say, you always come to the opposite conclusion."

"That isn't true and you know it, Mrs. Scotchsmith," the woman replied, hurt. "But I have my own opinions and I wouldn't care to stay in a house where I wasn't free to say what *I* think — after all I raised *six* children of my own and know at least a little something of the ways of the world. And I want young Perry to know that things aren't always what they seem like on the outside. I happen to know that Joe Preuga has had a running quarrel with the building commissioner over a completely different matter altogether so don't tell me that has nothin' to do with it, especially since they keep that house up real nice, at least I think so, and they keep that little girl real clean."

"It just seems," said Perry, "that something like that always happens to people who don't deserve it, when every other snotty kid in the neighborhood lives in —"

"All right, Perry!" Mrs. Scotchsmith yelled in exasperation. "I don't want to hear anymore about it! I know how you feel and I certainly hope you know how I feel. Now go upstairs and clean up and tell your brother and sisters that dinner will be ready in less than an hour and I don't want them eating any junk in the meantime."

Perry sidled off the counter, having completely lost his punch and verve and, with as disgusted an expression as he dared convey, went out of the room. Ella ran ice-cold water over the fresh raspberries, the very first of the season. They were to be a treat as both Perry and his father loved them so; the whole dinner was to be a little fancier and more festive than usual. She bit her lip; why should it be so hard to keep her temper down? It just seemed that Perry had sided with Fanny and that angered her. In fact, she was absolutely furious with the woman and somehow felt everything was her fault. She didn't look at her for fear she would say something nasty but she heard the peas being shelled — the sound of them dropping against the china bowl was enough to leave her with a headache. She shut off the tap and took a heavy, almost profound breath from someplace low in her stomach, then she counted to twelve and sampled a raspberry.

As Perry turned the corner of the hall upstairs he heard his sister, Patricia, screaming deliriously. It seemed as if her yells were coming from Fanny's room; he investigated. Ron and a friend from school had shut themselves in the maid's room and as Patricia walked by they had pulled her in and were busy frightening her with a garden snake they had captured by the tomato plants.

"Come on, keep the noise down," Perry warned as he rescued his giggling, kicking sister, who was really enjoying it all, from the fangs of the reptile. "What are you up to with that?" Perry questioned his brother.

It seems that after tiring of breaking in on Martha as she was taking her shower and assaulting her with squirt guns, Ron and his friend, Billy, had found the snake and decided to put it in Fanny's bed.

The boys ripped the covers down and stuffed the snake under them, then pulled the blankets up to the top so the snake couldn't escape, then they howled at its outline wiggling wildly under the comforter.

"Old Fanny's gonna scream her head off when she gets into bed with this!" Ron cried.

"Don't you think that might scare her a little too much?" Perry asked.

"Boy, your brother's a real sissy, isn't he?" Billy stuck out his chin and pouted.

"Yeah," Ron answered. "He's no fun. Spoiled crybaby."

Perry wasn't concerned about the snake really and he didn't particularly care if Fanny did have a scare. What bothered him was that in their enthusiasm the boys had knocked over Fanny's jewelry box and the broaches, the rings, the rhinestone necklace had all ended in a heap on the floor.

"Pick those up before you leave," Perry started out the door.

"Let Fat Fanny pick them up!" Ron yelled.

"She's fatter than your house and mine put together," Billy chimed in before Ron had finished his sentence.

Perry felt the blood rush to his head. His hand shot out to strike his brother across the face, but he caught himself in mid-air. Ron had been waiting just for that moment and he flung himself with all his might at Perry, butting him hard in the stomach with his head and Billy jumped on him too and they both began to kick him and call him names. Patricia joined in the name-calling and threw Fanny's cheap necklace over her blouse and hopped around the room like a stripper, sticking her stomach out as far as she could and pulling faces in the mirror. The fighting stopped when Patricia saw the snake glide through a hole in the sheet and slither towards her. In terror she pulled back, grabbing at the necklace, and it split in two. She threw it on the bed and rushed from the room as Ron and Billy began to hunt for the snake. While they were searching in the closet the creature shot from under a chair and Billy stepped backward on its head and crushed it but the rest of its body continued to twitch in agony.

"Stupid!" Ron shoved him. "See what you've done! Stupid faggot!" He punched Billy in the shoulder. The snake still shook as if drunk although its head was only a bloody pudding. "It's gonna die now, anyway," Ron added and his mind worked quickly. "I know," he produced a pocket knife. "Let's cut up its insides and see what it looks like."

"And get blood all over the room?" Billy whined, his

shoulder smarting from the harsh blow.

"There's blood all over the room already, you dumb ass-hole!" The snake suddenly spurted forward, as if it still thought it had a life of its own, but it was really a death sprint. The boys squealed. There was no time now to dissect it.

As Perry went to his own room he heard them stomping it with the legs of a chair. Perry washed his hands, carefully removed his shirt, wet a washcloth and massaged his chest. Then he put on a red and white checked shirt, a summer favorite, and sat at the folding table by his window where he kept his telescope and his notebook in which he charted the positions of the stars. He couldn't see any stars in broad day-light, of course, so he kicked himself for sitting there as if he could, as if he could look through the glass and see the mysteries of the sky beckoning him, challenging him, enchanting him. Venus was to be particularly splendid tonight, at around nine o'clock. It would not only be so for him, who would study it magnified through the telescope, but for anyone who, gazing upwards, could see it sparkling serenely with his naked eye.

The planet's craters, composed of smooth grey clay, rose grandly and precipitously into the dark where their ragged peaks were crowned by bursting blue stars erupting with x-rays. The atmosphere itself glowed in the ever present dawn caused by the continuous star explosions and every tiny rock and crevice in the stainless canyons could be seen as distinctly and fully as gems beneath microscopes. A beautiful perfumed fungus floated in the air near the molten lakes; a patch would sometimes loiter over the liquid flames waiting to attach itself to another drifting plant and together sprout new matter which would begin a life of its own.

The spinning never stopped above the lake of fire; there was a dangerous draught, a funnel that sucked anything in its path and drove it deep to the bottom; Perry was caught in the spastic, twisiting current and saw he was headed for a burning Hell. His body slowly sank into the gaseous red and yellow fluid and he felt himself pulled under much as someone might pluck him by the feet from a high ladder. His face became lost in the hellish liquor yet there was no pain — only a strong feeling that this was a transition; there was no sense of death — indeed, no idea of death; there was another finality awaitng him, a different fate.

The flaming water now seemed colder than the most frigid winter air and the yellow burning patches became chunks of hard ice and brushed against his cheeks and small bony fingers. He was swept into a new cavity, a thin passage that pushed him past hoary caves where giant insects dwelled and kept human babies as their prisoners and playthings. He saw young boys in blue diapers caught in enormous webs and a fat bee was busy licking a newborn girl's toes. Still he was carried further, though the water had evaporated and he was spinning along through the air, hundreds of fantastic birds his companions, fluttering ahead and behind him.

Now it was dark and he was rising beside the rough peaks, the mountains, dead, cold, yet so unyielding, so tough. Perry was glad to be protected by the breezy umbrella of billowy taffeta above his head. He clung fervently to the ends of the material as his feet slid along the dry, dusty rocks. Once one of the stones came loose and fell from the crag, but though Perry listened closely he never heard the stone hit home, there was only the sound of nothingness, of the long night that was never to know daylight or the bright and passionate sounds that the sun inspires and that the moon then quiets and lulls to sleep.

He was at the summit of the mountain now and he planted his feet firmly on its crest. The umbrella wafted down from over his head and he gasped to find that it was his mother's dress. In fact, it was his mother herself, standing there wearing the dress, a funny smile on her face, a smile that he had only seen once in his life, from his crib, at the very first moment he had been aware that she was his mother. She had leaned over the playpen and smiled at him, and while the smile was full of warmth and joy it also seemed a bit fearful and ignorant, as if she didn't quite know what to make of the child. She was in awe. And now she was smiling that same way, only she was twelve feet tall and her hands were fragile rubber and turned listlessly above her taffeta dress. Perry's mouth began to move and he realized he was trying to talk or at least make sounds but nothing came forth and he felt his lips and discovered that they were made from the same tactile composition.

A stream of blood began to flow down his mother's legs and formed thick pools before him, here, at the peak's meridian, at its utmost height, at the crown of its head. Perry was tortured by the most terrible thirst he had ever known. The blood glowed. A scream tore from his fevered throat and suddenly there was a burst of fire, the intensity of which he had never seen or felt before, much less imagined. His mother had exploded and become a blue x-ray star, pulsating wildly above the planet. And Perry, too, had become a similar star. They were two stars now, destined to reign in this part of the sky, two stars with souls, hungry, beating, giving light.

The dawn had come in slowly as if brought over the lawn to his house by the fishermen leisurely retuning from their morning catch. Perry opened first one eye, then, after surveying the room and gladly finding all his familiar possessions bathed in a rosy illumination and unchanged from the night before, opened the other eye and rubbed the sleep from the corners. He knew he had been dreaming but had forgotten the substance of his vision. He could only focus on the table across the room holding his telescope which pointed toward the sky. Perry sighed and shook his head in disgust as he got up and smoothed the wrinkles from his clothes.

Why was I so tired! he chastised himself. *To fall asleep so early with all my clothes on and not wake up till now. But the very worst, I didn't get a chance to see Venus on the finest viewing night of the year...* And he kicked the bedpost and prepared himself for a speedy breakfast to be followed by a bicycle run along the beach and perhaps a picnic at Beechwood Cove, that is, if Martha had made the vanilla fudge cake she had promised, and if Ron and Patricia wanted to accompany them to help carry the elaborate provisions.

Chapter Four

"What did I tell you?" Stewart Reggino sipped some port and arranged his legs so they would be in the sun.

"You were right," Jake agreed. "I wasn't prepared for that whole experience." They were sitting at an outdoor cafe in Greenwich Village, relaxing, watching the crowds. Jake had recounted his visit to the Hotel Dove but he hadn't mentioned that he had been back the next week-end in search of Renee Cloverman and that she had been gone. Nor had he mentioned that he was no longer planning to write a story about the hotel, now that she had usurped his interest in it.

"You know," Stewart mused as he studied their waitress's tanned thighs, "I read all the time now about the crime wave that's hit the area around the hotel . . . down into the Garment District, over in the 40s in the Diamond District . . . antique places. I don't know who's behind it, of course, but I tell you I saw some of that stolen stuff in the basement of the hotel."

"How can you be sure it was stolen?" Jake asked.

"Oh, come on, man," Stewart continued in disgust. "You're like Shirley Temple — a permanent rainbow stuck up your ass. You've got two eyes. Use them." He ordered another glass of port.

"Guess you must be getting the most out of your vacation," Jake changed the subject.

Stewart's lips seemed to tighten, almost imperceptibly, and his face became suddenly impassive. "Yeah," he replied. "Only — well, I've had enough. It's time to get back. You can only stand so much freedom."

A couple of bums begged some cigarettes from them and started talking incoherently, their words slurred and low in their throats. "We let you have the cigarettes, now don't bore us to death," Stewart gave them pats on the backs to send them on their way and the bums gave a cursory salute and wandered to the next table where two young girls were even less eager for their company.

"I've got to go," Jake stood.

"Can't even wait till I finish this glass?"

"Sorry. I have to report to work," Jake lied. He was edgy today and wanted to be by himself. He left Stewart some money, then walked sluggishly to the Washington Square arch. The maple trees were in the path of a firm breeze and their leaves were blowing so forcefully that Jake wondered why they didn't tear away from the stems.

In the shadow of the arch people were gathered around a man playing an upright piano. He was no younger than ninety, with shrivelled up little hands and dyed blond hair. But he was really swinging, throwing himself into the ragtime beat and getting the group to clap hands. His purple shirt shone in the polished mahogany of the piano on top of which were glued cheap statuettes of dogs of every breed and color. The man shook the keys harder then the maple leaves were trembling.

That night Jake returned to the hotel. It was not yet nine o'clock and he raised no suspicions as he sat in the lobby reading the paper. The teen-age boy came on duty replacing an old hag with balding patches who waved good-bye to Jake, it seemed almost out of pity, as he was the only soul in the room. The boy scrutinized Jake for a moment, then switched on his portable television, propped his legs up, opened a can of Coke and settled back comfortably.

Different women filed into the hotel and Jake recognized several as the perfumed whores of his first visit, only now they wore curlers in their dull straw hair and their shorts revealed cellulite in what must be advanced stages.

At around ten o'clock Renee Cloverman, struggling under some large packages, pushed the door open. At first Jake didn't recognize her, yet he knew from the way she walked with her belly thrust out and her legs bent back that it must be her. She paused near his chair to re-arrange her packages. Jake saw his opportunity. "I'll help you take those upstairs," he offered and without waiting for a response seized one of the bags that was filled to the brim with nuts and oranges.

"Very gallant," she muttered, avoiding his eyes. "Donny can

help me," she indicated the pimply youngster behind the desk who hurriedly turned up the volume of the television set so it would appear he hadn't heard her.

"No need bothering him," Jake removed a second bag from her arms. "I may not be his age, but I can still carry packages." He paused, examining her face. "That is — if you don't mind."

She resented this intrusion. She wanted to have a nice bath and rest for a few hours, perhaps listen to some classical music on the radio, but he seemed so earnest and insistent that she nodded in assent and entered the elevator. Jake followed, closing the door behind them. She pushed the button for the top floor.

"We rode like this once before," he said. "Remember?"

"No." Renee kept her eyes fixed on her own reflection in the glass. She liked her outfit tonight, a yellow and orange striped blouse, very bold, a black vinyl skirt and tan Greek sandals.

"Don't you remember me? Jake Adams. I spoke to you early one morning in the hall. You were giving the cat some milk."

She stared at him. "Oh, yeah," she pondered. She really hadn't remembered until now. "The cop."

He cringed, then answered with a succinct, "Yes." The memory of his masquerade was brought back to him; he still felt foolish that he had worn the uniform that night. Why couldn't he tell her he wasn't a cop? The elevator opened and Renee headed down the hall searching for her keys. She soon realized she had forgotten to lock the door; in fact, it was open a crack so she pushed it back and motioned for Jake to come in behind her.

"Shut the door," she ordered as she put her shopping bags on the large unmade bed. "Set yours there, too," she told him and he leaned his against the others. Renee lifted the blinds and the room turned as bright as day thanks to the light bouncing from the movie marquees, the car and bus headlights, and phosphorescent street lamps.

"The movies changed again," she said. "I can't keep up with them . . . there are new ones every three days or so."

Jake joined her at the window. There were perhaps a dozen theaters, most of them playing exploitation films — war veterans on dope and skilled in killing, Chinese martial arts quickies with blow-ups of men's tight chests exploding chains, or women in cages fighting each other in the Philippine swamps of World War II. One theater was showing a film about an obscene phone caller. An immense poster showed a big black glove picking up a cherry red telephone behind which a screaming young girl was tearing her hair with one hand and covering her tits with the other; but her face was smaller than the phone and it looked as if the instrument might crush her, like a truck had she run drunk or doped into its path. Below the marquee a black woman was pleading with three vice cops; she was in a rage, crying and shrieking and protesting that she didn't do it, but a white woman dressed like a whore was shoving a finger in her face while an undercover cop was fitting the cuffs on her. It seemed the white woman had been standing in the pay phone booth, her wallet dangling from her purse, and the black woman had taken the bait and snatched; unfortunately for her, the cops had stepped from the shadows and given her the bad news. As she was carried away she screamed at the woman who was already stepping back into the phone booth to wait for a new victim who was surely only a block away. Her yells could be heard even from the paddy wagon, "I'll get you, you white mother-fuckin' bitch, I'll be out on the fuckin' street tomorrow and you better believe I'm gonna come after you!"

Renee giggled and fell back on the bed.

"Jaded, aren't you?" Jake remarked.

"Oh, please," she answered. "It's a fact of life here. You'd come to miss it if it didn't happen all the time." There was no reply from him. She studied his quiet figure against the window, then blurted in exasperation, "Nobody's keeping you here anyway, so why don't you go on?" Jake heard himself breathing; he was in limbo. "You get off on it, too," she added. "Or else you wouldn't be here."

"May I sit down?" he asked and after she stretched and nodded he pulled a wooden chair next to the bed and continued, "I don't think I get off on something like that. I don't think you do either."

"Oh, all right. Let's not argue about it. It's dumb." She turned on her side and the bag with the nuts and oranges spilled onto the sheets, sending the cashews, peanuts and macadamias rolling the length of the bed. "Goddam it!" Renee sat up. "Oh, well," she sighed. "Have a nut."

But he lit a cigarette instead and watched her as she absentmindedly munched the nuts, occasionally shaking her hair from her eyes. He wanted to take her in his arms so badly; she was possessing him again like she did that first night, without trying, he supposed. "Hey, squirrel," he said. "What are you doing?"

Renee laughed in spite of herself. "A line like that should sound corny, but it doesn't."

He moved onto the bed and began to run his hands along her thighs. "I'm not a cop, you know."

Renee looked up disappointedly. "What do you mean?"

He kept his hands moving up and down her legs. "Just that. I'm a journalist who got in here on a crazy scheme and got hooked on you."

Renee felt flushed and she began to move her hand on top of his. "Hooked on me?" She was mystified.

"Kiss me," he pleaded softly. "Real slow on the mouth. I want to feel every bit of breath in that body." And he bent her over backwards and began to lick her lips. "Come on now, aren't you gonna kiss me like I asked you to?"

Renee fastened her arms around his neck and stuck her tongue into his throat. She was losing herself while he became more aware and more in command and soon he had taken her clothes off and was letting his weight crush her against the sheets. He kicked the bags off the bed; the nuts spiraled across the floor. Then he stood up to undress while she lay there shivering, waiting, with her eyes closed. When he lowered himself over her again he was naked and she clung fast to him, moaning. He entered her and soon they had found an exciting rhythm. They repeated this lovemaking three more times that night and each time Renee became softer until at the end she was something breakable that whimpered with a voice that was questionably human. He locked her toes in a vice with his hot feet and they slept.

They were awakened around eight by the rain and a clopping sound outside the door. Jake frowned. "That's Pandora," she whispered. "She has a wooden leg."

Jake stretched. Resting his hand on her stomach, he drummed on her skin with his fingers. "I'm not going to let you go . . . you know that."

Renee was perplexed and a little embarrassed. "But, you don't even know me."

"Yes, I do," he insisted. "I already know a lot about you. For example, the way you behaved in bed with me told me more than a week of conversation would."

Renee sat straight up and stared. "How did that tell you

anything about me?"

"With some people, you just have sex. With others, something more. You were terribly tender, Renee. That might mean you're terribly lonely."

She gasped and jumped from the bed. "And it might mean you misread me." She stormed to her closet and threw on a robe. She was shaking. "By the same token, I learned about you, too. You seemed terribly desperate."

"Maybe so," he shrugged.

"This is all shit," she coughed. "I've got to take my pills." And she opened a little Chinese vial, worked up some spittle, and swallowed several.

Jake propped the pillows behind his head. "This is the first time I've seen you in the daylight."

She watched the rain. "And how do you find me?"

"Very beautiful."

There were few people on the street although a procession of taxis was heading east.

"What do you want to do today?" he asked.

"With you?"

"Of course."

"Well, aren't you arrogant?" she laughed. "What makes you think I have nothing to do but spend the day with you?"

"Everything is a matter of priorities."

"Exactly," she snapped.

"There's the Circle Line cruise, I've always heard that's incredibly romantic or there's the World Trade Center, the view is unreal. There's a carriage ride through Central Park," he continued laughing. "Or a guided tour through the U.N. in ten languages."

She picked up a bottle of perfume and mockingly sprayed it in his direction. "Aren't you clever!" she cried. "Yes, you must think you're a marvelous wit."

"I wonder if they perform marriage ceremonies around here?"

Renee was suddenly angry with herself. She was beginning to like this man and it made her nervous. He stared at her as if he owned her, yet stared with the eyes of a slave, or so she thought. He came over and put his arms around her and kissed her. She liked his kiss; it totally relaxed her.

"When are we going to see each other?" he gently smoothed her hair. "Seriously. Would you like to come to my apartment for dinner, or may I take you out?"

"Jake," she said slowly. "You know, we're only playing. This is just a game."

He moved his lips against her ears. "Is it?"

"Yes, it is."

"We'll see."

The rain turned inward and beat the pane. He held her until she pulled away.

"Enough," she said.

"Well," he grinned. "Then you don't want to go out with me today?"

"Can't. I've too much to do here."

He dressed and she watched him in the mirror as she pretended to apply mascara and rouge. He certainly had a seductive figure, she thought. His buttocks were firm and seemed strong as blocks, as did his shoulders, and she loved the way his arms moved only slightly as he fastened his pants.

She gazed into her own face. Her eyes were surprisingly radiant this morning, an unusually deep blue, the shade of waves at sea, rough, just before a storm, or perhaps the awkward, unreal color of water in a fishbowl.

She dropped her head in her hands and she felt bluer than her eyes, bluer than the rain. When she looked up in the mirror again her eyes seemed less intense, the color a bit washed out, she recognized herself. She sighed.

"I'll be over tonight around the same time as last night. I'll knock on your door and if you want to see me, let me in. If you don't, that's O.K., too." He smoothed the top of her head. "Don't get up. I'll let myself out."

Throughout the day the rain increased steadily until by the time Stewart Reggino was punching his time clock there was an energetic downpour. He didn't like long periods of rain, though he enjoyed the swift lightning flashes and loud thunder. But when it poured without dramatic effects he wanted to curl up and sleep and never open his eyes until the air was dry.

"Fuckin' vacation over, huh?" It was Ed Ubal brushing behind him, ready to punch in.

"For another six months," Stewart declared. "Next time I'm going to take one of these cycles to the mountains . . . maybe the desert, say in Arizona or New Mexico, instead of messing around the apartment." But Stewart didn't like riding too well, though he felt he had to pretend to the other guys that he was the next greatest thing to a hell-bent stunt driver.

Once Ed Ubal had almost tripped him up. Ed, who was a fat man of forty, invited Stewart over for a picnic to meet his wife. Ubal sat around guzzling beer and Stewart didn't do too badly himself. Then Ubal's two sons, fifteen and seventeen, roared up on the new Yamahas their father had gotten at a discount at the plant and Ed bragged before them how Stewart was such a tough, hard rider.

Stewart had sat in a sweat remembering all the lies he had spread at the plant about racing in his teen-age days and now these boys were putting him to the test, shoving his back against the wall. He had finally pleaded drunkenness though Ed Ubal sensed his fear. Stewart walked back to his car at the end of the day, staggering with exaggeration, desperate to save his face.

The constant roar of the production line could be heard even through the supposedly soundproof doors. Reggino swung them back and took his post, acknowledging the friendly greetings from the other men. He worked on the Yamaha cycle moving assembly line. He had been a steady, serious worker for two years now and had been made foreman of the rubber tire and wheel sub-assembly line where he supervised the men and made sure that the wheel and tire alignment was correct and the assembly properly balanced. Not the most patient boss, he was very critical about the way the men installed the tires and he broke more than one worker's nerves by forcing him into a question and answer session about the technical aspects of the balancing equipment. It wasn't long before Stewart realized that the role of foreman was not for him and he requested a return to his original job which he missed very much. The request was granted.

Stewart went back to welding the body panels together, one of the very first jobs on the main assembly line. He loved the feel of getting down with his hands and the welding tools and actually forcing the metal together; this was the only way he could feel any sense of accomplishment. He needed to work with his hands, then stand back and admire the direct results of his labor.

Commuting from Manhattan to the New Jersey plant site took less then thirty minutes by car and Stewart didn't mind the drive. Working the night shift occasionally bothered him only because he found it difficult to fall asleep once the dawn had risen. But if he worked arduously with heavy concentration he usually was tired enough to drift off to sleep in the morning.

The plant had been converted from an airplane hangar shortly after World War II and prior to that had been a motion picture studio before Hollywood's glory. The glass panes had been painted black and the wood fireproofed and weather protected. The only thing that Stewart disliked was that it was so dark, even with the overhead bulbs and the jets from the torches. When he stared into the flames, then looked away, everything became black though he knew he should be seeing figures and the shapes of the cycle parts. It was better never to take his eyes from his torch; that way he wouldn't have to adjust his eyesight to the surrounding blackness only to experience those stabs of pain when he returned his gaze to the fiery, blinding jet.

Stewart spent a few hours crouched low on his ankles, welding maybe two or three cycle bodies before he took a coffee break. As it was, he shouldn't have bothered since the coffee tonight was instant and grainy besides.

He had to urinate; coming out of the bathroom as he was heading in was Al Blane, a fleshy black man who kept the others entertained during breaks by his constant stories, or his sleight of hand card tricks, or his expert throwing of jacks. Stewart went up to the urinal as Al paused in the doorway to welcome him back.

There was an incredible stench from the toilet behind him and Stewart felt his blood pressure boiling. He had had the misfortune to follow Al into the bathroom before and the smell the man left behind was always unbearable. Stewart held his breath so he wouldn't breathe the foulness. He blocked out the inanities Al was spewing. He quickly washed his hands and as he walked out the door Al patted him on the back while Stewart controlled himself from blurting, "God, your shit stinks."

As Stewart returned to his job he thought how he hated Al and the rest of the blacks on the line; they were always whining and wanting you to feel sorry for them just because of their color, because they had been slaves for hundreds of years. They always expected preferential treatment and talk was that they got better raises than the white guys. He only thought of them as niggers now. And that struck him as very odd because growing up on Long Island he had never been prejudiced, having had black buddies as close as any whites, but now he thought differently yet kept it to himself, not joining in the barbs with some of the other white guys.

The rain kept pelting the panes all through the night and into the morning when the dawn came grey and damp. The men pushed open the doors to the back yard and shivered and cursed; a wind had picked up which carried with it a chill that would have better befitted soggy November.

"Fuckin' Christ," one of them said, tossing his metal lunch-pail from one hand to the next, "I was gonna scramble some eggs out back this morning."

"The hell you were," came the response.

Stewart shut his tools in his locker, zipped his jacket to his chin and thrusting his hands in his pockets stomped through the mud to his car. There, leaning against the door, was one of the night accountants, Dorothy Pulley, a tiny redhaired girl whose glasses and clothes dwarfed her.

"Can you give me a lift? It's raining," she whined.

"I can see it's raining." *You dumb bitch,* he thought. "Get in." Dorothy had often begged rides from him, acting so mousy and demure, but Stewart had heard tales of how she threw her legs apart for the other guys who gave her rides home. It seemed just one or two drinks opened her up, then anyone could have her. One night, not long ago, she had been drinking before Stewart gave her a lift and she tried to get him to screw her right in front of her home almost before he had pulled the car to the curb. But he had shoved her out, disgustedly. And he had watched her crawl up the steps into the house. *That bitch has no pride,* he thought as he looked at the smokestacks along the highway. *I hate people without pride.* . . . Cars passed with their low headlights on and the factory smoke mixed with the clouds and the rain. Dorothy sat calmly with her hands folded in her lap and stared at the car in front of her.

She finally spoke. "Ever try to count how many license plates you see from different states as you drive home each morning?"

"No."

"Today we've passed Rhode Island, Pennsylvania, New York, South Carolina and, naturally, New Jersey."

Stewart didn't answer, but accelerated to cut ahead of the car in front whose driver, probably some salesman going to Manhattan, gave him the dirtiest look he'd had from another driver in months. He came to the exit which was only a few blocks from Dorothy's house and he swerved onto the ramp, then down to the first cross street.

"Look, Dorothy, you think you can walk from here? It's so much easier for me, if I just go through that underpass and get on the highway again."

"Yeah, sure," she sniffed disappointedly. "Anyway that Mr. Do-Nut place up there is just opening. I think I'll get some cinnamon twists and coffee before I go in the house." She slammed the door and Stewart pulled back onto the highway.

Renee returned to her room that evening at eight o'clock. She hadn't decided whether to open the door to Jake and, indeed, she hadn't thought about it all day as Bee had kept her completely occupied during their shopping spree for shoes. But now that she was back all she could think about was Jake Adams and as the hour passed and she finished making herself look as attractive as possible, she was overcome with the same anger she had felt earlier. Here she was, waiting — like a starry-eyed girl for her first date. What made this even worse was that while the date would surely appear to carry the starry-eyed girl to the dance, she wasn't sure at all that Jake would come as he said; there was no reason to come, no appearances to keep up, perhaps nothing to gain.

She had worn a loose fitting light blue cotton dress and had fastened a tiny red chain around her neck. The women on her floor had noticed that she looked prettier than usual and had been heaping lavish praise on her. This also made Renee uneasy. Why had she taken so much care to look softer, less flamboyant?

It was ten o'clock. Renee studied the traffic below, the headlights were like night rainbows, if she looked very closely she could see spheres of color around the bright white beams. She was suddenly hungry and thought of cheese and pears and cake. She switched on a lamp with a thin silk shade; her room might be small but the bed was sturdy, there was a nice bureau and dressing table, and plenty of closet space. There was even a book shelf filled with dusty old magazines which she hadn't bothered to investigate until now. She ran her hands over the titles and brushed away the dust, but they weren't at all interesting; a *Popular Mechanics*, three *McCall's*, several tennis magazines, and some *National Geographics* that were twenty-years-old. She wondered whose room this used to be. She paged through one of the *Geographics;* there was a story about camping in New England with faded photographs of boys hiking in the summertime in the Green Mountains of Vermont. They were carrying bulky back-packs, had crew cuts and were shirtless. She liked the chest on one of the boys; he had big nipples, firm and brown, as big as a woman's, perhaps bigger than hers. The color was so washed out, then she remembered that color photography wasn't very advanced twenty years ago, at least the colors didn't seem natural at all, but strained, as if you were seeing the world through the eyes of a visitor at a child's birthday party where everything was tinted pink, blue and royal gold, and she thought of the spheres of color around the headlights and she wondered what caused them and she wished she had paid more attention in science class years ago since there must have been an explanation, or at least a discussion, a lesson about color.

There was a knock at the door. Renee paused; her fingers nervously rubbed the edges of the *Geographic.* The knock was repeated, this time more loudly and insistently. She thought it must be Jake yet something stopped her from answering. She remained crouched. Renee heard footsteps moving away from the door and down the hall. Then she heard an exchange of muffled voices but she couldn't distinguish if they were male or female. Then there was silence. She replaced the *Geographic* on the shelf. A car honked twice outside her window, staccato sounds made by a furious driver.

Suddenly she ran out into the hall. Jake stood by the elevator talking to Bee.

They spotted Renee. "Can't you hear people knocking, darling?" Bee sniveled.

"Of course I can," Renee replied. "Why do you think I'm standing out here in the hall?"

Jake walked over and kissed her on the forehead. He laughed, "I'd given up, I thought you'd decided to go out for the evening on your own."

Renee resented his casualness. "People always seem to give up too easily, don't they? That's one of the facts of life you can count on."

"Cryptic," Jake murmured.

"Oh, she's in one of *those* moods," Bee cautioned him as she stepped into the elevator. "Glad it's you tonight and not me."

"Where's she going all bundled up like that, with a towel

around her head and a beach bag under her arm?" Jake asked
as soon as the door shut and the elevator began its descent.

"The communal shower. It's in the basement. Bee likes to
spend at least an hour gossiping down there each night and the
girls encourage her because the running water usually drowns
her out."

"Well," Jake put his arm around her waist and headed her
toward the room. "At least she warned me about you."

"No," Renee stopped him. "Let's not go back in there. Let's
walk."

"Where?" he asked with surprise.

"How about the 42nd Street pier? It's quiet there and we can
see if an ocean liner's leaving for Europe. You know, it's fun to
watch people throw the confetti."

Jake couldn't tell if she was being cynical or actually eager to
see such a spectacle. He decided not to press her about it but
just take the walk as she suggested.

"What shall we talk about?" Renee asked as she dangled her
legs off the pier and stared out at the dark Hudson River. "We
have to think of something since there aren't any boats leaving
tonight." She stared up at Jake who stood behind her playing
with the zipper on his summer jacket. "And for God's sake, sit
down. You make me nervous prowling around where I can't see
you."

"Let me alone a minute and I'll sit down, too. I'm taking
everything in."

"How do I know you're not some maniac who likes to
strangle girls and throw their bodies in the deep river?"

"*You* suggested coming here. I didn't."

"Ah, yes. Well, you got out of that one. . ."

Jake dropped beside her. "And I can get out of anything." He
paused. "There was a time when I couldn't be a part of anything that didn't leave me in a goddam mess. But now I've
changed things."

Renee pouted, as if she didn't believe him. "What messes?
You don't seem the type to get into messes."

"I was following everybody's advice — friends, parents,
teachers — trying to please the whole lot. My goals were theirs,
my life was theirs. And it took me a long time to start making my
own decisions about myself, only I still couldn't say 'no' to
people, I lied to them instead. Hence, the messes. But there
came a time when the dam had to break, when I had to stop

pretending to enjoy other people's dreams."

She moved closer to him so that their thighs met and began to stick in the humidity. "What kind of family do you come from?"

"Middle class. Maybe lower than middle," he admitted. "My dad was an electrician out on the Island and I was the oldest of six kids. Dad died when I was about sixteen and I had a lot of responsibilities — as you might imagine." He lit a cigarette and offered her one but she refused. She listened quietly. "I resented being the new head of the family. I resented it like hell. Some days I handled it O.K. and other days I blew it. . . Now, I'm on my own. My brothers and sisters are grown up, they've all left home, and Mom lives on the insurance policies Dad left and on what the rest of us send her."

"So it sounds like you have no worries now."

He shrugged.

There was a break in their conversation and each was appraising the other as far as they were able. Soon Jake began telling Renee about his job with the magazine; he described his apartment and some of his photographs. When he asked a few questions about her, she explained a bit of her background in terse, uneasy sentences.

"You don't like to talk about yourself, do you?" he finally confronted her.

"I don't mind," she rebuffed him. "It's just that it isn't too exciting, is it? I've told you all that's important to know about my family. What eles interests you?"

"How long have you been at the hotel?" he asked quickly. "And how did you discover it and decide to move there anyway?"

"I'm not sure I can answer the last part of your question; or at least I don't think I want to now. But I've been staying at the hotel for six months. Sometimes it seems more like six years."

"But you like it?"

"Yeah," she answered, making her eyes seem hard as diamonds and fixing her gaze directly on him. "I like it a lot."

"That's very strange," he commented in a low voice.

"Maybe not to me," she said defensively and moved her body away so that it was no longer touching his.

"Hey, wait a minute," he put his arm around her waist and moved her back against him. "Where are you going?"

She reached for his hand and one by one bent back his fingers until she was released, then she slid away again. But he pulled her against him. She only sighed this time as he bit her gently on the neck.

"What is it you want?" she said, exasperatedly.

He didn't answer but moved his lips to her throat and gave her a long kiss. She stared stonily at the black river without even a tug or small boat of any kind to focus on. Her hands gripped the dock. He opened her lips with his fingers, then kissed her, forcing his tongue to the back of her throat. But she remained icy. When he ended the kiss she said disgustedly, "Quit using me. I'm tired of it. You aren't interested in me. I'm just another trick."

Jake watched her with surprise, "I'm not using you, Renee. I thought you knew that. I could have left last night and never come back, but I wanted to come back, and I'll want to come back again."

"Yes, my dear," she responded sarcastically. "But there comes one morning when you don't come again. What then?"

"For Christ's sake, how do we know that?" he cried. "What's wrong with trying something?"

"Because it's never worth the effort," she replied. "It always ends the same way."

"What is it, then?" he stood up. "It's easier to take some guy up to your room for a night and then turn him out in the morning. Right?"

"You could say that," Renee stood as well and faced him. "And besides," she continued. "Who are you to criticize me or toss out disparaging remarks about my life?" A breeze stirred and her light blue dress rustled.

Jake thrust his hands in his coat pockets. "You're right," he mumbled. "I'm sorry. How about forgiving me for saying what I did?" She didn't answer. He put his hands on her shoulders. "Come back with me to my apartment tonight."

"No," she shook her head.

"Then let me go with you to the hotel. Let's not cut each other off like this."

She did want him to come back with her and, as suddenly and mysteriously as a lightning bolt will strike earth, an intense feeling crashed inside her, a desperate need for him to be with her tonight. But this need, seeming to appear from nowhere, was actually born within her, in her own heat and clouds, in her own untapped atmosphere. Her neck heaved. Jake studied the red necklace rising and falling with every breath she took. The red chain somehow touched him deeply. He brushed it with his thumb. "That's beautiful," he said.

There was a sudden intake of her breath. Then she unfastened the chain and held it, indecisively, then threw it into the water.

"It's because. . ." she responded to his astonished stare. "It's because," her voice quavered, "I never want to see it again. Never. . ." She brightened, even giggled. "Yes, come back with me to the hotel. We'll have a good time, that is if you think you can stand the heat. I don't even have a fan."

Chapter Five

Jake and Renee spent every night together for the next week. Some evenings they took long walks, joining the crowds in the Broadway theater district; other times they chose more isolated areas such as the well-kept streets around the United Nations and the East River or the empty stretches downtown near Chambers Street and City Hall.

As soon as work was over for the day Jake left immediately for the hotel and in the morning after a shower rushed back to his office; he didn't return to his own apartment until Saturday morning to gather some clothes which he needed for the new week. As he folded his shirts and put his socks in the suitcase pockets, he glanced at his mounted photographs. He wanted to take some pictures of Renee; he knew just the poses he wanted from her, the faraway expressions he hoped to catch. He saw them displayed on the wall before he had even pressed the shutter . . . he saw them cropped properly, the expressive lighting, the rich color, he saw the entirety of her face filling the frame. He shut his suitcase.

Looking outside he noticed Mrs. Block at her window across the way. Nothing had changed here. There was laughter from the park; the neighborhood children, engaged in pranks, were in their usual high spirits. So was he.

When he returned to the hotel room Renee sprang at him and pulled him down onto the bed, tickling and kissing him again and again. "Where were you?" she demanded. "What took you so long?"

Jake scoffed at her questions as he retaliated, digging into her ribs a little harder than was necessary until she screamed and begged him to stop. He lifted her on top of him and she nestled close, sitting on his waist.

"Now," he said. "Are you going to persist in asking these ridiculous questions so I can torture you some more or have you had enough and are you going to be quiet and behave?"

Renee forced his hands against the bed and pushed on them with all her strength.

"So you think I can't get out of that?" he asked.

"Of course you can," her voice softened. "But I'm going to tell you something before you do."

"What?"

"Can I tell you without being tickled?"

"Yes, if you'll only let me go." His eyes filled with mock tears. "Please, let me go, Renee."

She released his hands, then brushed his lips with her fingers. But she somehow couldn't form any words.

He waited impatiently. There was an uneasiness in the air. "What is it you were going to tell me?" He couldn't hide an eagerness, as in old movies when a man on the brink of being told where the gold is hidden continues to talk sweetly and act disinterestedly but the excitement and anticipation has crept into his body and the other person can tell. Renee could tell too. She played with the buttons on his shirt and wouldn't look into his eyes.

"Well, if you aren't going to say anything. . ."

She looked up. "I was just going to chide you again for taking so much time at your apartment."

"That's all?" He was disappointed.

"Yes. That's all." Then she added, "It was unfair of you to be gone so long. I missed you."

"And I missed you," he sat up and closed her in his arms. "But I was only gone an hour or two and I asked you to come with me."

They held each other and watched the bubbles of sunlight float through the air. The room was warm and cheery and the sun made the mirror on the bureau so bright that it seemed less a mirror than a silver shield, too intense to look into.

"How different things look in daylight," Renee mused.

"Sure. I don't know why it is, but at night you can be so depressed — utterly miserable — and you think the world or at least your world is coming to an end, and then with the first streaks of dawn you wonder what the hell you were thinking about. . . Funny the sun is responsible for making us feel better," he chuckled, "when it's an unfriendly, all-consuming fiery monster. . ." He ran his hand through her hair.

"Time for my pills," Renee searched in the bureau. The pill-box was in the bottom drawer under a stack of old letters. "If I would only learn to put it in the same spot each day. . ."

"What are the pills for?"

She swallowed several and in between mouthfuls said, "For nerves. They just get me floating a little."

"Well . . . you've taken your pills . . . you've rested and straightened the apartment. What would you like to do now?"

"I wouldn't mind something to eat."

"Renee!" came a voice from outside the door followed by five quick taps. "It's me, honey, open up!"

Renee shook her head in dismay and shrugged at Jake, forming the word "Bee" silently on her lips.

"Renee," Bee burst into the room. "Oh, hello," she noticed Jake, then seized Renee by the shoulders. "Pandora has to go to the doctor's and there's nobody to help me take her and I'm not strong enough to support her whole weight by myself. Feel like helping out?"

"Can't Donny help you get her into a cab? Isn't he behind the desk?"

"He is and I went to him first but you know what an unco-operative s.o.b. he is. He claims he can't get out of his chair or he'll get the axe."

"I can help," Jake offered.

"Good," Bee declared. "It won't take long. Renee, honey, are you coming too?"

"Oh, I guess not. Jake can probably manage better without me."

"Girl, that's not a healthy attitude," Bee scolded. "You let him out of your sight like that and next thing you know he'll be having a torrid affair with Pandora."

Jake and Renee laughed uneasily.

"Oh, maybe that wasn't the right thing to say," Bee searched their faces.

Jake blushed a deep red and Renee folded her arms and said angrily, "Don't be so stupid, Bee! Go on. You have to get her to the doctor, don't you?"

Bee winked at Jake. "Come on. See you soon, Renee." She led Jake down the hall and into the elevator. Renee closed the door after them and leaned against it. She felt numb. The room seemed incredibly empty. A mosquito was hovering over the pillows. She watched it glide for about five minutes, following it with her eyes so that she wouldn't lose sight of it and later have it bite her from its hiding place. It was only a matter of time before the insect was drawn towards her. When it was about to inspect her face she brought up her hand and grabbed it. When she opened her fist there was a tiny speck of blood and crushed wings.

Bee Crockett was a riddle. No one honestly knew if she was as dumb as she acted or as blank as she looked. In a group she would talk excessively and mindlessly and then become silent; her false eyelashes would flutter and she's itch herself and twist the strings of her dyed blonde hair and pull her tight, sticky skirt away from her thighs. If she caught someone staring at her she would scream at them, "That's right, nobody lives here."

Her reputation as the house clown was well founded and deserved. A favorite story the whores liked to tell was about the time Bee took some cops upstairs in the elevator. She was trying her best to be seductive and she murmured sensually, "Hey, boys, want me to cuck your socks?" No one could believe what they had heard and there was a deadly stillness. Then the cops began to guffaw and so did the other girls. Bee was mortified and her eyes became wild with fury and she spat at her friends, "Why do I always have to ride with a goddam carload of bitches?" But by the time the elevator doors opened Bee was laughing the loudest and she didn't calm down the whole night . . . at two and even four A.M. the laughter from her room rang through the halls.

Bee and Jake helped Pandora to the street. It was still painful for her to use crutches since her shoulder muscles had become strained, so Bee convinced her to leave them by the bed and to lean on the two of them.

Pandora was a slight girl with amber, curly hair which fell to her shoulders. She had freckles and crooked teeth, the combination of which was very attractive. Her room was filled with tables covered with long, hot cloths on which she and the other girls played ouija and Scrabble and on which she read their fortunes with her deck of special cards. Dim colored bulbs flickered beneath dense shades.

She had never said much about her accident and she was

always smiling. She acted no differently than usual although both Jake and Bee noticed her hands tighten on their shoulders when they approached the elevator and there was fear in her eyes when the door drew back. She was remembering.

At the curb Pandora clung to Jake while Bee hailed a taxi. "This is very kind of you, Jake," she said and patted his shoulder.

"Don't think anything about it," he assured her.

The doctor's office was located in New York Hospital which had all the x-ray and surgical equipment necessary to treat her. She was put on a bed soon after her arrival and wheeled to an operating room where several doctors could better assess her condition. A young intern held her hand and drew her into conversation as he pushed the moving bed past Jake and Bee waiting in the doctor's office.

Bee smoked several cigarettes and leafed through a magazine while Jake found the cafeteria and carried back some coffee.

"Did you bring cream?" Bee asked.

"Yeah. Just a second," he searched in his pants and produced the small packet.

"I can't stand it black," Bee made a face and emptied the cream into the cup.

Several hours passed and there was still no sign of the patient.

"Gosh," Bee remarked as Jake paced. "I had no idea it would take this long. Wonder what they're doing to her. I wonder what they can do."

"I don't know," Jake yawned.

"Poor Pandora," Bee continued, going to the window and watching the young nurses and doctors filing through the courtyard below, "her Box is a little hollower now than it used to be. Knock on wood."

"You certainly have a way of saying things," Jake sat back down and turned his attention to a nurse who was scolding a boy for delivering the inter-hospital mail late.

"Sorry," Bee whined.

It wasn't until sundown that Pandora was wheeled back to the office. Bee was up to the bed at once.

"What happened?" she insisted. "Did they do anything?"

"I come back next week," Pandora replied as the intern helped her to the floor. "Though it looks like this will be my permanent leg — if they can keep it on me and if it stays comfortable enough."

On the way home Bee rode in the front seat with a cab driver who was charmed by her, while Jake and Pandora sat in the back. Pandora stretched her wooden leg so that it took half of Jake's space and he had to cross his legs at an odd angle. But he didn't mind. Bee was discussing some city problem but Jake could only half hear her since the sound of the wind and the rushing traffic was drowning her out. Then from the woman next to him came a low drawl, "Reporter, huh?"

He turned to her. She was smiling at him almost suspiciously, her lips partly opened. It seemed she was laughing at him.

"Yeah," he answered. "That's right."

"What story are you working on now?"

"At the moment I'm on a photographic assignment in the Garment District."

"You should do a story about the hotel. I guess you know a lot about it."

"I don't pay much attention to what goes on around there." He watched the crowds pouring in and out of the cheap stores on 42nd Street and he noticed pushers and bums in the park next to the public library.

"I guess Renee keeps you pretty busy," her voice was lower than before and her smile was even stranger, only partly there.

"We have some breathing room."

"That's good. That's wonderful."

"It's working out."

"I bet Renee is really proud to be seen with you."

"How do you mean that?" Jake was becoming increasingly uncomfortable.

"What did you play in school? Football? Baseball?"

"A little of everything."

"A little of everything . . ."she repeated slowly. "A change has come over her. I mean, she must love to walk around town with you. I know her. It must be a thrill to hang on the arm of a nice handsome guy with a big strong build. I know her."

"She's very attractive herself."

"Oh, of course. . . But she's got problems. . . Who hasn't?" she laughed and tapped her leg. "This is my problem."

Jake didn't know whether to say it certainly was a problem or to say no, it wasn't as bad as she thought. Instead he said nothing and wished that they would get to the hotel.

"She's lucky, isn't she?"

"What do you mean?" he was losing patience.

"I just want to hear you say that she's lucky."

Jake turned and looked out the window. In a moment he felt her hand tapping his shoulder and when he turned she had it poised in mid-air, offering it to him. He shook it.

"My name is Angela Bowman," she said.

Suddenly the taxi swerved. It had come up too far on the tail of a truck and to avoid smashing into the back the driver had darted into the next lane forcing another car up against the curb. Pandora cried out as her wooden leg was thrust against the seat. The driver waited until the truck passed, then he crept back like a guilty animal into his own lane, wiping his brow with a dirty handkerchief.

"That's what happens when you look at women," he cursed at Bee.

"Oh, I see, you're blaming me!"

"You're goddam right I am!" He stopped abruptly across the street from the hotel. "I can't turn around. Impossible," he muttered. "You'll have to get over there on your own."

"Look," Bee quipped. "It's not my fault that your mind wasn't on your driving! You were too busy telling me about how young you feel even though you've been married twenty-five years . . . I got news for you, baby, you're only as young as you look."

Jake had only one regret about his relationship with his father. There had never been any real love between them or even much comradeship, but it had never mattered much to either one. There was no time. The family was too large; it was hard living from day to day attempting to eke out a living. But at his father's funeral there was a lump in his throat, not caused by the sorrow of death, but by the recollection of a shameful incident.

When Jake was sixteen he became, for him, daringly rebellious. All his life he had been a model child, dutifully studying the violin, eagerly preparing for his lessons and recitals; he had been a fine student and he was superior in sports. His mother spoiled and pampered him and his father, while not affectionate, bragged about him to his friends when the situation called for it. Ray Adams never saw his son as a separate person — only as an extension of himself — a worthier extension — and he took it for granted that Jake would always be concerning himself with setting a fine example for his younger brothers and sisters. But lately Jake had stopped seriously pursuing the goals he and his parents had set. He was staying out late with friends, questioning "the meaning of existence" on his way from one party to another.

One spring evening the family gathered as usual at the dinner table to find that Jake was not present. He arrived at the end of the meal and stumbled sullenly into his waiting chair without a word. His mother said nothing but kept her eyes on the food that she was serving him. But his father began to seethe, yielding to a slow building rage.

"Where have you been to stroll in so late and not let anybody know about it?" Ray spat the question at him. Jake didn't answer; he accepted his plate from his mother. "We waited forty-five minutes for you," Ray continued. "Is that fair to your mother? She's reheated your food three times — been up and down to the stove during the whole meal."

"Sorry," Jake mumbled across to his mother.

"It's all right," she quickly replied.

"It's not all right," Ray insisted. "Do you think you're the only child in this family? There are five others at this table who always are waiting for your every move like you were some queen. You always come first."

Jake slammed his knife hard on the table. He looked into his father's face which was a furious pink, the veins pulsating. "Look," Jake's words came embarrassingly slow like the water from a tap that keeps dripping. "I didn't know it was that late or I'd have called."

"What are you — drunk?" his father shouted.

"No!" Jake cried although he was light-headed and feeling the effect of a pint of gin.

"Who were you with just now? That Reggino boy?"

"What if I was? Is that a crime? I've know him all my life."

"Sure, but he's changed in the last couple years. He's turned into a bum just like his father. Is that the kind of guy you think is neat?"

"Ray, please," his wife cautioned. "Let's talk about this another time."

"No," Jake snapped belligerently. "If you have something to say, say it now." He was suddenly as angry as his father. They stared at each other across the table like two mortal enemies who had been waiting for this confrontation all their lives. There was no trace of the binding blood of father and son.

"Stand up!" Ray ordered as he staggered to his feet. "Stand

up, I said!" Mary Adams gasped and hid her face in her hands while her other children watched, transfixed. Jake made no move. His father grabbed him by the collar and pulled him forcibly to his feet. "You want to be a bum, be one, but not in front of your brothers and sisters, not in this house!"

He swung his arm back, taking aim at Jake's face. In a flash Jake threw his arm up to protect himself and stumbled backwards. Ray's swing missed, striking only the air. Jake backed into a corner, his arm still protecting his face. His father came at him. Suddenly Jake hissed and bared his teeth like a wolf at bay. His hand came down from his eyes and as his father reached him Jake swung back and belted him across the face.

All was quiet. Ray swayed, his head reeling. Jake stared incredulously. He realized he hadn't just slapped his father; somehow he had formed a fist and had hit him, hard. And what was worse he had no intention of helping the man to a chair, he almost hoped that the blow would bring him to his knees. But Ray steadied himself against a chest and threw a quick glance at Jake; his expression at that moment was not hurt or guilt or hate, but fear. His face was that of a man afraid, a man who would not go after his son again for fear of being beaten. Ray rubbed himself and a little smile came to his face as he looked at each of the children around the table with apologetic eyes, as if he hadn't been able to protect them from something. Jake uttered a hoarse cry and ran from the house.

He called Stewart from the pay phone booth three blocks from his house.

"I've got to talk," Jake stammered, out of breath. "It's really important."

"O.K., calm down, man, I'm available. I was only in the back working on my Riviera. I'm covered with all kinds of grease and shit, so why don't you come on over here?"

"No . . . no. I feel like getting away from the neighborhood. You know that hill above town? That high mound with the blueberry bushes? Let's meet there."

Stewart was silent, then after considering the urgency in his friend's tone replied that he would leave for the spot at once. Jake replaced the receiver and paused, panting for breath. He was thankful that Stewart would meet him. He left the booth and began running through the streets, past familiar homes and stores, down the roads of cement and bricks that he had run along all these years, but everything seemed slightly strange now and he had the feeling that the neighborhood had been holding something back from him, that it hadn't revealed its true, its whole character. He tried to stop his mind from wandering and he concentrated on running, following with his eyes one foot after another, appreciating the swift, light feeling of his gym shoes as they stroked the surface and carried him on.

At last he threw himself on the young grass at the very top of the hill just as in the distance the sun was sinking into the bay and throwing the town into shadow. Soon he heard branches breaking and saw Stewart emerge from a blueberry thicket, the last of the sun illuminating the car grease and grime covering his bare neck, his jacket and his pants. Stewart knelt by his friend to find him shivering, his attention focused on nothing in particular. He pulled him to a sitting position.

"It was terrible," Jake muttered, looking wildly into Stewart's eyes. "I punched my dad in the face."

"Is that all?" Stewart said reassuringly but he couldn't hide his surprise.

"Come on," Jake chided, agonized.

"How did it happen?" Stewart's voice was soft now.

"It happened so quick, it beats me. All I remember was him getting ready to belt me . . . and I thought, 'It's either him or me. . .' And I guess I decided it wasn't going to be me."

"Well, then, it was self-defense. You were just protecting yourself."

"But it was in front of my mother and brothers and sisters. I should have taken it," he said sadly. "I just should have taken it."

Stewart cleared away a muddy branch and a few rocks and sat down next to Jake. He studied the darkening landscape for awhile then said, "You know something. You're a man now. What you did, you had to do. A man has to make those choices. . . But you know, if you stand up and say, 'I'm a man,' you have to take the responsibility that goes along with it. Understand?"

Jake shook his head, "You mean I should go away now and live on my own money?"

"No, I don't mean that. You just have to be honest with yourself and let everybody know it. That way, nobody's going to mess you up. Ever since I've known you, you've been trying to please everybody but yourself. You see," his eyes narrowed, "I quit doing that a long time ago. Now people know where I stand. I come and go where and when I please. I earn my own way working on people's cars. My dad could tell me to get the hell out anytime, but he doesn't, because I'm taking care of myself. He hates my guts, but he wants me around. See, when you make yourself useful, people want you around, no matter what."

"Yeah, but I don't know where to find a job."

"Let me talk to the guys at the repair yard and see if they could use an extra hand in the afternoon."

Jake felt the first relief of the entire day. He responded gratefully, "Do you think you could?"

"Sure."

"Only . . . I don't know that much about fixing cars the way you do."

"I'll teach you the basic things you've got to know. Believe me," he started to laugh, "if I can do it, it's not that hard."

Jake laughed along with him, though his laughter was controlled and hesitant. "What would really be nice would be to do one thing well — one little, simple thing that no one else can do as good as you. The violin. It's not me. My teacher knows it and I know it. Nobody else knows or cares," he sighed. "If I could find one thing to be good at." A crescent moon appeared over the tip of some strong old oaks. "I want a camera so bad and I want to take pictures. All kinds of pictures. Pictures of that moon up there. I'd take maybe fifty, all in a row, and one of those shots, I promise you, would be good. It wouldn't even matter if there was nothing else in my life . . . if one of those pictures would turn out to be good."

"Well, get yourself a fucking camera then. There's no law against going into a store and buying one," Stewart scratched his shoulderblade, digging his nails deep into his skin. "You can take some practice shots of me working on my car."

"Sounds good," Jake agreed.

"All right, then leave this guilt behind you, right here on this hill. Don't carry it on your back. There's enough there already and there'll be more on the way."

They shared some cigarettes in the dark and drank some of the gin from the bottle Stewart kept in his coat.

"Don't that feel good going down?" Stewart chuckled.

"Yeah," Jake answered as he took another gulp.

"Hey, man, haven't we had some great times up here on this hill? Plenty of ghosts around."

"Some I wouldn't mind seeing again and others — no way!"

Rocking with laughter they fell onto their backs. They worked themselves up into hysterics as they reminisced about the times they used to hide up here from Jake's brothers and sisters; the time they blindfolded a classmate they hated, then disappeared after telling him not to remove the cloth for twenty minutes; the time they put up a tent and huddled inside, braving a fierce electrical storm all night long; the time they coaxed two girls up here and made them kiss them; the times they would come up and talk about the world in general or their own problems and relax, safe from the town.

When it was almost midnight and they had nearly talked themselves to death, Jake stood. "If I'm not back by twelve, I'll probably get locked out of the house. Or maybe they've already sent the cops after me."

Suddenly there seemed to be a mystery to the night, some riddle. There was a faint scent of crushed blueberries; both of their shirts were brightly stained.

"God," Jake concluded. "We must have rolled into the bushes!"

Stewart pushed his hand deep into Jake's and kept it there, pressing harder and harder. Then he marched away and Jake, very moved, trudged down the hill towards home.

Within a year Jake's father died of leukemia. Several weeks after the funeral, when Jake realized that his father knew that he was dying at the time of their fight, he was overcome with misery and didn't leave his bed for an entire week. Eventually he decided that his father would want him to be on his feet, looking after the family, so he badgered Stewart about a job in the repair yard and Stewart, in a sluggish, lazy mood at the time, was at first very annoyed, but within a few weeks procured an afternoon job for Jake who in the next several years never missed a day of work and was never late to the job even by a few minutes.

On Sunday Jake and Renee woke at noon after a dronish morning of half-hearing the bells peal every hour from dozens of churches scattered over Manhattan's West Side. This enduring clamor only made them determined to sleep longer and to snuggle against each other more closely.

In the early afternoon, since the air was dry and the sky blue, holding a few puffy, harmless clouds, they decided to find a cafe

tucked away somewhere and have an omelette and some wine.
But too many others had the same idea and after fighting
through swarms of pedestrians and discovering that all cafes,
even the tucked away ones, were crammed, they grabbed a
sandwich at a deli and returned to the hotel where Renee, hit
with a brainstorm, decided to give Jake a tour of parts of the
hotel he had never seen.

"Well, come on," she implored him. "You act as if you don't
want to see!"

The stolen merchandise was stockpiled in the basement.

"I'm one of the few with keys to this room," Renee confided
in him as she opened a rusty spiked door adjacent to the
elevator. "Back of us, down the hall, are showers and lockers for
the girls. But in here, nobody goes. . ." She felt for a switch on
the wall and light from about ten naked bulbs on crisscrossed
strings glared down on wood crates and cardboard boxes
loaded with silver, and expensive clothing, sophisticated video
and motion picture equipment, television sets, even microwave
ovens.

Jake whistled.

"You won't tell, will you?"

Jake gazed at her, perplexed. "I suppose not. If you ask me
not to. But did you steal some of these things, Renee?"

"Oh, no. I've never stolen anything. I'm just keeping a
secret, that's all."

"Keeping it for whom?" There was no response. "Who are
you protecting?"

She ran her hand along the top of a television set. "Just
someone. He trusted me with a key. And I check the supply for
him sometimes, to make sure that the cops aren't taking too
much of it home, you know, for their own friends and families. I
think Pandora's the only other woman in this place that he let
have a key. *She* takes things though, I've seen them in her
room."

"But you don't?"

"Oh, no," she said lightly. "These things don't interest me.
None of them." She walked over to a far corner and pulled a
shedding red rug off the top of a box. "Look," she motioned for
him to join her. "It's a small safe. It's unlocked." She swung
back the metal door and there was a succession of small drawers
which she pulled out one by one. "Jewelry. . ." The variegated
selection of gems was astonishing: rubies, diamonds, sapphires
cast into rings and necklaces, adorning watches, even loose and

alone. "I could steal any of them, if I wanted. But I don't like jewelry. Never have." She slammed the door.

"Who stole these things?" he asked.

"The cops. About seven are in on it from what I can figure out. I sometimes hear them moving around down here at night."

"Renee," he dismissed her remark in exasperation, "it's impossible to hear them moving down in the basement from your room on the fifth floor!"

"I guess I must dream I hear them. In the dead of night. But I have seen them loading the stuff on the elevator. It's because they forgot to unlock it and send it back up that Pandora had her accident."

"Well, what's in all this for you, Renee? You don't join in the thieving, you aren't in on the take. . ."

"I don't know," she was confused. "At first it was a little exciting. But now. . ."

"Frankly," he said. "This has the earmarks of an incredibly petty organization. It's very small time." He wanted to make her feel foolish. His words produced the effect.

"It does seem dull now. Stupid." She passed her hand over her brow. "Maybe it seemed so different because I didn't know you then, Jake," her lips trembled. "I waited at night hoping one or two of them would find their way to my room after they'd finished unloading. . ."

"What — so that you could feel degraded?" His tone was harsh. "So you could despise yourself afterwards?"

"Let's get out of here." A strain of confidence had returned to her voice. "It's so goddam hot. You've seen it all."

Later that afternoon, Renee sat by the window painting her toenails and Jake lay in bed cleaning his camera and accessories. While holding one of his lenses up to check for grease spots, his eyes happened to fix upon a discolored square on the ceiling.

"Ever noticed that square right above your bed?"

"What square?" She rested the polish on the floor and lay back on the bed. He tilted her face so she would see it. "Oh . . . that? I don't think I ever noticed. It's probably just a stain."

Jake removed his shoes and stood on the mattress. "It's not," he tapped the ceiling. "It's hollow. Can't you hear it?"

"I suppose so."

"It's been carefully cut. It must be an access to the attic."

"I never even knew there was an attic."

Jake pushed on the square. "All these old buildings have attics." But his weight didn't move it.

"Maybe you shouldn't do that," Renee suggested. "The whole ceiling might come down on us."

"No," he shoved the square disgustedly. "This is just a light piece of wood. It's stuck. But it's budging." He worked for several more minutes trying to dislodge it. Finally, with an adrenalin-filled thrust, he pushed the square out and layers of dust showered down on him.

"Look at the mess!" Renee cried.

"It's all right," he insisted. "It's light up there. The sun must be coming through a window, though I can't quite get my head high enough to have a good look."

"There's a ladder in the basement," Renee said and Jake went in pursuit of it. On his return he pushed the bed to one side and stood the ladder against the hole in the ceiling. Then he climbed through the square and Renee could hear his steps creaking above her. He called for her to come up, held the ladder tightly and lifted her as soon as he could reach her waist.

It was a pygmean space, where a window on the west permitted light to fill the little area.

"This place is for dwarves," she said, astonished.

"No," Jake corrected her, "I imagine it's for pigwidgeons."

"Pigwidgeons? You made that up."

"No, I didn't. It's an elf, a sprite. Somebody like you."

Renee sneezed. Thick dust was the carpet, and white cobwebs hung from the window. Against one wall was an old bed without a mattress, the iron rusted, the springs drooping, and next to it a chest of drawers. There was no other furniture.

"It was someone's bedroom!" Renee exclaimed.

Jake laughed. "You thought you were so smart showing me through secret rooms. You had no idea that one was above your very head."

"Don't tease me."

"Why shouldn't I? You deserve it."

"Bastard," she pulled open one of the drawers in the rotting chest.

"That's an old sailor's mug," Jake declared, peering over her shoulder at the contents of the drawer. She handed it to him. "I haven't seen one like this for years. It's probably worth something."

"No one's been up here for years." She studied several coins.

He took them from her and rubbed his spit hard on their surfaces so he could try to read the dates that were obscured by muck.

"These are filthy as hell," he remarked. "They've reached the stage where they're green and powdery. Wait a minute. The date's coming though on this penny . . . 1909. Incredible." He found that this first penny was the most recent coin, the half dozen others marked with dates a few years prior to it.

Rummaging through the bottom drawer Renee found a child's bedcap and pyjamas. And to Jake's delight she also found a kaleidoscope which still worked. As he held it to the window and rotated the edge, enjoying the frenzied colors and designs, he told her how, on his sixth birthday, his grandfather had given him a beautiful kaleidoscope. Within days he had lost it. He had hurried to the dime store to buy another but all he found were cheap paper jobs. It had been a terrible blow to find that his misplaced toy had been an antique.

"I've been trying to find an authentic one ever since. They just aren't made anymore."

"Well, you have one now."

"Yeah. I think I'll have this one insured. Or put in a bank vault."

"It would be safer up here than anywhere. Who else could find this room?"

He set the kaleidoscope on the chest. Then he carefully studied the surroundings. Finally, "Don't you see?"

"See what?" she crossed her arms suspiciously.

"That bed. Look at the size of it. And look at the items we discovered."

"It's a child's bed," she answered. "And these were his things."

"Right! But why would anyone keep a child up here, hidden above the ceiling? The family must not have wanted its existence known. The child must have been deformed or sickly or retarded. The poor thing probably spent its days holding this very kaleidoscope and running its fingers through these pennies." Jake was satisfied with his theory.

"It does make sense," Renee bit her fingernails. "At least I couldn't think of a better explanation . . . and the sailor's mug . . . do you think a seaman's family lived down below?"

"Hard to tell." He laughed. "Someone could have bought that mug at a five and dime store on any odd Sunday."

They continued a spirited exploration of the room until, at last, the fiery, dusty air overpowered them, forcing them back down to her room. But it was hardly more comfortable there. For several days Jake had been promising to buy a fan, just to move the air around the bed. "It'll still be hot and sticky tonight," he warned. "I'll go out and try to find one now. I think that appliance store is open down the block."

"All right," Renee replied. "I'm going to put some milk down for the cat." They walked together to the elevator.

"I may take a short stroll as well," he announced.

She paused. "Don't be too long."

"I won't be."

"You know, you were gone forever yesterday when you and Bee took Pandora to the hospital."

He stepped into the elevator. "Couldn't be helped."

"Of course not," she answered as the door closed. "I just wondered, that's all."

As Jake inspected each fan on the shelf he thought of Renee and how good she made him feel; he imagined her waiting for him now, how satisfied she would be when he returned and how beautiful she would feel to him as he took her in his arms.

He selected an inexpensive model, paid the salesman in cash, waited for the man to tie a handle to the top, then wandered into the Garment District, deliberating about which photographs to use with his article. . .

He returned to find the bedroom empty. Jake called Renee but she didn't answer. He wondered if she had gone out or if she could be visiting one of the other women. Then he heard sounds from the attic: feet moving swiftly. The mystery was solved. He plugged in the fan, then carried it with him into the attic where he set it on the floor. The room was filled with a lustrous gold light — the sun was setting and its perfect orb was framed by the window. Renee had swept dust from some of the floorboards and she was dancing, naked, on the dull wood, her carmine toe polish looking like continuous blood drops spraying the floor. In front of her chin she held a tired old silk Chinese fan which depicted mountains and rivers and flowers. Renee's expression was petulant; she forced Jake to look deep into her eyes.

The fan stirred the unhealthy air and froze the sweat patches that were drifting down both of their faces. Renee continued to whirl about the room and Jake sat down on the floor in front of her, watching, his hands clasped behind his head. Once when she stepped close to him he reached out and grabbed her ankle; then he bit her heel, then her knee, then her stomach. She dropped down across his shoulders and pulled his shirt up from behind and touched her tongue to his hot back; as he waited in silence she moved her tongue from the nape of his neck to the small of his ass, then back up through his blond hair.

Chapter Six

"What do you know about electricity, Renee?" Roger Fourne inquired casually as he removed his silk sport shirt and hung it thoughtfully in the closet.

"Absolutely nothing," Renee finally replied, lounging on a sofa reading a fashion magazine, her back to him and her voice remote. "I know how to plug in a lamp. That's about it."

"Exactly. . ." He slipped out of his white cotton pants and inspected them for stains. Finding none, he placed them on a hanger and stored them at the back of the closet. He then examined his legs; their whiteness made him wince. He couldn't remember the last time he had exposed them to direct sunlight. Heavy black hairs traveled down his calves and gave the impression of new tar highways in snow country as seen from the air. He shrugged capriciously at the image as he dropped his shorts and packed them tightly in a laundry bag filled with dozens of other pairs. He poured himself a shot of vodka and downed it.

"Want something to drink?" he called to Renee who waved a refusal.

Fourne screwed the top on the bottle and replaced it on the shelf, then moved to the sofa and stood nude in front of her. He removed the magazine from her hands and placed it face down on the table so that all that was visible was the back cover displaying women of Paris running in the spring rain bearing multi-colored vinyl umbrellas.

"Ready?" he asked.

"Yes." She stretched sluggishly, then followed him through his vast penthouse which ostensibly overlooked the East River yet provided views of all corners of Manhattan. As Renee drifted through the corridor she caught a glimpse of the Chrysler Building radiating in the dark through one of the southwest windows; it was the skyscraper she preferred to any other . . . it was majestic, symmetrical, perfect.

Fourne switched on the mild overhead lights in the bathroom. The room was incredibly chic, spacious, decorated in black and white except for the somber lemon tiles imported from Yugoslavia. The wall was a world of solid mirrors. A standing steep white tub supported by minute ivory legs graced the center of the room. The toilet, clean and shiny, stood opposite against the wall. Several thick dark carpets had been scattered on the tiles, seemingly dropped at random yet in reality purposefully arranged for maximum aesthetic value.

"Everything in here is so easy on the eye," Renee checked her long red garters and spiked high heels in the mirror.

Fourne, as if reading her mind, reassured her, "You look perfect, Renee. Don't give your appearance a second thought."

But it was him she was studying. Even though she met him at least once a week, at each encounter she had to reacquaint herself with his appearance since in the interim she had forgotten his features absolutely. To Renee he fell into a bland, somewhat dreary category; there was no sharpness either in his figure or personality. The only thought she ever had about his body was that his ruddy eyebrows and pale complexion seemed incompatible with his black chest hairs. His age was unclear and, she reasoned, unimportant.

Fourne had picked her up in an East side bar one late afternoon last autumn. They had talked for several hours quite superficially; he making asinine statements and she, in an argumentative mood, nastily refuting everything he said. But he coaxed her into a rendezvous the next afternoon . . . she was to be waiting by the fountain in front of the Plaza Hotel at three o'clock.

Out of boredom Renee kept the appointment, though throughout the morning she had debated visiting her mother instead. Unfortunately at three a thunderstorm struck and Renee, in blue jeans and a sweater, with a morning newspaper over her head, danced from one foot to the other in tremendous agitation, watching the rain swell the water in the fountain, until a limousine driven by a wizened chauffeur pulled to the curb and Fourne himself threw open the back door. Renee, soaking wet, crawled onto the seat next to him.

The remainder of the day was spent dashing from shop to shop, furnishing Renee with a new wardrobe. To her astonishment he insisted on buying her as many expensive articles as she desired; her whim was rule and as she selected evening gowns which she would never wear, or negligees to fill three closets, or enough shoes that she need never buy another pair in her lifetime, she remained very cool and purposely acted blasé and fatigued. He spent between five and ten thousand dollars on her and she never thanked him as she realized he was benefiting from this exploit more than she.

She had then become a kind of mistress to him. His sexual appetites were nearly as unusual and bottomless as her own, so one night each week she arrived at his apartment to play a fantasy, always of his choosing. She asked little in return. He gave her the room at the hotel which he owned and saw that she had credit cards and enough cash to survive. She refused to accept gifts beyond these offerings. It had always been a source of pride to her that she didn't need the material extravagances that others searched for all their lives or were furnished with at birth. If Fourne were vastly rich she wished for none of the fortune, though she sometimes contemplated the strange enterprises with which he was involved. She refused to discuss his dealings, but from overhearing some of his phone conversations she realized he owned much property and was involved with judges and policemen in theft rings. But this business held no attraction for her and she rarely gave his activities a passing thought. She held his trust, perhaps because of her overwhelming disinterest.

"Have enough money these days?" Concerned, he faced her, his hands on his hips. "You're getting along O.K.?"

"Yes," she mumbled. "Everything's fine." Her eyes fell to the tiles which were gleaming just enough to cast soft reflections of her high heels. "But these goddam tiles are so slippery, I wish you'd install a bar in here so I could hold onto it."

"You mean something like girls use for ballet exercises?" he snorted.

"Why not?"

"That would be interesting," he laughed. "I think I'll put one in."

She had no ingenious response. She just stared. He adjusted the light so that it became quite delicate, and Renee, as tired as she was, found that her face glowed and her head seemed to hover apart from her body.

Again he read her thoughts. "Nice, isn't it? The light in here . . . is beautiful." He added, "When I'm with you, I let everything out." He placed his hands on her shoulders and pushed her firmly to her knees. He tossed his head back. A lengthy groan of relief, much as an athlete gives at the end of a grueling race, escaped from his lips. "You're such a wonderful slave, Renee." His voice choked. "I thank God He sent you to me."

Renee would usually laugh hatefully to herself to hear him utter something so ridiculous, but for some reason, tonight, it embarrassed her, the words haunted her, and she wasn't able to immediately forget them.

"The cabinet . . ." he motioned and she leaned across the tiles and opened the bottom drawer of a vanity chest and rummaged until she found a slender piece of rubber. She turned on the tap of the high tub and let the water run until it became the right warm temperature, then she rinsed the rubber patch and scoured it with soap. Yet she felt she was working in slow motion; she couldn't decide what was wrong. It had been previously decided that there was to be no sex tonight; that was why she had allowed herself to come. Otherwise she would have offered some excuse to Fourne as she was determined to sleep only with Jake.

The sunny water soaked her hands. She felt she was sleeping with Jake now; she saw him looking up at her from the splendid tiles below; his face was everywhere; she could feel his warmth take the room, his breath stir the water. Fourne propped his foot on the rim of the tub. "Don't forget to spend a lot of time between each toe."

"I know," she said and began to clean his foot with the small rubber piece. There . . . as she rubbed . . . the feeling which had momentarily fled her fingers and hands was returning, the normal sensations of her body were coming back. Her mind cleared and she made herself as comfortable as possible on the hard floor, shifting weight to her thighs so her legs wouldn't go to sleep.

"I'm tired tonight," Fourne admitted. "I thought too much today, that was the problem. There are some days when you should never think."

"This should help relax you," Renee stated matter-of-factly.

"It does. But my mind is wandering. It keeps twisting and whirling. I wish to hell it would stop."

"Close your eyes . . . just try being quiet," she recommended as she massaged his ankle.

"Put more soap on that, will you? And keep your leg stretched out on the floor where I can see it."

Renee leaned back over the tub and wet the patch once again. The phone beside the toilet began to ring and she gave him a questioning look.

"I'm not going to answer it. Not even if they stay on the line till Christmas."

The sound echoed harshly, the high electronic bell pleading to be released from the room, if only through a chance open window, instead of continually reverberating painfully against the hard mirrors. Fourne had closed his eyes and his head was tilted towards the ceiling. For the first time this evening, since she knew he wasn't watching her, Renee felt brave enough to peer into his face — it seemed made of clay. She brought the rubber against his thighs.

"Take the phone off the hook," he commanded dreamily.

She crawled quickly and removed the receiver and a felicitous peace flooded the room. His eyes were still shut. She resumed the massage. A few minutes later she looked again into his face. It bore the troubled expression of a child battling a nightmare; his muscles twitched uneasily and his eyes were screwed up as if glutted with tears.

"I'm doing what you said," he announced. "But it's not working."

Renee swore under her breath. "It's not enough to keep your eyes closed," she entreated sweetly. "You have to empty all your thoughts as well."

"I can't." His eyes opened wide. "I'm afraid of my thoughts. I must never let my mind lose control like this. You know what I'm talking about?"

"No," she replied honestly, attempting to work the last bit of lather from the patch as she shifted to the back of his leg.

"You remember . . ." he began gravely. "The horrible thing I said I'd like to do once with electricity."

"Yes, of course," she murmured but she didn't remember. She wasn't even certain that he had ever mentioned it to her, though at the very back of her mind she thought perhaps he had admitted wanting to do something awful once, something hideous, but it was only an obscure notion. At any rate she didn't want to be reminded now so she remained silent hoping it might discourage him from continuing.

"Man first learned about electricity over two thousand years ago," he informed her. "I think a Greek philosopher named Thales was the first to conceive of the possiblity of producing it. An ironic twist, isn't it, that a philosopher, not a scientist, was able to discover something about it."

Renee tried to concentrate on her own thoughts but his words broke through with the same strength as hammers beating against glass.

"Thales saw that amber, produced by the hardened sap of trees, when rubbed against a material like wool, attracted light threads and fibers to it. . ." He watched the glowing bulb above his head. "When you think about it," he mentioned slowly, "electricity seems very simple. Rubbing. That's all it is. Look at what you're doing, Renee."

"You mean, rubbing you?" she asked.

"Of course. That's electricity. It's true you need two different electrically insulating materials. My skin wouldn't do. But that patch in your hand . . . that certainly could be used for rubbing against say, fur or wool. . ."

"Do you want more soap?" Renee shattered his train of thought. She had not even finsihed washing half his body. The long night lay ahead. He would never permit her to speed the process; she was to labor slowly, cleaning every crevice of his skin perhaps dozens of times, and then at the end she was to cover him with powder scented with roses and tuck him gently between the sheets.

On Friday afternoon Jake paused on the steps of the hotel's front entrance; he noticed Renee and Bee winding their way down the street and waited to join them.

"Isn't that a friend of yours up ahead?" Bee pointed.

Surprised, Renee grabbed Bee's wrist and checked her watch. "Three o'clock," Renee said. "He's not due back until five-thirty."

"Oh, well, maybe he's been fired," Bee suggested. Renee narrowed her eyes at Bee who defended herself, "Those things happen, you know."

"Jake," Renee said in sotto voice, to conceal her concern, "this is unexpected."

He kissed her. "This morning I finished the Garment District story and I spent the afternoon in a meeting with my boss which just broke up now."

"And he sent you home early?"

"Believe it or not."

"It was a good meeting?" Renee was wary.

"I was going to tell you about it later but since the subject's in the air —"

"Oh, yes, tell us now!" Bee interrupted. "Come on. I'm dying for my daily morsel of gossip."

They were jostled by a group of fat men who insisted on passing through the gilded front door in a tight cluster. "Single file, fellas, single file!" Bee yelled after them and the last man swung around and gave her the finger. Bee returned the gesture and held her nose as the odors from their cigars and armpits still stung the light afternoon breeze. Renee aggressively shoved the hair from her eyes. She blew one last free strand out of the way, then crossed her arms waiting for Jake to continue.

"I got handed a new assignment, thanks to the superior work I turned in the last few weeks. This one is a photo essay about the job boom in Colorado — the sudden growth of the towns there and the effect on both the long-time citizens and the newcomers. . ." His voice trailed off. No one spoke. Bee glanced at Renee who stared straight ahead. "Well," Jake continued, laughing. "It's a fucking great assignment! How about some congratulations?"

"It's fine," said Renee. "But does it mean you have to go there or what?"

"Naturally. For about two weeks. I have to cover twelve little towns."

"My, my," Bee pursed her lips. "Can you take me with you? I'm free the next two weeks."

"Oh, no," he answered. "Sorry. I can't take anybody. Not this time at least."

Renee realized these words were for her benefit — they meant *you need not ask either* and this infuriated her. She felt foolish standing there contemplating it in the heat with the constant scream of the traffic in her ear and the boundless procession of faces distracting her.

"That's marvelous, Jake!" Bee cried, rubbing his back. "Maybe next time you'll get to cover a few hick towns in New Jersey. I bet you'd take me along then, wouldn't you, you son of a bitch!"

"You have me figured out, Bee."

"Let's go upstairs," Renee said, flushed.

Over dinner Jake assured her, "I'll only be gone two weeks. The time will pass before you know it."

"I know," she responded, but the manner in which she lazily picked through her food told Jake that she was upset.

He held her hand. "I don't plan to fool around or anything. I'm faithful to you, Renee."

She felt then like asking why he couldn't take her. They could pay the extra expenses themselves. But something in his expression startled her and she was afraid to ask and all she could do was repeat, "I know." Perhaps this was his test to see if they could survive two weeks apart. He admitted as much during dessert, "It will be good for us."

But Renee had trouble falling asleep that night. She listened to the buses as they rumbled around the corners, the tremblings of their huge motors rising above all the other night sounds; and she watched the colored lights flash somberly from the giant marquees. She thought continually about Colorado; she wasn't even certain where it was or why people visited there, but she considered it an enemy.

Jake would occasionally stir, open his eyes. He could sense her tautness and mumble, "I don't like to leave you here all alone." Then he would drift into sleep and Renee would once again listen for the overpowering cries of the midnight buses.

Jake was bothered the next day by the idea of Renee remaining at the hotel for two weeks without him. When he returned that evening he presented her with a solution.

"Get ready to pack," he announced, flopping onto the bed and loosening his tie.

"Pack?" she replied sarcastically. "Where am I going?"

"To the seashore. I've arranged everything and it's impossible for you to say no."

"What is this all about, Jake?" she pouted as he grabbed her by the leg and pulled her down on top of him.

"I don't think you should stay here by yourself anymore." He kissed her forehead and smoothed her hair back. "You're going to stay with my aunt in her house on the bay until I come for you myself."

Renee tried to wriggle from his grasp. "Your aunt? What are you talking about?"

"Stay put," he pinned her arms behind her. Then he care-

fully explained how he had spoken with his aunt, Ella Scotchsmith, that morning . . . how he had told her about his job and
Renee. She had asked him to visit the family as soon as possible
and when he told her that he would have a few days free after his
Colorado assignment, and that Renee was staying behind, she
suggested that the girl come stay with them while Jake was
gone. Renee would have her own room and the summer sun and
all the sea air her lungs could hold.

"No, Jake," Renee stated emphatically.

"Why not?"

"It just wouldn't work. Moving in with strangers."

"Why should they remain strangers? They're my family and
I want you to meet them. Aunt Ella is very warm and friendly.
And I'll be up at the end of next week and we can all have a nice
vacation together."

Renee stared doubtfully into his eyes. "Oh, I don't know."

"Renee," he pulled tightly on her fingers. "I insist."

Martha was the first of the children to actually see Renee. She
called her brother to the kitchen window so he too could watch
the woman crossing the front lawn with their father.

"What's her name?" Martha wondered.

"I forget," Perry replied, munching an ample stalk of celery.
"She's Jake's girlfriend though, isn't she?"

Martha hesitated, then stammered, "I guess so."

"You're sweet on Jake, aren't you?" Perry chided. "I bet
you're jealous."

"I'm not either!" she cried shrilly. "Don't ever say that
again, Perry! I'm not sweet on anybody and even if I were, Jake
Adams is much too old." Her face was flushed and she brought
her hand to her cheek as if she could feel the actual heat and the
rush of blood. "If you tease me like that again, I'll tell Mother
and she'll put a stop to it." Perry simply shrugged as he poured
himself a glass of milk and helped himself to a handful of ginger
cookies.

Peter Scotchsmith paused on the garden path. He had met
Renee at the train station and they had driven directly home.
He set down her two small bags, which he had made a gallant
show of carrying, and began familiarizing her with the grounds
that surrounded the house — the smooth expanse of newly
clipped grass that stretched like a shifting carpet towards the
sea . . . the different flowers close at hand in the rambling

garden that his wife so anxiously tended.

"You'll meet my wife later this afternoon," Peter said, then explained apologetically, "She's at one of those godawful ladies' teas."

Renee gave a quick laugh, knowledgeable and light; she felt this kind of response was expected. She smoothed her dress and focused her attention on the profuse clusters of sweet peas and gloxinias that had eagerly strayed from Ella Scotchsmith's prized garden and were crossing the brick wall and brushing her feet. She veiled her eyes with her hands as the brim of her white summer hat wasn't quite wide enough to do the job.

"Look at those monkeys in the window!" His voice broke with laughter and Renee followed his pointed finger to see two small heads nimbly disappear beneath the kitchen window-panes. "My son and daughter," he announced as he led her to the kitchen door. He abruptly changed his mind and stopped so suddenly that Renee stumbled into him. "Sorry," he steadied her. "What was I thinking of anyway? You'll meet them later. First I'm sure you want to see your room and get some rest."

Her room, until a few days ago, had belonged to Fanny whom Ella finally had to "let go" as she had pushed the family to their "wits' end" by her constant complaints and general stub-bornness. Scotchsmith waited uncertainly for Renee's reaction to the cramped and shadowy room, the only natural light admitted by a row of small window slits which didn't fully open. He was relieved when Renee switched on the lamp beside the bed and began to unpack, apparently pleased.

"You'll find plenty of closet space," he confidently indicated the room's one strong feature.

"Good," Renee kept her eyes on her suitcase.

Scotchsmith took the hint. He left her to herself, encouraging her to come downstairs and meet the kids when she had fresh-ened up.

Renee sank onto the bed, disturbed and truly bewildered. How had she let Jake convince her to visit these people?

She couldn't remember staying as a house guest with anyone before in her life. It was unnerving. Sighing, she removed the hat which was fastened to her hair with a long, straight silver pin, the kind that fashionable ladies used at the turn of the century. She enjoyed the ritual of the unpinning. She placed the hat gently on the bedside table. Then she peered through the window slits. All she could distinguish were billowy green leaves, but whether these leaves robed trees planted close against the window or in a far away field she couldn't decide. *Goddam bastard,* Renee dismissed Peter Scotchsmith. *He sticks somebody in a fucking hole like this and expects them to be grateful.* She slammed her fist against the slits which only served to shut them tight, dispelling the meager daylight.

She felt calmer after a bath. Tightening her Chinese robe around her, she started for her bedroom but was startled by a presence at the top of the staircase. It was a figure plunged into blackness by the brilliant light from large oblong windows behind it and its shadow fell the length of the corridor, ending at her feet.

"Hello," the specter finally spoke. It was the voice of a boy echoing through the air. She nodded as he approached, his shadow shrinking, his features lightening until his handsome face was perfectly clear and almost eye-level with hers, as he was only an inch or two shorter than she. "My name is Perry." He took her hand in his and shook it hardily.

"I'm Renee."

"We're so happy you could visit us. It's always so much fun when Jake comes to stay. And we always like whoever he brings along."

"That's good," she answered, wondering whom Jake had brought here in the past.

"Would you like to see my room?" he asked. She paused, her hand on the knob of her bedroom door. Renee viewed all children with distrust and her first impulse was to ignore them totally; but then Perry hardly seemed to be a child and he was affable and she felt she must sooner or later become acquainted with the entire household. "It's directly across the hall," he persuaded her with a grin.

His room, in contrast to hers, was breezy and soaked with sunshine. Everything was orderly. She realized at once that he made his own bed; not even a mother would have smoothed the coverlet and fluffed the pillows with such a deft touch or kept the schoolbooks dusted and in alphabetical order on the shelves or protected the table by the window against clutter so that a lone telescope, looking majestic and important, could rise toward the sky, a spiral notebook the instrument's sole companion.

"Sit down," he pulled a rocking chair to the center of the room for her, then settled onto the edge of his bed wrapping his arms around one of the mahogany posts. At once he began to giggle.

She eyed him sharply. "What's funny?"

"You look like Grandma rocking in that chair." For some reason this observation sent him into convulsions. Renee abruptly stopped rocking. "No, no!" he insisted. "I was only teasing, don't stop!"

"And have you make fun of me?" she said.

"You don't look like Grandma. How could you? You're young and pretty. My grandmother's pretty too, though, but it's not the same thing, is it?"

"It is the same thing," Renee answered.

He made little rhythmic taps against the post. "I'm glad Jake found someone like you."

Renee stared hard at the boy, trying to figure him out. But the more she examined him the more mystified she was. She was surprised by his sensitivity and intelligence, by his quick blue eyes which changed when he spotted something new and seemed to grasp the essence of things automatically. He seemed to be penetrating her essence without the least effort or care.

"And you, I suppose, have no time for girls?" she questioned him closely.

"Me? No time or interest. That comes later," he added with assurance. He lay back on the bed and drew circles in the air. "Right now I'm busy with school."

"You like it?"

He laughed. "The sixth grade at Faun Creek School is not the most challenging environment to find yourself in. We never study anything that I want to know about at least. We haven't had any lessons in law or health or science. Nothing practical. The last day of school, in fact, we were reading silly stories. There was one about Martha Washington's dress! I mean, that's such a waste of time, isn't it?" He sat straight up and looked at her so imploringly that she felt she had to nod in agreement, after which he relaxed and fell back on the bed tracing circles once again. "And they emphasize sports too much. When you play everyday it's almost like sleep — you're just playing the game by rote, never learning anything new. One time a week might be good to keep you loosened up. But too much sports is like a drug. I read that in the papers."

"What do you know about drugs?"

"I know they're bad. They make you forget your name and

where you are. You don't even remember where you live and you can wander around the streets like a zombie."

His voice rang with such certainty that Renee was convinced. "Well," she sighed. "Things are different now than when I was your age. No one ever thought to criticize anything connected with school. It just wasn't done."

"Only a few of us evaluate school now," he said. "I'm one of them. The climate probably hasn't changed much." Perry was spinning circles so furiously and seriously that Renee had to ask what he was doing. "Oh," he replied. "Drawing galaxies. I'm putting the stars where they belong and trying to remember their names. There's so much to remember."

"I noticed your telescope," Renee remarked. "Are you interested in astronomy?"

Perry sat up and glared at his telescope. "That thing? It's a baby's toy." He blinked at her, forgetting for a moment that she wasn't aware of his future plans. "I'd like to make a serious study of the universe and perhaps, with luck and patience, make some startling discovery someday." He jumped up. "But," he added disappointedly, "I can't go far now with that small telescope. If only Mother would understand and give the go ahead. . ." He motioned for Renee to follow him to the window behind his bed. "See that?" he inquired. But all she saw were massive fields, broken and untidy, crammed with dying vegetables. "Dad owns those acres. I've offered to help clear them myself if he'd let me use them for my experiments."

"What kind of experiments?" Renee was becoming increasingly confused.

"Nowadays you can't study the stars that well with optical equipment. But radio telescopes can carry us far into space, into regions of the universe we've hardly dared think about. Take pulsars, for example — you know," he added, "stars brighter than the sun, that can flash on and off thirty times a second — well, some people in England discovered them just by stringing wires across a field! I could easily build my own radio telescope. And if I had the patience of those people in England, who knows what I might find? . . . Just think," he murmured excitedly, "we could hear sounds from millions of miles away, from millions of years ago throughout the galaxies. In fact, they say we can actually hear the hiss through the wires from the explosion that formed the universe . . . the very noise of creation. . ."

"It sounds awesome, Perry," she stated. "How is it that you know so much?"

89

"I don't. I hardly know anything. And I hate to run on like I just did, because people start to think I'm crazy or that I have a swelled head and think too much of myself. That's not it at all," he bit his lip and walked across the room, but his step now seemed heavy, even guilty. "I didn't mean what I said about this telescope." He patted it gently. "I love it." Then he laughed. "We've been together for years."

Renee folded her arms, a little stunned by this conversation and feeling left in the dark; she realized that she knew next to nothing about any specific subject — she existed in a world of ignorance. Even in her personal life she wandered continually through fields of emotion, never sure of her own feelings, never knowing what other people's real feelings were towards her. Suddenly she didn't even know whether Jake really loved her — loved her deeply and wanted to remain with her. She sat down hard on the bed and held her head in her hands.

"Are you O.K.?" Perry asked. There was silence. "I said, 'Are you all right?' " He nearly shouted at her.

"Yes. Fine," she replied, looking with concern at the boy whose fingers tightly gripped his telescope. She blocked the torrent of unhappiness that was pouring through her; she constructed a strong dam just before the sadness was to break into her bloodstream. "My God, yes. I'm certainly O.K."

"Knock, knock," came a voice from the doorway. They both turned, startled, to find Peter Scotchsmith grinning at them. "I'm going to pick up Ron and Patricia at school. Anyone want to come along for the ride?"

"Naw, Dad," Perry answered, flipping the pages of his book of star charts. "I think I'll stay and get some work done."

"Renee," Scotchsmith continued. "Why don't you join me? I'd like you to see the school and meet the kids."

"Sure," she answered, then, realizing she was still in her robe, said self-consciously, "give me a minute to dress."

The road to the school was hardly more than a country lane. Luscious purple cherries sparkled in the dirt. The car jolted.

"We could have used the highway," Scotchsmith adjusted the rear view mirror. "But I thought we'd have more fun this way. You don't get to see much of the countryside where you live."

Of course not, she almost snapped. This man irritated her. He seemed to be wanting something from her, nothing sexual; yet she sensed he was the type that sized a person up to decide how best to use him. Beneath his bland easy talk was something ice cold.

"Perry's a fantastic son," he reflected. "I couldn't ask for any better. Did he tell you that he's one of the state finalists in this national contest?"

"No, he didn't," Renee answered, her interest piqued.

"Oh, yeah," he kept his eyes on the choppy road that looked and felt like a river. "Hayden Planetarium up in your part of the world is sponsoring it. Scientists are selecting the five most promising astronomers of tomorrow from thousands of kids under fourteen from all of the fifty states. They chose the finalists on the basis of reports the kids sent in on astronomy related subjects. Now they're weeding out the best of those. The five winners are to be honored at a luncheon at the planetarium where they'll read their papers to the scientists and receive an order of merit and a sterling silver star pin. Naturally I'm keeping my fingers crossed for my son, but I don't like to bring it up to him and raise his expectations when it's not at all a sure thing. I don't want him to come crashing down too hard if he doesn't get selected. . ." Scotchsmith paused, then blurted, "Do you want to hear a terrible admission?"

Renee frowned.

"Something quite serious which I'll never forgive myself for."

"What?" she asked cautiously.

"I fell asleep at the exact moment the astronauts stepped onto the moon. Can you imagine?" he lowered his voice, laughing nervously. "I was in a crowded room and I was right up close to a big color set. I'd been eagerly anticipating the event yet all of a sudden — wham!" He snapped his fingers. "I was out like a light and nobody bothered to wake me up. When I pulled myself together an hour or so later, it was all over. Now how could I admit that to Perry?"

He parked the car in the lot which overlooked the baseball diamond. "Summer school," he remarked disparagingly. "All they do is play baseball. That's where all the money goes." But his eyes twinkled mischievously. "There he is!" he exclaimed. "Number Forty-Two. Red and white sweatshirt." Renee strained her eyes to locate the boy he was describing but there were so many of them running about in mass confusion. "My son, Ron. He's the best slugger this team has got!" Renee thought she caught a glimpse of a wiry little blond boy wearing Number Forty-Two dashing in circles and swinging a bat threateningly at his teammates.

The car door opened and Patricia slipped onto the back seat. "Hi, Dad."

"Hi, honey." Scotchsmith introduced his daughter who nodded blankly and offered Renee some gum which she refused. "What kind is it?" asked her father. "I might like some."

"Dad," she groaned. "It's the kind you hate with that real fruity taste."

"Oh, all right, forget it then. How was school today?"

Patricia played with a long strand of amber beads that hung almost to her waist. "Wonderful!" she cried ecstatically. "Mrs. Gardner was sick! And we had the dreamiest substitute with wavy black hair and these incredible blue eyes. Oh!" She squealed and fell against the back seat. "I'm glad I wore these jeans today, they're so cool." She explained to Renee, "Martha and I spent all week-end embroidering them." The sides and cuffs exploded with hearts and bees and flowers in multi-colored threads. "And, of course, he didn't give any homework to us since he didn't know what Mrs. Gardner was teaching! Though the kids in the fifth grade say he gave them a whole lot to do —"

She was interrupted by the arrival of her brother, about a half dozen of his friends and their coach, John Ryan, a prepossessing red-faced man with golden curls who had five sons enrolled in Faun Creek School. Ryan and Scotchsmith greeted each other warmly but Ron pushed his way between them and leaned in the window so his face almost touched his father's.

"Dad, Mr. Ryan is taking everybody to McDonald's. Can't I go too?"

"No, no. Mom's planning a big supper tonight. Renee Cloverman here is our guest."

"But we'd only be gone a little while," he pleaded. "I'd just get a milkshake. *Come on,* Dad."

In the back seat Patricia had locked the door and was rolling up the window furiously as some of the boys were trying to get inside to tease her. She screamed as she realized several more were on their way to the other side and she lurched across to lock the door and raise the window. "Get your hand out of the way, she warned. "Or I'll roll it up too and break it off!" But together two boys punched hard enough on the glass to stop her from moving it. "Dad!" she called. "Make them stop!"

"Hold on!" he yelled at her.

"I can't hold on!" she whined. "They're getting in!"

"No, Ron," his father was emphatic. "Climb in back. You can't go today."

"Please, Dad," he set his mouth in a pout and a determined look crossed his eyes and he started bending his father's fingers.

"Watch it," Peter Scotchsmith cautioned.

John Ryan, laughing, pulled Ron backwards. "Just think if you had five like me!" The men whistled in exasperation. "Ron, the team will go out this Friday after practice too," Ryan slapped him playfully on the rear. "You can wait till then."

Ron, realizing he was defeated, pulled on the door handle. "Patricia, let me in!"

"I can't! They'll all get in too!"

Ron pounded on the window while Ryan yelled at the other boys to stop. "Enough is enough," he called. "The last guy into my van is gonna be stuck on short stop on Friday for the whole afternoon!"

As Peter Scotchsmith started the car he grinned to himself. "That John Ryan is some guy." He turned onto the narrow asphalt that ran the length of the school building. "Show Renee your rooms."

"Mine's right there, third grade," Patricia announced. Renee made a pretense of looking and her eyes went right through the windows but she didn't see anything.

"We passed the *second* grade," Scotchsmith coached, staring at his son in the rear view mirror. No response. "Don't sulk." These words only made Ron turn away and face the window. He mechanically tossed a baseball back and forth in his glove.

His back was to Patricia who eventually shoved him. "Move over, you're taking up too much room."

"I am not."

"Yes, you are," she said angrily. "You're taking up more than your half!"

They evidently worked this problem out quickly as there was silence in the car for a short stretch, giving Renee a chance to study the passing scenery for the first time. There were a few old brown barns, neglected and silent, but cows still grazed in their neighboring pastures. There were acres of beans, columns of cherry trees, both red and black cherries hanging in abundance from the burdened branches. Giggling came from the back seat, muffled at first, then breaking loudly.

"What is it?" Scotchsmith insisted.

"Nothing," Patricia howled.

"It has to be something or you wouldn't be acting this crazy," he winked at Renee.

"It's her hair," Ron blurted. He and Patricia held onto each other so they wouldn't laugh themselves off the seat. Renee glanced back at them. "Does your hair always stick out like that?" he winced.

Renee turned to Scotchsmith, breaking into a wild, nervous laugh.

"Aren't they terrible?" he chuckled good-naturedly. "Of course, they don't mean a word of what they're saying."

Renee's mouth was still open, a tender smile playing at the corners. The laughter calmed down in the back. Renee sat up straight and closed her mouth. A feeling of utter astonishment crept over her. She slowly turned and fixed her eyes on the children.

"What are you starin' at?" Ron asked in an ugly tone.

Renee's gaze became harder than ever. She began to smile at him, then slowly changed the smile into a sneer. She held this withering, devastating expression for a moment or two longer, then calmly turned back to the front, smoothing the pleats in her cotton skirt.

Ella Scotchsmith prepared a superb meal that evening: moist lamb with baby turnips, delicate potatoes evenly fried in butter, spears of asparagus. For dessert Martha whipped up a black bottom pie from scratch. Martha insisted on candlelight to the protestations of her brothers who complained they wouldn't be able to see their food and she lit two slender tapers on high silver holders.

Renee was placed next to Ella and found her pleasant, but Ella found Renee a bit strange: reticent, shy. Throughout their conversation about New York, the country, the children, Ella's mind wandered. She hated to admit it to herself but she thought of her own sister, Mary, Jake's mother, as the black sheep of the family, the only one of the five girls who had married below her station. They were not close at all. But Ella had always had a soft spot for Jake whom she had kept for many summers of his youth because his own mother and father were in financial straits and floundering in exhausting jobs. She had enjoyed taking young Jake on excursions before her own children were born, on tours of fine homes in New York's Hudson River Valley, to time-worn Connecticut villages, on boat rides along

Cape Cod Bay. But now she really wondered about him. His girlfriend was nice enough and, she supposed, pretty enough, but she didn't seem to come alive or have much spirit, qualities she assumed Jake would be after in a girl.

"Mother," Martha chided. "You haven't said a word about the pie."

"It's like tasting a little corner of heaven, my sweet." And to show her enthusiasm Ella took another bite.

"It is very good," Renee complimented her.

"Yes, but not as good as the banana cake you baked last week," Perry sniffed.

As the days passed Renee kept mostly to herself. She would sit and read mysteries in the garden. She would take prolonged naps in her room. And she spent hours helping Ella with household chores. Ella's first impression of Renee changed somewhat: now she enjoyed and respected the girl more, found her easier to talk to. As they washed dishes together after each meal Ella relished being able to share confidences about that silly creature Fanny whom she had to fire, about the terrible time she was having with the PTA, about her youngest sister's problems with her husband who was an alcoholic and beat her. Ella realized it was the first time in years she had been able to confide in an adult woman; after all, Martha was just twelve. She could discuss her sister's problem and it would be understood.

Renee was a good listener, but she was only biding time, waiting for the moment that Jake would step through the door. She had sent him several letters to his hotel, but after four days no reply had come. The only time her body felt any sensation was when the mailman came in the kitchen door, exchanged a few words with Ella, dropped the mail on the butcher's block. The rest of the time she slumbered, whether asleep or wide awake.

Finally, on the fifth day, she thought she saw part of her name scrawled on a letter which was stuck under some bills, and, ignoring the chatter between Ella and the mailman, she hurried to the block. At that moment Ron rushed through the kitchen, saw Renee moving toward the mail, whipped up the stack of letters and carried them off.

She flew after him, following him into the den. He switched on the T.V. and made himself comfortable on the couch.

"I'll take my letter," she said.

He flipped through them quickly. "Nothing for you. Will you turn up the sound?"

Renee was livid. "Give me that mail!"

He began to shove it under the couch but she clutched him around the neck with one hand and tore the mail from his fingers with the other and after removing her own letter from the stack, threw the others back at him. He rubbed his neck in surprise, furious at himself for letting her have the letter so easily; her action had come out of the blue.

"I'll tell Mother you threw the mail on the floor," he threatened.

"You do that, baby," she cut the last word short — making it staccato — and climbed the stairs to her own room where she could read the letter in peace. She sat on the edge of the bed.

> *Dear Renee,*
>
> *There is nothing much to report as it is my first night here. The room is nothing to write home about but at least I'm not paying for it. It's lonely here so far. Funny to open the curtains and see mountains and so much sky. We'll have to go here together sometime.*
>
> *I hope that you're O.K. and that you like my aunt. I worry so about you and miss you.*
>
> *This is just a quick note and I'll write a longer letter tomorrow. I have to get to bed early as I have to be up at dawn clicking my camera to hell and back. I'll go to sleep dreaming about certain portions of your anatomy. Are you thinking about mine?*
>
> *Renee is always in my dreams.*
>
> > *Your Jake*

Renee re-read the letter several times, but she was still seething from the scene of a few moments ago and felt she couldn't fully appreciate it. She would read it again tonight. She folded it carefully and slipped it in her drawer. That little bastard. He was a boy who would grow up into the kind of man she knew so well. A tormentor. An oppressor. At that moment Perry crossed in front of her door on the way to his room. He waved quickly to her. And he, Renee thought, though she couldn't be sure, would turn out to be a victim like her.

Chapter Seven

Jake came by train on Saturday morning and checked his watch as the wheels ground to a halt. It was not yet seven. He didn't wish to bother the Scotchsmith family at that hour and wanted his arrival to be a surprise to Renee, so he hired a cab to take him to the house. Before going inside he paused on the path to enjoy the spectacle of the sun beginning to smolder against the wood, drying the dew and chasing away what remained of the sea mist. Though he had a key, he didn't need to use it as the door was kept unlocked. Peter Scotchsmith maintained that if a thief wanted in, a bolted door would not discourage him; there were, after all, nearly thirty windows that provided access.

Jake heard sounds in the kitchen. Martha, in her robe, was preparing some hot chocolate. She almost tipped the pot over when she caught Jake smiling at her. "Want some company?" he asked.

She embraced him eagerly. "How on earth did you get here?"

"Taxi."

"We didn't think you were coming today. Why didn't you tell us!"

"I wasn't sure myself. Anyway I wanted to surprise everybody. Where is Renee sleeping?" He asked a simple question yet it seemed to hang in the air.

Martha took the pot from the burner and began to stir the chocolate. "She's in Fanny's old room, Jake." She poured the liquid into two mugs. "I didn't put much sugar in. It might not be sweet enough for you."

He sipped it slowly. "It's just right. Delicious."

Outside the window birds called to each other. "It's mar-

velous, isn't it. . ." Martha commented. "I hear them every
morning, very early . . . sometimes from my room . . . sometimes standing right here where we are . . . oh, well, I should get
dressed!"

After Martha's footsteps had faded, he climbed the stairs to
Renee's room. The room was completely dark; even the wan
light drifting through the hall hardly relieved the dimness. He
closed the door behind him and moved forward, bumping into
the bed.

Renee woke, startled. "Who's there!"

Jake bent down, putting his hand across her mouth.
"Shhh . . . it's me. I'm back."

She felt his face, running her fingers anxiously over his
cheeks, his eyes, through his hair. He kissed her fingers,
lingering over each one. She pulled him next to her onto the bed
and they held each other for a long time, without speaking.

Finally, "It's so good to be with you," he murmured. "It's the
only thing I've thought of all week. Waiting for this moment."

Renee didn't answer. How could she explain that every
second she had spent he had been within her, almost weighing
her down to the point of exhaustion? Her only response was to
rub his chest as tenderly as she could.

Naturally the whole family was delighted by Jake's arrival. It
was a fine day — the air light, the sky turquoise and clean,
clouds with striking shapes blowing by now and again. The
family put up a table outside by the garden and fixed an
impromptu buffet lunch. Jake was plied with all kinds of
questions about his job, his trip to Colorado, his apartment
where the children wanted to see his wonderful photographs.

"That's right, Jake," Peter Scotchsmith suddenly remembered. "You take all those pictures. Ever had a showing in New
York?"

"Not yet." He felt embarrassed. "But hell. You might see
them in a gallery someday."

"I'm waiting to see the pictures you took last summer," Perry
declared, licking his fingers, his plate filled with bones of cold
fried chicken.

"What pictures?" Jake demanded.

"What pictures?" Perry repeated incredulously. "All the ones
you took on the boat when we went out fishing that morning.
Don't you remember me holding that giant sea bass?"

"Oh, yes," Jake replied guiltily. "I'll send them along."

"Bet you never do!" chimed in Patricia.

Jake helped himself to seconds. Ella joined him at the table and lowered her voice in a confidential manner, "Renee is such a nice girl. We're so glad that she could come up as well."

"It was great for her to get away," Jake winked at his aunt and she slipped her arm around his waist.

"I do believe you've put on weight," she surmised.

"I have not," he insisted, laughing.

"You have," she laughed back. "Just a little and it's flattering. You were too thin before."

After the meal Scotchsmith took Jake on a stroll, explaining how he expected his recent business deals to be incredibly profitable. As they had promised, Martha and Patricia cleared away the dirty plates and dismantled the buffet table so that their mother and Renee could relax for once. Making quite a show, Martha pulled two lawn chairs to the edge of the garden and insisted that the women rest there. Perry, full from lunch, lay quite still at their feet, enjoying the softness of the grass and watching the circles of clover twist away from his fingertips into the flower garden before disappearing beneath the riotously colored petals and the broad, low leaves. Ron changed into his Little League uniform and waited impatiently for his father to return from his walk to take him to practice.

"I was just telling Jake about my plans to buy a small turbo jet," Scotchsmith appeared behind his wife and began to rub her shoulders.

"Yes, Dad, you have to!" Ron was enthusiastic.

Ella laughed indulgently. "Don't be so silly."

"Why shouldn't I?" Scotchsmith knit his brows. "After all, I can afford two or three."

"It's ostentatious," she declared, knowing full well that her husband would eventually have his way.

"Wow, think of the kids at school, how jealous they'll be when I tell 'em my dad bought a real jet!" Ron shouted as his father chuckled and ruffled the boy's hair.

Perry flipped onto his stomach. He wished instead that his dad would help him clear the field in back and buy some wire so he could begin to construct his radio telescope. *Oh, what's the use?* "Come on, Jake," Perry suddenly looked up. "Let's go out in the rowboat."

"Jake just arrived," Ella chided. "Let him rest a day or two."

Jake's face reddened. "Might as well go out today, Perry," he confessed. "I have to leave on Monday."

Renee froze. Here it came again, this message, like before, not given to her privately but blurted out in a group for immediate discussion.

"Monday?" Scotchsmith touched Jake's shoulder. "Why go back so soon?"

"They need me in Colorado again. There's a lot more to this job than I thought." He gazed sheepishly at Renee but she stared at the ground and nodded swiftly, pretending that this news was no surprise.

"Then Renee can just stay on with us until you come back," Ella said.

"That's wonderful," Jake brightened.

Renee stood. "Oh, no, don't bother," she stuttered. "I'll be fine in New York."

"Nonsense," Ella insisted. "I was only beginning to get to know you. You can't leave."

Renee's eyes met Jake's; his look implored her to accept Ella's offer. Perhaps this odd insecurity he had about facing her first with his plans was beneficial to them both. She didn't have time to mull over his decisions, to be plagued with uncertainty or anguish, to worry or argue or to chew her nails in some corner. What did it matter anyway? She was caught off guard but there was no deeper concern. She would stay. The matter was settled.

Ever since he could remember, Perry had imagined himself an explorer. Not only now as his mind journeyed through the known and unknown dimensions of the world beyond the earth, but also in years past as he and his friends had guided his boat along the shoreline that stretched from his house to Sandy Creek. He had reveled in examining the rocks, the trees, the cliffs and caves that appeared behind each new curve of land and he would bestow names on any unusual formations that might serve as landmarks along the way. To the amusement of the other boys, a handful of apple trees crushed together on a narrow embankment became The Sacred Grove of Apollo; the dry brown palisades that scanned the open sea on one side and provided a backbone for a cheap housing development on the other was transformed into The White Cliffs of Dover. The small dark grottos into which Sandy Creek, the narrow, slithering stream lost itself, were in reality The Caves of Hercules whose miraculous spurts of water were the pride of

ancient Morocco and kept the populace in awe and fear of the
majesty of the god. And the boys would have it no other way.
They urged Perry to lead them, to change the ordinary landscape into something rich and exotic and make it seem as if they
were discovering it all for the very first time.

Now a faint smile was on his lips as he rowed at the narrow
end of the boat, Jake keeping a steady pace at the other, Renee
between them, dipping her hand from time to time into the
water.

"What's on your mind?" Jake had caught Perry in his
reverie.

Perry was remembering the past days of exploration but he
was too embarrassed to reveal his boyhood preoccupations to
Jake, especially to let him know the special names he had for the
commonplace trees and groves that were drifting by.
"Memories," was all Perry said and Jake laughed at how
solemn the boy seemed.

"I could put all the memories you've had in your young life in
a glass jar," Jake told him. "Now me. I have memories. Wait
until you've reached my age."

"The wise old man," Renee quipped.

"Don't pay any attention to her," Jake cautioned.

Perry respected Jake whom he pretended was his older
brother when they took excursions together. They had a special
rapport and Jake was always so cheerful and helpful. Perry
couldn't think of anybody he would rather spend the afternoon
with or anything that he'd rather be doing than riding over the
tiny green waves with the ever-changing sea and sky as his
silent allies. He couldn't resist throwing his head back and
giving a loud yell.

"Now why in hell did you do that?" Jake spoke angrily and
pointed his oar threateningly at the boy, then suddenly he
threw his head back too and gave a loud, sustained cry like a
war whoop. Renee refused to be outdone and let a piercing
scream fly through the air.

"That's not fair!" Perry shouted in delight.

On the shore a group of children, so far away that only their
shapes could be made out, raised their arms and waved.

"We'll be arrested," he continued. "Disturbing the fish. A
nuisance to all marine life within a twelve mile radius!"

"Renee," Jake edged menacingly toward her. "Didn't you
tell me once you didn't know how to swim?"

"I don't remember ever conveying that bit of information to you," she refuted him. "As a matter of fact, I'm a very good dog paddler, expert water treader and my butterfly isn't bad either. And since you had the bad taste to bring up matters of physical prowess, I will tell you that the very first time I fell in love was when a boy rescued me at the community pool one summer day when I was younger than Perry. I had jumped off the diving board and landed at a funny angle so that the wind was knocked out of me and I was just leaving this world when a beautiful lifeguard in a bright yellow swimsuit jumped in and pulled me out of the water. I opened my eyes — and you won't believe this — I looked straight into his face and he beamed down at me, then his head moved and there was a rainbow in the sky."

"Right over his head in the middle of the sky?" Jake challenged her.

"I told you you wouldn't believe it. Yes. Running right across the middle of the sky. This glorious rainbow. It only lasted a few seconds though, then disappeared. I was saved."

"Do you believe that?" Jake asked the boy.

Perry regarded Renee skeptically. Then a cursory "no" came from his lips. He changed the subject. "Do you want to help me build my radio telescope when you come up again?"

"Oh, Christ," Jake muttered. "I can't do anything like that."

"You can too. It's easy. You've helped me do lots of things before."

"The only thing I've ever done for you is chase a bat out of your room with a wastebasket over my head when you were about five years old and bawling your head off, scared to death."

"You were more scared," Perry remembered.

"I was not."

"You were the one with the basket over your head!" he insisted.

"Well, you wouldn't know that unless I told you, since you stayed under the bed and wouldn't come out until we promised you it had flown away to Never-Never Land."

"Jake, you're terrible," Renee scolded.

"He's just pretending to be mean," Perry assured her. "He's helped me with a lot of things. He's scouted stamps for me for my American Collection, and cleaned my telescope, even built my bookshelves."

"You are handy," she admitted. "You're doing a great job

turning that room above our bed into a darkroom." Then she giggled suddenly at being reminded of the hotel. She stared at Jake with mild confusion.

He sensed her discomfort. "You'd better take over," he shifted his weight. "My back is ready to break. And I think we should put you to work anyway."

They carefuly changed places and Renee began to row. She gripped the oars tightly. "I'm not real good at this."

"We forgive you," Jake announced as he lay down and rested his head in her lap.

"Oh, wonderful, additional weight."

He opened one eye and stared up at her. "Is it really too much?"

"No, it isn't too much. It's never too much."

"Sorry about the Colorado affair," Jake kept his eyes closed. "But a living is a living."

"Oh, don't even discuss it," her voice rang sweetly.

"Well, I may be going back and forth a couple of times." He stretched. "I really don't know."

"What does it matter?" she said. "I'm pleased that it's good for you."

"I'll call you a few times this week and let you know how things are going, how long I might be this trip."

"Fine."

Jake yawned and Renee felt him relax completely. He was asleep. She noticed that Perry was watching her with curiosity. Had she been looking at Jake in a certain way? Was she rowing badly? Then Perry's eyes went to Jake's face, then back to her and he smiled. She knew then that he had been studying her expression as she watched Jake fall asleep. What was it he had seen. . . She did not know herself.

They rowed for a long time. Renee watched the scenery along the shore for awhile, then her eyes fell onto the floor of the boat and her thoughts wandered: she wondered what her mother was doing these days . . . she pictured her sitting quietly on the porch; for some reason she thought of Henry Wess languishing in prison and of his sister Anna and she remembered the day on the bus when Anna had seemed so forlorn. She saw her mother cross the porch and go into the house and turn on the television and sit motionless on the sofa. The voices from the television screen became louder. Renee looked up. "Perry!" she exclaimed. "What is this!"

"I don't know. This just blew down on top of us this instant!"

"Jake!" Renee shook him, fear in her voice. "Jake! For God's sake, wake up!"

Jake sat up to find himself facing a grey wall of fog: sheer, impenetrable. Turning around, they found they were hemmed in by sheets of it, though only an ice thin mist trailed across their faces.

"Where are we?" Jake was anxious.

"Near Sandy Creek. It was within easy view just a minute ago," Perry said. "Then suddenly — *this*. . ."

"Well, stop rowing," Jake instructed. "No telling what direction we'd be going." The horrible thought occurred to them that they might row the wrong way, out into an invisible sea; it was bad enough to lay the oars down inside the boat and hear nothing but the water lapping against the sides and realize they could be drifting away from land anyway. Jake made Perry change places to balance the weight of the boat more evenly. Perry crouched low. Stunned, he waited with Jake and Renee for the haze to lift.

"This is a hell of a thing!" Jake made his voice as strong and confident as possible. "Bright blue skies and then a solid blanket of fog."

"I *guess* it's fog," Perry interrupted. "It looks more like a black wall."

"Of course it's fog," Jake insisted. "Weather changes. It should blow right over."

But there was no wind. The fine vapor now covered the water and turned it into a realm of strange, wicked shadows. Jake wanted to say something cheery but his voice failed him and he realized it might be better to say nothing.

"Maybe we should all hold hands?" Perry suggested.

"Maybe so," Renee echoed and she reached for the boy.

But suddenly there was a funny sound like a corncob splitting and the world became black as pitch, then overhead the sun appeared and seemed to push the fog down into the bay; it was as if a wall was being dismantled quickly and easily, brick by brick, before their eyes and they were soon once again in the even daylight with the brilliant blue sky above and not a trace of mist remaining in the air.

"Goddam," Jake swore.

They were glad to find they had drifted inland with the tide and they all commented on their own stupidity not to have realized that it was high tide at this time of day. Perry especially was relieved to see such a familiar sight as the caverns which housed the fork of Sandy Creek which, after rushing in from the sea, formed deep pools of crystal water in the depths of the caves, cold springs which reminded Perry of the name he had given the grottos — The Cave of Hercules. He even mumbled the name aloud, thankfully.

"What's that? Caves of Hercules?" Jake questioned. "I'll say!"

They decided to pull the boat ashore and rest awhile before tackling the now arduous voyage back to the house.

As the week passed Renee became more and more bored with her existence at the Scotchsmith's. The pranks and noise of the children preyed on her nerves. Ella's breezy conversation became increasingly difficult to tolerate; Renee finally made no pretense of listening. Her mouth turned down in a surly manner and her eyelids half closed. Ella noticed, of course, and let up a bit, thinking Renee might not be feeling well.

Renee was battling insomnia, though in the day she didn't feel tired. Even if she only managed to fall asleep just before the dawn she felt refreshed when she woke a few hours later.

What bothered her was the fact that she had not heard from Jake for six days. There had been no letter, no phone call. Twice she had tried to phone him but he had not been in his hotel room and though both times she had left him a message to return her call there had been no response. Depressed and irritable, she spent most of the week shut in her room.

One night, after coaxing herself to sleep, she woke minutes later in the clutches of a nightmare, the substance of which she could not recall; but she knew it had been terrifying because she lay on a mattress soaked with her own sweat, her teeth were clenched tightly and it hurt to relax her jaw, her fingernails had ripped into the wrist of her right hand and had almost broken through a vein. She pushed open one of the window slits and gasped for a breath of air, holding her mouth against the screen as if it were an oxygen tent. The rush of air revived her, but the final effect was one of bringing a corpse back to life just to kill it over again. The nightmare returned and with it waves of nausea so that when she woke next she was choking on her own vomit. Still she had no clue as to the nature of the chilling dream.

She was determined to remain awake until morning. She felt

the quiet desperateness of insomnia was preferable to the violent, mysterious sleep.

The next day she was exhausted; she could hardly drag herself to the kitchen to toast some bread and fix some coffee.

"You're very calm today," Ella observed with a pinch of sarcasm, but Renee didn't answer, only stared blankly into her face.

She spent the rest of the day sitting by the garden, her wide hat shading her from the sun. She thought about nothing in particular. It was as if she had stopped herself from functioning for a purpose — as one would stop a clock suspected of running incorrectly and go off to check the actual time elsewhere; later, at the appropriate moment, the instrument would be rewound, the hands would begin to tick again.

"Are you going to sleep so early?" Martha asked as she passed Renee at the bottom of the stairs.

Renee, her hand on the bannister, nodded briefly. "Yes, I think I shall sleep forever."

"You'll get your chance," Martha glanced at her wristwatch with the pink velvet band. "It's not even eight o'clock."

Naturally, the instant her head touched the pillow she felt wide awake. She tossed and turned in the dark. She swallowed three valiums but her mind remained charged, a place filled with energy even as her limbs begged for sleep. After two hours had passed she heard the whole family prepare for bed; she knew the habits of each member, how they would walk, how long they would remain in the bathroom, what, if anything, they would say to each other as they closed their bedroom doors. Their noises drove her to distraction. She had gone to bed first . . . it wasn't fair to be kept awake by them as they seemed to flounder haphazardly toward sleep. Renee pounded her fists against the wall. She was inordinately jealous of them all for being able to sleep.

She couldn't stand it. She sat straight up, then like a sleep-walker, but one fully cognizant of her actions, left her room and crept down the stairs. Her own reflections in the arched windows made her think of ghosts, of spirits dying in a burst of pale light against the black night sky. She clutched the hem of her short lavender nightgown. The material was so thin it didn't protect her from the dank air that hovered at the bottom of the stairs and yet the night was warm. She picked up the phone and put a call through to Jake's hotel. The desk clerk asked her to be

patient as he dialed the room. She listened with intense anticipation to the shrill ring . . . but Jake did not pick up the
receiver. The clerk apologized. Mr. Adams was not in. Would
she care to leave a message? No. It was conceivable that Jake
could still be having dinner at eight o'clock Colorado time, but
she had phoned him last night at midnight his time and there
was no answer. Where he had been she could not imagine; nor
did she want to try. But she would not call again. That much
was certain.

Her room was empty, her bed beckoned her with a mocking
air, knowing full well she would not be able to sleep. Something
in her was crumbling. She bit her lip till she tasted blood. Then
suddenly, instead of submitting to another depressing night of
insomnia, she decided to fight. She slipped on her sandals and
located her small gold lamé coin purse, then she glided silently
across the hall into Perry's room and sat beside him on the bed.

"Wake up," she urged. He opened his eyes to find her head
bathed in a somber ray of moonlight that glided down across
the vacant field to pierce his window. Her hair was wild and
twisted, her countenance intense and stubborn , her lips parted,
blood-red, quivering.

"What is it, Renee?" he asked, rubbing his eyes.

"We're going to do something very daring," she announced,
pulling the covers from his thin body. "We're going to go to
New York."

"What! Now?" he could not believe it.

"Get dressed." She hurried him out of bed. "We'll be back
tomorrow before they miss us."

"But you aren't dressed!" he blubbered.

"Yes, I am," she calmly replied. "Dressed enough." She was
too edgy to even consider changing her clothes. "Hurry," she
picked a shirt at random from the closet and held it to him. "We
have to make the next train."

Perry dutifully followed Renee down the stairs which creaked
slightly under their weight; at the bottom she turned and
cautioned Perry to close the door gently behind him. Renee flew
down the garden path toward the country road that wound
through towering elms and poplars to the train station. Perry
nervously glanced back at the windows to see if anyone was
watching their sudden flight but only moonlight fell there and
the world seemed suddenly barren and lonely as if he and the
woman running ahead in the skimpy purple nightgown, her

hair like a flame in the darkness, were the only two inhabitants in a land filled with death and sleep.

The train was virtually empty and they arrived at Grand Central Station by midnight. Renee jumped onto the platform and took deep breaths as if she were suddenly in a country grove on a young spring morning. Then she grabbed the boy's hand and yanked him along behind her all the way to the subway.

It was Perry's first ride in a subway car. The bright lights hurt his eyes; the dirty pink and orange seats intimidated him. The din of the wheels striking the track was ear splitting, the fetid air rushing in from the black cement walls blew their hair and carried pages of newspapers from one end of the car to the other. An obese woman across from them was finishing an ice cream cone of soft chocolate and vanilla swirl. She suddenly gasped as if she had tasted poison and dropped the cone on the floor. She had hurt her gum; she opened her mouth and massaged the gap between two pointed teeth in the center of the bottom row. The gap was large and bruised and there was dark blood pumping to the surface; tears filled the woman's eyes and she muttered something in a foreign language, then threw her hands into the air with a cry of grief. Two young men next to them stared at Renee. She did her best to ignore them. They had ugly faces; one had a rash of small open sores running in a figure eight down one side of his face. The rash continued on his arm. His T shirt was black with dirt, there were drops of blood on his pants. Next to him slumped his wiry friend with wavy ebony hair; he was dressed in a cheap matching dark green polyester outfit. His pants were so tight they had begun to split down one side. His shirt was covered with black silhouettes of women. A black heart on a chain hung around his neck. A sharp-toothed comb was placed just so in his hair. His breath smelled of stale spice and wine. He and his buddy nudged each other and made lewd comments about Renee. The din of metal bruising metal increased. Stagnant water dripped from the ceiling, Perry tried to shake it off his shoes. The fan above them groaned, then stopped. The woman across the way picked up the ice cream cone and brushed away the dirt. She began to lick it once again. Her gum felt better. The train rushed on. A band of boys in baseball jackets raced screaming from one car to the next, swinging around the iron poles, falling, picking them-selves up, their laughter dying several cars away.

"Cigarette?" one of the young men extended his pack to

Renee. She waved a refusal without looking over. Then, determined not to give up, they offered one to Perry who shook his head no and this sent them into hysterics. Then the one with the bad breath and comb in his hair asked Renee to come home with them.

"No," she said coldly.

"Why not?" he slurred his words. "We got a big bed. That is if my pig of a girlfriend ain't in it."

"No."

They got off at the next stop, the man with the rash grabbing his cock through his pants and shaking it as he passed Renee.

A cop got on at the other end and stood staring at his reflection in the glass door opposite, fixing his moustache. The train screamed. There was a jolt. The cop fell a little to the right, then steadied himself against the door. The lights faded, then burst back with a silver intensity. Renee pulled Perry off at the next station.

At the exit some black youths had a small white woman trapped in the turnstile and were demanding money. She was a tiny, mousy woman with cockeyed glasses and she was sobbing, pleading with them to let her go but they demanded she empty her purse into their hands. Ignoring Perry and Renee who were passing through the nearby stile, the tallest boy tried to intimidate her by slapping the air in front of her just missing her face by inches. He pulled little tufts of her hair and repeated rapidly, "Come on, white cunt, hurry up, hurry up, hurry up, hurry up, white cunt, hurry up." His words rang in Renee's ears even after she reached the street which was shadowy and empty, the low storefront windows hushed and filled with dust and machinery, bits of wool and thread, and above these shops rose skyscrapers whose tips were sometimes masked in a veil of humid clouds. Occasionally there would appear a patch of dry open air and a few stars would glisten; Perry took heart to see his friends in all this strangeness even if he could not immediately identify them, separated as they were from the complete map of the sky.

They headed north. At times a taxicab would pass, slow down and the driver would give them hopeful glances but Renee wanted to walk. She felt like walking to the ends of the earth.

"You aren't tired yet, are you?" she questioned the boy.

"No, not at all." His apprehensiveness was fading and he was enjoying the adventure.

They passed rows of small stores selling tropical plants and exotic fish confined in phosphorescent aquariums, their gills and fins pronounced by the magnified glass, their pink and blue flesh delicate and shimmering. The heat poured down from the sky. Though it was after midnight the pavement was fiery and one longed passionately for the dawn with its cool softness. A dog, howling with pain, limped on three legs across their path; its fourth leg was bundled up with several bandannas and the animal kept it raised with all the strength it had. Loaves of bread dumped from the back of a truck lay scattered in the street; broken glass glistened on the sidewalks. The sound of gospel music blared from a loudspeaker over a record shop that was locked tight with a metal security gate pulled across the front, four heavy padlocks attached to it. A few record jackets of old Broadway musicals were displayed in the windows. The voices belonged to men, perhaps four or five men, and ranged from the most sorrowful bass to the most shocking soprano, singing in sweet harmony, traveling together on one long passage to God's Kingdom.

"It's only a little while before we reach the hotel," Renee assured Perry. And within fifteen minutes they found themselves at the crowded Broadway-Times Square area, the men and women of the late night shoving and jostling for the last rush of honky-tonk, squeezing the juice from Friday night. Perry grabbed Renee's hand and she pulled him through the mob at her own hectic pace.

"You aren't sorry you came?" she shouted back to Perry. "After all, it's better than lying in bed at home."

"It's fine," he answered though he felt he was at a carnival where everyone wore grotesque masks to hide their actual faces, where no one was allowed to smile, indeed a smile would have seemed an obscenity, a gross departure from the norm. But it didn't matter because the people were fascinating. His hand sweated a little in Renee's palm.

"Hungry?" she stopped at a pizza stand and bought him a slice. An old bum in a wool coat kept rubbing the boy's head, talking about his dead son and swearing before God that he was going to find the person responsible and slit open his belly. Renee bought some pineapple ice which dissolved in the sweaty night before she could finish it. She insisted that Perry have another piece of pizza while she sat in a doorway and stared at the crowd, her alert eyes taking in everything.

"This is too much to finish," Perry complained. "I'm getting a stomach ache already."

"Then throw it away. You don't have to finish it."

"But where should I throw it?"

Renee looked bored. "Behind me, in the doorway."

"Renee, you can see up your dress when you sit that way," he whispered discreetly in her ear and she shut her knees together tightly but her face was tired and weary.

Across the street a white woman with a thick Germanic accent screamed out the window at some black whores who were huddled below in a doorway, "I told you never stand there again! Get out! Get out from there!"

"Shut up, old mama!" one of them screamed at her while another invited her to call the cops.

"I'll call them when hell freezes over! Now, you filthy nigger bitches get away from my window!" And she hurled a pot of geraniums through the air with all her strength, but she was a terrible shot and it crashed yards from the target against a lumbering meat truck that was creeping along the street, gears grinding. The whores laughed and the woman slammed her window shut.

Renee and Perry moved on. Her pace had slowed, she was dripping wet and she tugged at the sleeves of her nightgown, clutching her coin purse tightly. A dance was letting out, some benefit for a housing project on the Upper West Side, and a crowd was gathering to hoot and jeer at the couples as they left. The women, mostly heavy set, of all races and ages, swept the long trains of their rented gowns from the sticky, unpleasant sidewalk. A toothless man tapped one of them on the shoulder and croaked, "Can you give me a penny to get back to hell?" And the crowd roared in approval.

The Hotel Dove was dark and shuttered with no lights in the windows. Renee hugged Perry around the shoulders and kept her arm there as they took their final steps. The sky was clear to the east and over downtown Brooklyn the Pleiades sparkled; Perry excitedly pointed them out to Renee.

"You know, the seven sisters! The famous cluster!"

"Oh, yeah," she shook her head doubtfully.

A woman hopped by them on one foot; she was bald, her white head speckled on top with red patches. A giddy smile was on her face and she bounced her head from one side to the other as if she were balancing it on her neck and any moment it would fall off. "My Lord Jesus Satan," she rushed her words. "My Lord Jesus Christ Satan don't come no more." She stuck out her tongue at Perry and danced on.

"Wait here," Renee positioned Perry in front of the steps. "I have to go around the side and knock on Donny's window so he'll let us in."

Perry, left alone, realized there was something in the shadow of the steps. A stench drifted from there, so putrid, he wanted to retch. His eyes pierced the darkness, trying to find its source. A man was leaning against the pillar, smoking. In the flame Perry could see gigantic nostrils, the size of a horse's, but there were no other features. The rest was blood and bones. Blood that didn't drip but was held in place by invisible tissue. When Renee returned she too saw the man and gasped. She seemed to be looking at a giant heart pumping red and purple instead of a human face and yet he was smoking a cigarette. How could it be. The doors to the hotel swung back and Donny stood in the entrance motioning them inside. Again Renee put her arm around the boy's shoulders and together they ran up the stairs, refusing to breathe the monstrous odor, refusing to glance back at the figure leaning quietly against the column. Donny shut and bolted the doors behind them, then pressed the button and the steel trap slid across.

Renee brushed Perry's face. "You're exhausted. You've walked for miles."

"My stomach's a little upset, that's all." He surveyed the draughty lobby, interested in the murals of the Grand Canyon and Niagara Falls.

Renee shook some water from her hair. "Such a miserable, hot night." She pulled the lavender material from her body. It had especially stuck against her chest where there was a giant wet patch. She pressed Perry's hand against it, made a face and he gave a shy laugh. "Well," she said. "Time for bed." She led him to the elevator.

Donny sat behind the desk closely watching them, but when Renee caught his eye he swung his legs onto the counter, tipped his chair back and switched on the T.V. set propped in front of his face. The elevator opened. Perry waited for Renee to go in first but she was shaking, a distant expression in her eyes. She ran her fingers along the wall, then patted Perry on the back. "Go on," she said. "I'll be up in a minute. I have something to do. Press the button for the fifth floor and walk to the end of the hall. My door is the last on the left and it's unlocked. Wait for me there." Perry nodded, understanding, and he waved as the door shut. Then Renee straightened up. She stretched her muscles. It was a good feeling. She stared at the wall. Sounds of laughter, applause from the television. Then it stopped abruptly. She turned around. He had flipped it off. Donny was still leaning back in his chair; he rubbed one foot against the other as he lit a cigar. He was a skinny, homely boy whose T shirt drooped against his frame like a bedsheet and whose blue jeans were starchy and too big. His arms were long and gangly. He didn't look her way.

Not knowing what she was doing, she turned and walked to the end of the corridor and down some old wooden steps to the basement. She rubbed her hand along the shaky bannister until she realized she might get splinters and quickly removed it. Reaching the bottom she stepped into a pool of water that had run in from the showers which some woman had just left. A dampness lingered in the air. She moved into the shower room. Light filtered in from a naked bulb hanging outside the chamber where the stolen merchandise was stored. Renee counted the nozzles. There were fourteen. Three were still dripping. She watched the drops splash onto the tiles. An open vanity case was in the corner. She knelt down. Someone had forgotten to take it back upstairs. It looked like Bee's case, with a pack of pink cigarettes, tissue paper, a half-used jar of cold cream, a vaginal spray, a hairnet. It made her sick. She slammed down the lid. Donny was standing in the doorway. She had half-expected him. She stood up. She counted the nozzles again. Only two were dripping now. She was suddenly so drained, she felt so dissipated, that she began walking without even experiencing her own movements. At the door she passed Donny who reached out and touched her gently on the waist. She smiled at him and walked on. But he moved behind and now she felt both hands close ever so lightly around her waist. She shook her head weakly to discourage him but that only made him tighten his grip. She tried to pull away but he pinched her there as hard as he could and it made her cry in pain. She turned angrily and slapped him across the face. That was what he had been waiting for. He shoved her roughly into a corner and slapped her a few times on the upper part of her body; he tried to get her to fight him, to try to wear her down. She ducked under his arm but he caught hold of her and with one hand pushed her face down against an old wooden table and with the other reached up her dress and slowly, effortlessly worked his fist into her ass. Though she thrashed and cried, she was powerless, a victim of the impaling; he was too strong, there was nothing for her to do, she couldn't even turn her head around to bite him. Suddenly he swung her around and stuck his other hand up her cunt and then with both arms he pummeled her insides, his fists battering hard. She screamed in agony, she pulled his hair and scratched at his face and bit his forehead, but he took it, he withstood her blows, never stopping the power of his fists, her resistance only making him shove harder. She could no longer hold herself up and stumbled and he went with her as she writhed violently on the floor by the stairs in the pool of stagnant water. The pain was so intense, so horrible, she prepared for death. And still he came at her, his fingers now clawing her insides. All she could see was a gush of blood running down his face. A last tired scream tore out of her. Her eyes were twisted. They closed. He thought she was either dead or had fainted. He gave a quick tug and both hands came out but Renee thought she was on an operating table and that her heart, liver and lungs had just been sucked out by a plastic tube that had been inserted inside her brain. Finally she opened her eyes, remembering where she was. Donny crouched beside her, peering intently into her face. His hands were on his hips. She tried to sit up, but the pain was so intense that it was impossible. As long as she was lying she could stand it. But he wasn't finished. He leaned over her face and his teeth came down on her lips and he bit them as savagely as he could, then moved back and stared at her again. She flipped over on her side and began to crawl upstairs, her legs cooled by the foul water. She pulled herself up slowly. If she could crawl into the lobby maybe someone would help her. Donny pulled out his lighter and flipped it, running the flame along her leg to try to scare her. Terrified, she flinched and as much as it hurt her she jerked back out of the way, then continued her slow crawl. Next he put the lighter to her breasts. She saw his face: though bleeding, it was impassive, calm. Next he held the flame close to her face and she had to turn her head and shut her eyes. It was no use begging for mercy, that would only goad him on. She dragged herself along with all her strength. At the top of the stairs he stooped over her, still torturing her with the flame which he waved viciously around her hair and eyes. She felt its horrible white power. Then he stood straight, giving her one last look, stuck the lighter back in his pocket and returned to his desk where he flung himself once again in his chair. Renee staggered to her feet and felt her way into the elevator. She pressed the button for her floor. She never thought the door would open again and she died many times from the pain within her before she felt herself moving dreamily down the hall, her door in sight and slightly ajar. Suddenly she couldn't hold herself any longer and slid to her knees. She crawled the rest of the way, sometimes stopping to gasp for breath. She had an intense desire to cry, but no tears came. Once she lowered her ear to the hall floor. She thought she heard sounds from below, a tapping, perhaps Pandora pacing, but no, it must be mice in the wood, or air that had been trapped in the planks hissing with release.

After Renee had shut herself in her room, she noticed Perry, startled, sitting in the corner, the light from the street playing on his face.

"Where were you?" There was fear in his voice. "I waited for a long time."

"Didn't I tell you . . . I . . . I had something to do," her voice was hollow.

"But your nightgown looks like a dishrag! . . . You're all wet and filthy!" He still sat, a prisoner in the chair, afraid to come any closer.

"I am?" she was confused. Her mouth turned into a pout. There was an awful pressure inside her. She forgot for a moment why it was there. Then she flung herself onto the bed and covered her face with the pillow. She was possessed by a series of dry sobs. Then she heaved the pillow across the room where it knocked her lipsticks and make-up off the table.

"Are you going to sit there all night, in the corner," she cried angrily, "or are you going to come lie down with me where at least you can be comfortable!"

Perry rose and tentatively edged his way toward the bed. He stared down into her impatient eyes. Then he kicked his shoes off. Renee felt his body flattening the space next to her. He moved sensitively towards her until his toes were against her ankle, then she felt her own body collapse.

Chapter Eight

The air conditioning had broken down for the third night in a row and most of the men considered this the last straw, threatening to bring the union down on their plant manager's head. But he was clever and decided to inform them tomorrow night that it was fixed and working to capacity whether it was or not; after all, it was the *idea* of it being broken that irritated the men . . . normally it was impossible for them to feel the cool air since it dissipated so rapidly on its journey from the high recesses of the hangar to the hot working spaces on the factory floor.

Stewart, for one, didn't miss it. He had learned to live with flame in his face, with a mask of heat covering him head to toe. "Learn to adjust," he said simply to one of the men who was bitching the loudest. The man, struggling under a wheel he was trying to attach to a big cycle, glared at Reggino but was reluctant to come back with a smart remark since Stewart was a strong guy and had never been afraid to take a punch at somebody.

Stewart made his way to his locker. There his dinner was waiting, two ham and turkey club sandwiches covered with foil. He smiled to himself as he unwrapped them, recalling how he had kept his nose between two books all afternoon, forgetting to eat, even getting a late start to work. It was so uncharacteristic of him. . . Yet when he had passed a bookstore that morning he had been fascinated by its window display illustrating the history of western civilization; on impulse he had stepped inside and bought two books — one about Hannibal's dramatic attempts to conquer Rome and the other about warring religious factions during the Middle Ages. And he hadn't been able to put either volume down. Transported as easily and as totally as a child with a book of fairy tales, he left his room to wander with his sword along the simpler paths of past centuries.

"What's on your mind — if anything?" Ed Ubal snapped, leaning against the locker.

"Nothin'." Ubal would never understand the enjoyment he had derived that afternoon.

Ubal continued, "You keep eating like that and you're gonna wind up with a belly like me."

"Not on your life, Ed. Not on your life."

"No?"

"Are you kidding? If you saw the exercises I went through each day you'd know better. I'm fit." His face darkened.

"Yeah, yeah. I know you are. Don't let it worry you."

"You ought to do a few sit-ups each morning, Ed. Might get rid of some of *that*—" and he pushed Ed's stomach gently where an open button revealed a chunk of pink flesh.

"I'm just at the age now where if I started with these exercises I'd have a heart attack. Already got a hernia and a weak kidney. Couldn't stand nothing else, boy. Don't want my sons burying me yet."

The image flashed through Stewart's mind of the two boys roaring up to the gravesite on their Yamahas to pay their last respects to Dad— the thought amused him and he walked back to his job in a good mood.

He stooped low at his spot on the assembly line, pulled the goggles over his eyes and energetically began to weld the cycle panels. The harder he went at it the more the sparks flew and the more immersed he became in the rhythm of the work. He let his mind go blank until he felt almost the same sensation as when he was sleeping. He woke himself around four A.M., put down his tools, wiped the pouring sweat from his cheeks and took a long look around the plant.

He found the men at their stations, hardly moving, making deafening noises with their high-powered tools . . . Dorothy Pulley stood in the distance pouring coffee for the guys on their breaks, sharing a joke with them, pushing her glasses higher on the bridge of her nose, occasionally casting an awkward glance in Stewart's direction, wondering if he was coming over for some coffee too. He was on the verge of returning to work instead of taking his break when a loud yell came up the line about seven men away. Stewart saw a guy stagger and fall on his back, his hands clutching his eyes. From nowhere men gathered round and there was the eerie sound of machinery being halted in a chain reaction along the line. . . Bees in some dense garden stopped buzzing and suddenly deserted the flowers one by one. . . The men formed a circle around the moaning figure whose throaty sobs echoed in the silent hangar.

"Let me through," Stewart cried urgently, breaking the circle, kneeling beside the injured man. "What is it? What's wrong?" his voice was soft, pleading. But the man shook his head and the only sound he made was when he cleared his throat of phlegm and took deep breaths.

Stewart glanced up at the quiet onlookers for some kind of encouragement but none came. He was on his own. He tried to coax the man to take his hands from his face . . . but there was resistance. "Let's have a peek here . . . come on," he soothed. "It might not be all that bad. . ." And his fingers, working gently and insistently, were able to pull the clenched hands away. Now everyone recognized the sprawled figure of George Koppfler, a new guy who had started his job less than a week ago, who was just a kid really and scared to death.

"My eye, my eye," George whispered excitedly.

"Yeah, I see," Stewart gazed hard into Koppfler's right eye and brushed some fine red hair that had stuck to the lashes back to its proper spot on the forehead.

There was a piece of metal, perfectly round and about half the size of his orb, lodged in his eye — it had sliced it and there was blood, but the metal had not pierced through the surface to the retina . . . it was just stuck on the filmy skin of the eye, blocking his vision and causing pain.

"I bet it hurts like hell, but it's going to be easy to get out. You aren't injured," Stewart smiled.

"But I can't see out of it. It's burning. . ."

"No, no . . . it's caught in your eye and has cut it up real good but it's all on the exterior. . ." He motioned to the men to carry the boy, who was over six feet, to the coffee table where they could lay him underneath a strong lamp. "George," Stewart shook his finger as a warning while Al Blane and two other big men lifted the boy horizontally by the feet and shoulders, "you should always protect your face. That's the first thing you learn around here. You've just got one face, George, buddy, and you don't want to mess it up."

Beneath the light, it took only a moment to extract the metal. Blane held the eye open while Stewart eased the piece out with his thumb and index finger. "Keep it shut," Stewart commanded and pressed down on the lid. Dorothy had called the doctor who was due any moment to flush the eye, check it for lye and give the boy penicillin. He would decide whether there was serious damage that might require emergency treatment at the hospital.

George forgot to thank Stewart as he lay on the table in a kind of nether world, but Stewart's actions were not lost on the other men who patted him on the back, congratulating him for his quick handling of the situation. Stewart felt a sudden exhilaration. He shrugged as if he had done nothing and stalked back to the line. *Christ, it's what every one of them should have done . . . but I guess they didn't have the guts.* As Stewart pulled his goggles down over his eyes he decided he was made to be a leader — it seemed some men could take the pressure when it broke the door down and he was one of them. Nobody else had lifted a finger. The other men looked up to him, just as the boys in his home town had done when they had flocked around him like a group of trembling birds, revering his every thought, always ready to follow his orders. What was he doing here without a mind of his own? Wasn't he made for better things? Wasn't he built of stronger stuff?

Once he glanced back at the coffee table. The doctor had arrived and was examining young Koppfler . . . the men watched anxiously . . . Al Blane hovered over the boy following the doctor's movements with a sincere and steady interest. . . Suddenly Stewart felt a grinding at the pit of his stomach and a creeping sensation that he had gone through this exact experience at an earlier time . . . he had seen them all, quite still, leaning over this boy somewhere before. . . But no, it was impossible! . . . Then what was it that the tableau suggested? . . Ah, he knew. . .

His father lying on his hospital bed one early spring . . . the light crashing from above in a solid white ray. . . Doctors, concerned, pressed around the bed and Mrs. Clark unbuttoned the coat which enclosed her massive body, brought her fingers carefully to rest on the footboard of the bed and hunched forward, her eyes seeking those of Stewart's father. . . Stewart had collapsed in a corner of the room and was studying the scene before him, imagining his father was going to pass away momentarily from the mysterious respiratory ailment . . . he heard labored breathing . . . he studied a bowl filled with daffodils on the nearby table . . . Mrs. Clark still searched desperately for eye contact. . . He didn't die . . . with the aid of oxygen, with constant care, he survived and in the ensuing weeks gained back much of his strength . . . Stewart visited him every day . . . Mrs. Clark was always there by the bedside, knitting, or reading mysteries or westerns. . . She had a ragged, a brutal, hard face yet her words were always kind and encouraging. . . She had been his father's "companion" for about five or six years, coming to live with the man after Stewart's mother died. . . Stewart had never wanted to know her . . . he didn't like her. . . One night as he left his father's house a carload of boys whom Stewart didn't recognize passed him as he was getting into his car. One of the boys yelled out the window as the driver gunned the motor, "Your father re-married a nigger." Stewart was too surprised to be irritated . . . but he was possessed with a need to discover the truth. . . One afternoon, after Mrs. Clark had gone into the bathroom, Stewart noticed some photos in her open purse . . . noiselessly, he examined them . . . they were of her children in their Phil-adelphia home . . . the children were black . . . so Mrs. Clark was either black herself or had been married to a black man. . . If his father knew, Stewart reasoned, he would have killed her. . . On this afternoon in spring he watched Mrs. Clark reading by the window which the nurse had allowed her to open a crack as the hospital room was like a hothouse . . . a new bunch of daffodils stirred in the stiff March breeze . . . Stewart shared her secret only the woman didn't know it. . . She was always so condescending to him, and his father always took her side . . . but he could put an end to that in a flash . . . just by telling what he knew . . . Stewart's father nodded at him . . . he was feeling better . . . his mouth was set in a scowl . . . his jaws held in an unyielding vice . . . it was a face Stewart knew so well . . . pitiless, breaking with self-pity. . . "Still think you'll be a cop, son?" . . . "Don't know, Dad. The tests are pretty tough. . . I don't worry about the physical part, but I hear the multiple choice questions are confusing, you have to be familiar with a lot of police procedure —" "Hold on," he interrupted, his voice cracking. "Hold on a minute. I suggest before you go around being so eager to help other people you look out more for your own dad. I've been lying here in the hospital . . . why ain't you done more for me?" Mrs. Clark was on her feet. "Daddy," she scolded gently, "Stewart can't do more than he's been doing, coming to visit you, inquiring after your health to the doctors and nurses. . ." He paused, staring hard at the woman. "Oh, all right," the old man grumbled. "Then tell me more about this test you gotta take. . ." Stewart hated her . . . why should his relationship with his father depend on her words? He sat down slowly, his cap in his hand, and explained for the next twenty minutes everything he knew about the upcoming examination. . .

The factory doors opened and dawn streamed in. The coffee table was empty. Stewart guessed George Koppfler had eventually stood up and walked out, just like his father had done the day he left the hospital.

When Renee woke the next morning she found Perry sitting in the chair by the window, his eyes fixed on the sparse Sunday morning traffic. She calmly changed into a dress. Then they hailed a cab which took them to Grand Central Station. The train ride back was swift, the cars gliding easily on the sun bruised tracks. The two did not speak.

They arrived before noon. They had not been missed; Ella had assumed that Renee was still sleeping and that Perry was in the countryside on one of his routine bicycle outings. The pair never discussed the midnight incident; Renee felt no need to apologize, Perry seemed to suffer no ill feeling toward her. But they were wary of each other, avoiding close contact. They were uneasy when they were left alone together in a room or when they passed by chance on the stairs.

Jake arrived in the middle of the week, a few days after Renee's night in the city. He had phoned on the afternoon of her return to the Scotchsmith's and she had been very relieved to hear his voice, yet somehow she felt cheated that he had not called a day earlier . . . it was all wrong, his call coming when she needed it least. She anticipated his visit with excitement, dying to confess to him the frightful trip back to the city taken at a moment of exhaustion when sleep was a phantom always a few paces ahead of her, leaving only a veil of loneliness on his trail. But when Jake actually came through the door and kissed her with longing, she felt afraid in his presence and believed she could never share the memory of that night . . . he would not understand. It would only create a chasm between them instead of pulling a thread together. It must remain dark, buried. He must not know. If she was cheating herself of the comfort that would come to her with a confession, at least she felt assured that nothing between them was changed, that he wasn't scanning her face, staring into her eyes with a strange or reproving manner.

As for Jake, he was in a positive, cheerful mood. He seemed more composed than ever before. He took Renee for a walk on the beach. They strolled slowly, lingering over an unusual shell imbedded in the sand or a jellyfish dying near the crest where green weeds rushed forward to meet the colored pebbles of the shore. Jake wore blue jeans which had just been laundered and the smell of the bleach and powder stung the air more deeply than the scent of the seaweed torn from the sea depths which surfaced now and again.

While Jake talked about his job Renee found herself only half listening; she was acutely aware of how his face changed from moment to moment. A face never held the same expression; it changed constantly like the sea. Today the sea was like a patch of wild emeralds which darkened momentarily when a cloud cast down its thick shadow. Today Jake's face was charming and carefree as if a drug had drawn the eventuality of pain and worry from the muscles and his mind had been filled with contentment. Boats floated on the emerald sea. Jake's pants felt rough and pleasant to touch.

He pulled her down next to him on a scrap of driftwood. "So," he said. "I'll be gone this last time for only a few days. Just to finish things up."

"And then?"

"I come back for you and we find a new place to live in the city."

"A new place?" Her voice quavered.

"No more living in the hotel," he insisted. "Oh, I don't mind for a week or so until we find something suitable. But it's only temporary. My apartment is too small for us. And anyway, I don't think you'd like it much, you wouldn't be comfortable there. It isn't you."

She laughed. "I'm not sure what you have in mind then."

"Oh, it doesn't matter. Just keep your arm around my waist like that. That's all."

Her hand moved slightly from the jeans to his ribs, feeling the stomach beneath the cool shirt. She was holding onto something. Something tangible. She was suddenly overcome by nausea and she leaned over and a pool of vomit streamed from her mouth.

"My God," he said, startled. "What's wrong?"

"Nothing. Not a thing," she replied as he brought out his handkerchief and she wiped her lips. Soon the stains were gone and she kicked sand over the tiny pool of sickness at her feet, sank to her knees on the sand before him and rested her head in his lap. She remained like that for some time. Her hair turned in the wind. She closed her eyes.

"Renee, my darling. . ."

"It's no use," she looked up at him. "It's no use trying to drain all the sickness out of me. You'd never get that last drop."

"If you're talking about what's past, you can forget it."

"Don't you see? I've been wounded . . . like someone in a battle . . . only mine is a wound that never heals. It's a wound of memory."

"Come on. Stand up," he said and he drew her to her feet. "We're made for better than this. There's not going to be any of this talk when you're with me. I like to think I'm in control of myself, of my life. You are too." They walked back to the house, arms entwined, but not lingering any longer over the shells or jellyfish. He gave her a strong squeeze on the waist. They took a nap together before dinner.

The plant was closed every Sunday and Stewart could think of nothing he particularly wanted to do on his night off. A couple of guys downstairs had invited him over for drinks but he didn't feel like sitting around having to keep some boring conversation from its rightful place in the grave. It was all bullshit. He threw the paper down in disgust — no decent movies were playing and the only sports event that seemed interesting, a U.S. invitational track meet, had been sold out for months and there were rumors that it would be cancelled at the last minute anyway due to some political controversy. He shut off the radio, drowning out a woman who was reading the weather report in such clear, icy tones. *Fuck it, just say it might rain.*

He cleaned his firearms for awhile, but his mind was not on the polishing. His eyes kept falling to the night street below. He didn't like the idea of caring for his collection in a haphazard way . . . he felt guilty unless he was devoting his undivided attention to the assorted weapons spread dark and cold on the table. He was more interested in the life on the street, in the endless shadows passing beneath the skeletal girders of the West Side Highway.

He considered taking a drive . . . up around the Cloisters maybe or to one of the beaches where he could sit and watch the tide pull out. But the idea of planning a specific destination wearied him before he started. He should just get in the car and drive . . . it didn't matter where . . . just follow one road into another, take it easy, get some peace out of the night.

Before he knew it Stewart was crossing into New Jersey, following his familiar route to work. It seemed natural, the car almost drove itself. But he cursed himself that he didn't have any better imagination. He was a creature of habit he guessed. Fog spun across the bridge like a cloudy web. The vehicles seemed trapped in it, struggling to escape, lights blinking off and on in a silent plea. Sometimes the heavy white mist provided a surprising illusion — the cars weren't moving at all. They were frozen in a blanket of snow which would never thaw. Only the tires spun. . .

He turned off at the usual exit. He was only a few blocks from Dorothy Pulley's house. He generally let her out of the car right here, against this very curb. Up ahead was the Mr. Do-Nut shop but it was closed tight now. Across the street was a Roy Rogers roast beef palace. The fog was lifting . . . he saw that the restaurant was filled with people. He pulled in. He didn't feel like a roast beef sandwich but he wouldn't mind a Coke.

"Large or small?" the girl behind the counter questioned him.

"Large with a lot of ice."

Stewart thought the girl looked a little like Dorothy Pulley . . . hell, she looked a lot like her, same dumb face, same monstrous glasses. He thought she might be Dorothy's sister.

"You aren't a Pulley?" he asked as she handed him his Coke.

She was embarrassed as she had no idea what he was talking about. She looked back to the manager, a plain, bleached out looking guy who was sweeping the floor.

"You aren't one?" Stewart grinned.

"Hey, mister, leave her alone. Take your drink on outside," the manager indicated the door.

"What did you say?" Stewart demanded, livid.

"You heard me. I'm the manager here, bud, and I'm telling you to get out."

Before he knew exactly what he was doing Stewart bounded over the counter and seized the man by the scruff of his neck and pressed him back against the counter.

"Take your hands off me or I'll call the police!"

"Don't bother. I'm a policeman," Stewart answered in a rage.

"Let go!"

But Stewart, to give him a scare, inched him a little toward the vat where the French fries were bubbling. "Look out!" the manager panicked. Stewart contemptuously released him, then whipped his wallet out of his back pocket and produced an officer's I.D. card.

"Yeah, I see it," the manager was gruff but humbled.

"If you beg for trouble you're gonna get it," Stewart assured him. Then he clenched his hands, "The iron fist of the law's on my side, buddy. Don't forget it."

The man rubbed his neck and the girl who looked like Dorothy Pulley burst into tears.

"I should take you in for assaulting an officer," Reggino spat on the floor. "But I'm gonna let you off this time. . ." His eyes strayed to the girl. "Now I'm gonna ask you again, are you a Pulley?"

"Yes," she cried doubtfully. "Yes!"

"What's your name then?"

"Margaret Fisher."

"Oh, shit," Stewart said under his breath as he swung back over the counter. He grabbed his Coke and strode cockily back to his car, putting on a real show for the other diners. He doubled up with laughter when he thought about what a fool he had made of everybody. *Stupid buggers. . . You can fuck anybody over and they won't say shit. . .* The guy had fallen for his I.D. that had expired a couple of years ago. He'd passed for an off duty cop. He lit a cigarette but for some reason his fingers were trembling. He stared at them with surprise. He could make a lot of trouble for people if he wanted to and get away with it. That thought burrowed into his brain as he sat staring out into the night. He finished his Coke and began to lethargically chew the ice. In his trunk were a red flashing light that attached to the front dashboard, his .38 Smith and Wesson revolver in its holster, his handcuffs, his nightstick. Wouldn't he get a laugh if Dorothy happened to drive by on her way home and he followed her with his flashing red light and made her pull over. He'd make her sit waiting in her car, scared shitless, until he sauntered over real slow and told her she was under arrest. Of course then she'd recognize him and have a good laugh too. But that situation hardly seemed likely.

He drove past her house to find her car in the driveway and her silhouette against the shades. She was in for the night. He drove on. Without warning he pulled into the deserted parking lot of a Sears Roebuck store. Like somebody under a spell and without the trace of a grin on his face he opened his trunk and brought all his police apparatus into the front seat. He hooked up the red light to the dashboard. It sent strong flashes against the dull cement of the store. He switched it off.

He began to drive again. He covered the same ground, passing Dorothy's house. The silhouettes of two women crossed in front of the living room window. The other one was probably her mother. The Roy Rogers restaurant was closing. The lights along the front window went out and the big neon board announcing the specials for the day dimmed slowly as if it were sinking into sleep. Four farmboys in bibbed overalls were arguing in front of a broken down pickup truck. One gave another a shove. *I wouldn't take that, man.* But to Stewart's surprise the boy made no effort to defend himself. He turned his back and began to walk away when the other jumped him. They crashed onto the cement and started punching each other. Their friends tried to break up the fight but with no success. Stewart had a crazy desire to run up and put a stop to things. They'd listen to a cop. He'd line them up and chew them out and if one of them talked back it would be too bad for the kid. He'd give him a whack across the face that he'd never forget. There — the guys were able to tear the tiger off the mauled victim. *He thinks he's a real tough Mother.* They held him tight as he struggled, eager to keep the fight going. *That's right, hold him just like that . . . until I get there . . .* and Stewart began to sweat . . . his blond beard became moist and his lips went dry. He'd have loved to break that guy's face open while the others were holding him back. Break it wide open with his fist. Abruptly he accelerated and the car jerked forward, leaving a patch of burning rubber on the street and the startled gazes of all four boys following his vanishing taillights.

He had to get away. He wanted to be home, locked between his sheets. The ramp to the freeway was just ahead. He waited at the last red light. A small green Datsun passed in front of him.

It stopped at a little house beneath the shelter of the highway. A boy climbed out of the car, opened the passenger door and helped a girl to the sidewalk. The light turned green. Stewart stared as the couple, arm in arm, walked leisurely to the house. The car behind him honked. Stewart, instead of going onto the highway, turned left and idled his car a few houses from the one where the girl was standing on the porch, kissing the boy good night. The door opened. Her father joined them. He vigorously shook the young man's hand. Then he and his daughter disappeared into the house. The boy got into his car and started down the road. Stewart followed.

There was no traffic now and there were few houses. They were passing along a wooded area, shifting away from the highway, turning down into a kind of ravine choked with underbrush and ragged, sooty pine trees. Without thinking ahead Stewart switched on the red light. It showered its blood red radiance as far as the eye could see. It bounced, as between two mirrors, from Stewart's front window to the rear of the boy's car. The boy pulled to the side of the road. Stewart drew up behind him. He sat for a few moments, then walked to the Datsun. The air seemed cold.

"Can I see your license please?" he asked, banishing all emotion, as the boy rolled down the window.

Visibly shaken the boy fumbled in his glove compartment. "Is something wrong?" he stammered.

There was no answer. Stewart waited, standing erect, feeling powerful. Another car cruised by on the lonely road, sending its weak headlights into the spruce forest. When it had rounded a corner all was still again and dark except for the flashlight Stewart was using to examine the license and the grave red bursting behind them.

"You can call in on the radio and see I don't have any tickets or violations," the boy said, gaining his composure. For the first time he really took a good look at Stewart. He was shocked to find him in civilian clothes. "You *can* call in, can't you?"

"I'll keep this for awhile," Stewart announced, sticking the license in his shirt pocket. "So you're Jeff Murphy. Age sixteen. 27½ Greely Street."

"That's right."

"Let me introduce myself," Stewart produced his badge and flipped his identification in front of the boy. "I'm a detective who noticed you were driving pretty erratically back there."

The boy studied the I.D., then looked up at Stewart. "Erratically," he repeated slowly, unbelieving.

"You go to school, don't you? You know what the word means?" Stewart leaned down, his elbows on the window. He stared at Jeff.

"Yes, of course, I do." Murphy had a dim moustache which he rubbed thoughtfully. He was a nice looking boy, tall for his age, a member of his high school basketball team. He was wearing his letterman's jacket now even though it was summer and much too warm for the wool material.

"Out of the car," Stewart ordered.

"What for?"

"Look Murphy, I don't have to tell you a thing. But you've got to obey every command I give you. You got that?"

Jeff Murphy cautiously got out. He waited for Stewart's next words, his eyes cast down on the cement. A mixture of shame and fear invaded his body.

"See that yellow line in the road. I want you to walk along it a little ways for me."

Jeff walked out to the middle of the road and stood on the line. "Now?" he turned back to Stewart.

"Yeah, go ahead."

Jeff began to follow the line, slowly. He knew he wasn't drunk, he could walk perfectly along the line, and a wave of horror gripped him because he realized that Stewart knew that too. He might as well have been walking this line stark naked in front of a thousand girls. He would have been less embarrassed. He walked on and on until he thought he might be reaching a point in the road where Stewart could no longer see him. Soon, however, he heard the cop call for him to come back.

"No, keep on the line!" Stewart shouted to Murphy who was returning along the side of the road.

Stewart's face loomed closer and closer as the boy approached, one foot stepping carefully in front of the other, each step touching surely on the yellow line. But Jeff took his eyes away from the cop because there was something in his face that he dreaded. He came to a halt by the front fender of the Datsun and stared uneasily at his tennis shoes.

"That was the worst job I've ever seen! You're drunk and you know it!"

Jeff looked up startled. "I'm not," he insisted.

"The hell you're not."

"But I'm not. I'm really not," the boy protested. "I don't think I've had more than two or three drinks in my entire life!"

"Then what kind of drugs are you on?"

"None! I swear it to you!" the boy pleaded, his voice cracking. Stewart wanted him to plead, he wanted him to beg. "Please believe me!"

"There's one way to tell. Come closer." Jeff only took a half step forward as he was practically standing on Reggino's feet already. "Open your mouth."

He followed the instructions but nothing happened.

"Keep it open!"

Tears filled his eyes as Stewart leaned over and sniffed into his mouth. Stewart made an expression of incredible disgust. "What are you talking about, man, your breath stinks of liquor, it's foul, man."

Jeff's mouth shut slowly, seemingly of its own accord, as if it were an appendage apart from the rest of his body. Another car passed along the road. Stewart's eyes followed it out of sight.

"There has to be some other test . . ." the boy said quietly.

Stewart flinched. The boy noticed. He mustn't panic. He mustn't mess things up now. It might mean trouble.

"I'm going to have to take you in and give you a breath test at the station."

The boy was somewhat relieved. After all, there was safety in numbers. Somebody would see how cracked this cop was. He would be vindicated.

"Get in the car. . . No, not your car, my car."

"What about my —"

"It'll be fine right where it is. You're in no shape to drive it now."

Once inside, Stewart commanded the boy to put his hands behind his back.

"What for?"

"Shut up and do what I tell you."

Jeff tentatively slid his hands behind his back and Stewart deftly slipped a pair of handcuffs on him. "Why?" Jeff whined.

"Routine," Stewart started the motor. He shut off the red light and the night was once again its normal black color. Stewart headed down the road. He had never been this way before. He had no idea where the road led. But he was overcome with a sensation of potency; he was no longer susceptible to foibles. The idea of the boy unable to move, powerless before him, made him joyful. He felt the tightness of the handcuffs burning his own wrists. He veered to the right, up a steep incline that led to a cul-de-sac surrounded by trees and picnic tables. Stewart cut the motor. He stared at the pale boy whose eyes were glazed and focused on the invisible wind like a zombie's. Suddenly Jeff struggled and tried to force the handcuffs off. Stewart laughed. Then Jeff was still again.

Stewart jumped from the car. "Get out," he said.

Jeff slid across the driver's seat. Standing, he towered a full head above Stewart.

"Get on your knees and put your face against the car. . . Go on. . ."

Jeff felt his weight falling and nothing else except a coolness in his head, an emptiness.

"Put your fucking nose right up against the metal. . ." Stewart brought out his revolver and held it against the boy's head . . . he pushed it hard in a spot above the boy's ear. He cocked the gun. "Pray," Stewart said softly and drove the gun deeper into the boy's skull. Stewart felt Jeff go limp and fall into a faint against his legs. Stewart moved back and let him slump to the pavement.

Alarmed, he watched as the boy began to twist and groan, coming back into consciousness. He leaped into his car, threw it into reverse and tore down the road. He was terrified that the boy would report the incident and that they would come after him.

As he sped along the highway he tried to reassure himself that the boy would be too afraid to say anything . . . he wasn't the type to stir up a hornet's nest . . . he wouldn't go to a cop to complain about another cop. And if the boy did go to the police they would never find him. They would never know where to look. They would scrutinize members of the force if they bothered to do anything. He would never be identified.

The minute he got back to his apartment he fell across the bed. He had to quit scaring himself. He wasn't in any danger — after all, the boy had come to no harm. He would block it from his mind. And by morning, after a dark, absorbing sleep, he had forgotten the whole incident. There were other things to think about, there were jobs around the house to do, there was a hard night's work at the plant waiting for him. A peacefulness returned that was broken only once. At the end of the week he found the boy's driver's license in his shirt pocket. It was an ugly reminder.

"I don't know what's been getting me down lately," Reggino pushed his half filled plate of Chinese vegetables to one side. "I swear to God I don't." He lit a cigarette, then held the match for Jake. "I was in here one day last week," he swept his arm in a semicircle to indicàte the restaurant where they were the only customers except for an old man in a booth by the window, "and I must have been in one hell of a mood. Oh, Jesus, I don't know what got into me, maybe I was loaded, I don't remember, but I started giving Jimmy Chen a real hard time. I bitched about the food, the service, the specks on the water glass, the whole works. I was a regular bastard all right. At one point I just picked up the edge of the tablecloth and let it rip. Everything went flying straight up in the air. And you know what?"

"What?" Jake blew tiny smoke rings in elaborate patterns against the corner wall.

"They all rushed over to me with such respect, as if I'd just tossed down a hundred dollar bill for a tip instead of breaking every fucking plate on the table."

"That's because they're good people here."

"I couldn't figure it out. . ."

"Sure," Jake encouraged him. "That's it. They care about you, man. We've been steady customers for years, haven't we?"

"Yeah, I guess so."

"Why, I remember when we discovered this place. We stumbled onto it one night during a miserable rainstorm. And we loved it."

"It was fantastic!"

"And Jimmy — remember — he even helped us off with our wet coats and gave us some dry waiters' smocks from the kitchen."

"And you looked so damn funny because yours wouldn't have even fit a ten year-old boy."

"Right, but it was warm and dry, what there was of it."

"So . . . what does it all add up to?"

"They've come to know you. They ain't gonna call the cops and bust you because you smash a few old teacups. They're concerned."

"Bullshit."

"Then you explain it."

"They were afraid of me — that's what! Afraid I wasn't going to stop there. Afraid I was going to push their timid faces in. . .

Concerned . . . *shit.*"

"Have it your way," Jake sighed disgustedly. "You're only going to believe the worst tonight. You're in a morbid mood.'"

Reggino checked himself from answering back. After all, he could bicker all night; but he really wasn't out to annoy Jake. "I want to behave," he said. "Believe me." He downed his apple brandy and called for two more.

The windows were more decorative than usual; the glass was especially shiny and displayed on the sills were fiery wooden dragons and thin paper birds in the seven shades of the rainbow. From time to time figures pressed their faces to the pane and frightened the old man dining alone and lost in his evening reverie. A boy appeared at the glass like a ghost and to Jake and Stewart's amusement the man tried to shoo the harmless child away with complicated hand signals, as if he were being irritated by an obnoxious fly.

"That kid looks just like you did," Reggino insisted. "Same funny ears sticking out. Same goggle eyes."

"Thanks a lot," Jake replied. "As I remember, you didn't treat me very well in those days."

"What do you mean?"

"You teased the hell out of me. Made it next to impossible for me to join your gang. You were unmerciful on the rest of us kids. You demanded the world — and you usually got it."

Reggino's eyes glazed over and an odd smile appeared. "I did, didn't I? . . ."

"Naturally."

"Jake . . . Jake, I'm glad you called me up tonight."

"Well, why not? I had to swing down to New York today anyway to confer with my boss. I was free tonight. The only thing is I should get some sleep since I have to catch an early plane tomorrow to Colorado. But this is the last trip. Then I'm coming back for good."

"That's wonderful. I haven't seen you since the first of the summer. We'll have to get together more often."

"Sure. We will."

"This job you've got sounds pretty good . . . traveling to Colorado. Chasing the girls out there, I suppose?"

"Don't start that."

"You're a Don Juan. You can't keep secrets from me."

Jimmy Chen brought them a plate of tangerine rinds with two fortune cookies along with their apple brandy.

"No fortune cookies, Jimmy," Stewart said reprovingly. "No need to ruin a pleasant meal that way."

"I don't like those goddam things either," Jake agreed as Jimmy disappeared behind a golden screen to compute their bill.

"My problem is I believe everything I read," Reggino lit another cigarette and polished off his brandy.

"Gullible bastard, aren't you?" Jake chimed in.

"Yeah . . . maybe so . . . sooner or later you even end up believing you're a different kind of guy than you really are. . . Tonight you said I was in a morbid mood —"

"Look, I didn't —"

"Well, you were right," he leaned forward. "Only it's been my same mood for a long, long time. And it scares me to death. Sometimes . . . sometimes I'm not even sure who I am. You know me, Jake. I'm the guy who always wanted the best for everybody. The guy who cared. That's what I thought. But there's somebody else in me. A lot of. . ."

A chill went through Jake. He began to sweat. He sipped his brandy. He could hear Jimmy Chen moving behind the partition. He hoped he would hurry with the bill.

"That day," Reggino stammered. "That day you came by and I showed you my new SMG and my other weapons and we had a good time, some nice laughs, and I told you I wasn't the type to lose my head over them. I'm not sure that was true. . . Sometimes . . . sometimes I get this terrible urge to just burst into the plant and shoot everybody in sight. . ."

"We all have those thoughts," Jake brushed it off. "I've dreamed of killing my boss. . . It's a release."

"Only I'm serious. Sometimes it seems like I'm just an inch away from really doing it." Stewart watched Jake shake his head in disbelief. "Yes, it's gone so far as me sitting, planning how to kill each guy, what weapon to use on them. Rip that fat slob Ed Uball's stomach open with a machete and watch his guts spill out . . . take a blowtorch to that nigger Al Blane and see if he's black through and through! And Dorothy . . . and the others . . . I can't tell you about them. . . Oh, it's a nightmare all right!"

Jake Adams stood. "You're drunk. That's all. Drunk and tired. You need a good sleep. You're drunk. It makes you crazy."

"I am drunk. I'm sorry."

"Come on, let's get you home."

Jimmy Chen waited, perplexed, holding the bill on an ornate ivory tray.

"No, no. I can make it home O.K.," Reggino was embarrassed. "You go on. My apologies — and I'll see you when you get back."

"Get some rest, buddy," Jake patted him on the back, hurriedly dropped a twenty dollar bill on the tray and left the restaurant. He was certain he had overpaid. But it would have been worth dropping a hundred dollars to get his release from that restaurant a few seconds sooner. His muscles ached, his head spun. He was incredibly angry with Reggino for speaking so irresponsibly and didn't believe him for a minute, but if he did there was not a damn thing in the world he could do about it. If Reggino had threatened to kill the President of the United States that would have been his own affair. Jake was tired of people dumping their problems on him. He felt like a sponge used to soak up everyone's sorrow. It was too much to ask of anyone. He felt it on his job, with Reggino, with the Scotch-smiths, yes, even with Renee. Sometimes she really expected too much. There was no room for him to relax. But it would change for the better when he was back to stay.

He found he was walking at a breakneck pace, north into the artists' district of Soho. But this aimless ramble had been good for his nerves; he'd let off steam, if that was possible on this sultry, starless night. Young couples were gathered around the gleaming windows, commenting on colored canvases or pieces of sculpture. Jake slowed his steps and from nowhere an image glimmered in his brain of Stewart sitting all alone in the restaurant, staring at the walls, ordering another then another glass of apple brandy.

Chapter Nine

By the time she was ten-years-old Renee Cloverman was the talk of the neighborhood. Why, she was an out and out tomboy whose treacherous escapades rivaled those of the boys . . . and it was a disgrace that her mother let her run wild in those soiled blue jeans, black sequined cowboy shirt and ten gallon hat. The child never wore anything else! And it wasn't just her mad pranks or unconventional attire that "put people off" . . . it was her attitude: that expression of polite defiance with which she met all disapproving glances.

One day she unnerved a woman in the supermarket. Renee, who was shopping with her mother, was dashing through the aisles, punching the boxes of cereals and pinching the fruits and vegetables. The woman, who lived down the block from the Clovermans with her seven sons, glared at Renee but found something so intimidating in her expression that she turned to Milly who was meekly clutching a shopping cart and went so far as to say, "Excuse me. I didn't mean to stare, but I thought your little girl was a boy! She was carrying on like my Edward or Frankie. . ." At which point Milly, dying of embarrassment, grasped Renee by the shoulders and brushed her scraggly hair and patted her sallow cheeks, trying to puff them out and turn them pink while Renee, quite an obedient child, whispered, "What's wrong, Mama? What in the world is wrong?"

It was a well known fact to everyone in town that Milly had no money. Yet she was sending her daughter to a private girls' academy. It was true she had received an insurance premium after her husband succumbed to cancer but it was not large and could not be expected to see the family through too many years, much less pay for Renee's expensive education. Milly had spent every moment scrimping and saving and killing herself to raise the tuition, literally searching under the bed for pennies. For two years now she had managed to find the funds to keep Renee in school, depriving herself and her younger daughter, Sue, of everything but the barest essentials. Sue attended the public school and there were times when her mother refused to buy her the books she needed if that money had to go to Renee's tuition. Of course, Milly would have liked to have sent Sue to Green Bough too, but it was absolutely impossible. Green Bough. . . The very name sent Milly into an ecstatic state, left her wandering on a religious plane. . .

Milly had first seen Green Bough when she accompanied her neighbor from across the street to the school's yearly rummage sale. Fay Montgomery had driven her up the crooked drive which opened onto an elegant, oak-filled cul-de-sac, above which towered the century-old, four-storied schoolhouse of cumbersome brick and limestone, resembling a medieval fortress rather than a posh elementary school.

As Fay ransacked one box of winter coats after another she paused and declared to Milly, "This place is for the cream of the crop I tell you. It's for the best and only the best." And their eyes searched the leaded glass windows, hoping for some sign of concurrence. The wind whistled all the way to the top of the hill and the trees swayed gently. Milly made up her mind at that very moment.

It was a jubilant evening indeed when she crept across the street to inform Fay that she had enrolled Renee in classes at Green Bough for the fall semester. Fay was surprised and somehow annoyed, but the beaming, pleased look on Milly's face softened her and she patted her friend's shoulder, "Wonderful. What a wise decision you've made." Then she added, giggling, "And won't it be a change to see Renee in a nice green and white checked uniform instead of that wild west rodeo shirt!"

As for Renee, she seemed ambivalent about the school. She never discussed it. Her grades were very good though no one ever saw her study or as much as open a textbook. There was an even temper to each school day.

Renee kept a secret list in her red vinyl notebook on which she had pasted stickers of Superman, Sky King and the Lone Ranger. She had divided the girls in her class into two groups and under a heading of *Girls I Like* she listed Cynthia C., Frieda, Ann, Katie, Jill Prenger. Under *Girls I Hate* she had pencilled in the names of Belinda Smith (ugh!), Gloria, Yvonne, Anne Ewing.

She had composed a similar list on the opposite page. Under the column *Teachers I Like* came Mr. Payne, Mr. Lindorff, Miss Crane. *Teachers I Hate* consisted of only two names: Mrs. Kennedy, and underlined dramatically, Mr. Jennings.

Renee perused the list now and as she glanced up at Mr. Jennings, her home room teacher who sat grading papers at his desk, she gravely underlined his name once again, then flipped her notebook shut and began to read her history assignment along with the rest of the class. It was all she could do to concentrate; only the glossy illustrations of white settlers being scalped by Indians or lantern bearing turncoats in the rain-soaked streets of Boston were mildly interesting. Actually, she was transfixed by the black sailing clouds outside the window; their shadows passed over the floor, covering her shoes and dulling the silver buckles which usually were brighter and sharper than swords. Oh, if the clouds would only break and shower the earth with snow! Then they would all be dismissed and wouldn't have to return until after the Christmas holidays. It had happened just last year; the weather had been on their side. A similar occurrence two years in a row would require a miracle and Renee didn't know anybody whose life was touched by miracles. She yawned.

The girl behind her tapped her on the shoulder. Renee turned sideways and the girl surreptitiously slipped her a note. It was from Jill, one of her best friends, who sat in the back row. Jill was a large, shy girl who was good at drawing and on the note she had sketched elaborate snowflakes beneath which was a gnomic scrawl: *Maybe we'll get out early if it snows and we can go down to the pond and try to skate in our shoes! Cross your fingers, toes and eyes! Love, Jill.* And to Jill's amazement Renee whirled around and crossed her eyes right in front of the entire class! When Renee turned back she found Mr. Jennings staring at her. Yet it was as if she were transparent and he was actually watching the air beyond her. His gaze was that empty. She shivered. He adjusted his glasses and continued to grade papers.

Later Renee discovered his eyes were on her once more. Yet again he had created a strong impression that he was seeing nothing at all. He had turned in upon himself somehow and his

eyes were focused on his own brain and his own blood. *Stop it.* . .
She began to chew her nails. And still he watched her. *Relax* . . .
go on . . . look out the window . . . that's it . . . don't let him see you're
scared. . . To her disappointment the dark clouds had given way
to a brilliant blue and the sun was coming out all fiery and
splendid.

As it was, the fine weather did not keep the girls from the
pond. They decided it would be an interesting diversion even in
the absence of ice and snow. As they left the classroom Jill
purposely stalled directly in front of Mr. Jennings' desk. Jill had
once confided in Renee that she thought Mr. Jennings was a
dream. Renee could not agree. True, he had a solid, athletic
body and hair that was spun from gold but that was not enough.
His stiff, precise manner was intolerable. And those heavy
round glasses on his round baby face made him resemble an
owl. Not a handsome owl either. But Jill had been bitten,
perhaps because he was so much younger than the other
teachers — he couldn't have been past thirty — and perhaps
because he teased the girls so unmercifully, making them laugh
and, more often, blush. Jill was always playful around Jennings
and today did not prove to be an exception. The two of them
bantered back and forth, strewing the conversation about the
upcoming Christmas party with strange, almost sexual in-
nuendoes. Renee, patently ignored by them both, stared at her
shoes. It was so odd for her to be shy. With the other teachers
she was incredibly spirited. They found her witty. They complimented her work. But Jennings always made her feel un-
welcome. He cast a shadow on her figure which was meant to
make her doubt her worth. And she had no idea why.

In drama class he seemed to pick her to read the most
impossible soliloquies, then asked each girl to criticize her
performance. But when it came time to give an actual performance in front of an audience she was given the smallest part
with no lines at all. Jennings, supervisor of the girls' sports
program, complained about her wretched posture and pointed
out more than once that her gaunt frame worked against her in
a competitive team sport such as softball or basketball. She was
underfed. She should pay more attention to diet. Yet she knew
she was as healthy and as strong as the other girls. It would be a
relief to reach the end of the year and move on to a different
teacher.

"Be a good girl, Jill. Stay away from trouble," Mr. Jennings

winked coyly. Jill almost swooned and Renee had to direct her
from the classroom.

The pond lay at the foot of a steep hill which slept beneath a
slender bed of frost. The girls were joined by Gloria and Ann
and the four of them raced through the bare trees, kicking the
dead twigs high into the air and screaming through the cold to
hear their voices echo this homage to the winter sky. They could
barely stop themselves at the bottom. Ann, in fact, went over
the edge into the shallow water. She cried unhappily, "Oh, my
feet are soaked! Whatever shall I do?"

"Oh, Ann, it's not so bad," insisted Gloria, a vain girl whose
father was said to have made millions in the up and coming fast
food industry. "Just dry them with your sweater then change
your shoes when you get home."

Stumbling from the pond Ann discovered a dry spot and sank
down despondently. "It's easy for you to say. You didn't fall in.
Just think if you were the one with frozen toes, Gloria. I know
I'll get a horrid case of frostbite."

"Oh, shut up!" Gloria tossed her head in a bored manner.
"It's not even cold enough to see your breath."

"It is too!" Ann almost burst into tears.

"Can't you see, it's bad for her," Jill sympathized. "She
might catch cold and not be able to sing at the Christmas
party." This observation really drove Ann, an aspiring opera
star, to tears. The girls were so lost in this sudden drama that
they failed to notice Renee had disappeared. It was Ann who,
much later, blinked through her tears, "Where's Renee?"

The others were startled. There was no sign of anyone
around the quiet pond.

"My God, you don't think she could be. . ." Gloria's voice
trailed off as she gazed with terror at the icy water lapping the
hard ground. Suddenly from overhead came a familiar laugh
accompanied by the shaking of a bough which sent acorns
tumbling onto the heads of the girls below.

"You devil!" Jill shook her fist at Renee who towered above
them on the limb of an oak.

"She scrambled up there just like an ape and now she's acting
like one!" Gloria said disgustedly.

"If you fall and kill yourself, you can't blame us. It's your
own doing," Ann warned.

"Don't be such a scaredy-cat!" Renee was still laughing.
"I've climbed these trees a hundred times and I've never fallen
yet."

"This is the day for accidents," Ann moaned, still rubbing her wet ankles with her sweater.

"I can get all the way across the pond — from one side to the other — without touching the ground," Renee bragged. "Watch." Slowly, confidently, she hoisted herself from the sturdy arms of one tree to another, sometimes hanging sideways over the center of the pond, sometimes leaping dramatically through a small space between dense thickets, to finally drop victoriously on the opposite side of the heart-shaped pond. But her triumph was barely noticed as the girls had forgotten her by then and were squatting in a semi-circle discussing the events of the day. Renee amused herself by tossing flintstones at the poliwogs and carving her name in the mud before she headed home.

Still full of energy, Renee refused to let the remainder of the afternoon go to waste. She donned her Lone Ranger mask and forced her sister to play the victim of a daring stagecoach robbery. Renee, battling the invisible villains on the street, rescued the hapless lady and carried her safely to their front yard. This game continued until dark. Milly sat watching from the porch and occasionally a neighbor would pass by and exchange a few words with her in the gathering dusk.

Across the street, Fay Montgomery pulled into her driveway with her aging, ailing mother beside her. Milly knew that Fay had taken her to the doctors and she sent Renee and Sue over to help the elderly woman into the house. Fay was grateful. Seeing that her mother had two strong young escorts she was free to gather up two grocery sacks. She called across to Milly, "Getting cold."

"It's supposed to go into the teens tonight," Milly answered.

"It doesn't get to me, personally. But Mother with her arthritis . . . ah, well. . ."

The girls ran out of the Montgomery house and Fay gave them each a penny for their help. Renee wanted to re-stage the stagecoach robbery but Milly put a stop to it. "You've got to have supper now because Sue and I have an errand. Remember?"

Mrs. Howard six blocks up the street was recovering from a terrible tragedy. Her young daughter had died from a blood clot on the brain after a nasty fall down the stairs. Mrs. Howard thought that Sue might be able to wear some of the child's clothing, including the new winter coat she had just bought, and so she had phoned Milly suggesting that she bring Sue around for a fitting. So after supper Renee watched her mother and Sue, hand in hand, march north on their dark street. She had promised to finish the dishes and dust the living room in the meantime. She made quick work of her duties, after which she stepped into the bathroom and posed in front of the mirror in her Lone Ranger mask, pulling her hair back with tight rubber bands so that she looked more like the real man and not a schoolgirl. The phone rang.

"Yes?" she answered breathlessly.

Silence.

"Hello?" Her voice was unsure.

Finally — a familiar male voice — "This is Mr. Jennings, Renee."

Her fingers went to her mouth. "Mr. Jennings?" she repeated.

His voice was stern. "I'm afraid I saw what you were up to in class this afternoon. You know, we teachers see a good deal more than you girls give us credit for. I must let you know that the passing of notes is unacceptable behavior."

"I didn't pass any note," she said hurriedly.

He laughed. "Of course you did, my dear girl. You surely won't deny it."

"Maybe one of the other girls. . ."

After an eternity he spoke again. "I don't have to keep my eyes on the other girls like I do you. You are the class trouble-maker. You are the one I've got to watch out for."

"I didn't do anthing! I didn't pass a note!"

"Please," he said sarcastically. "Don't degrade yourself further. It's indecent. Aren't you intelligent enough to realize I have that note you exchanged with Jill? It slipped from your notebook when you left the room."

But Renee was staring at her open notebook, and lying on top of the first page was the very note she had received from Jill. To refute his claim would be an admission of her own guilt since she would have to confess that she held the note. He was preparing a trap for her and a very clever one at that for she would lose no matter what.

"So you see," he continued. "I know you for the little liar you are. You can thank me for not asking to speak to your mother about this. But I am going to have a private talk with you tomorrow. You will remain in your seat when the others go to lunch. Understand?"

"Yes," she answered sadly.

"Good." He hung up. Paralyzed she held the receiver a few inches from her face. The house seemed incredibly empty, too desolate to bear. For the first time in her life she was frightened to be left all alone. She replaced the receiver but his voice still filled her ears. When she returned to the kitchen she imagined she saw his face at the window, those large glasses of his magnified many times. If only Mother and Sue would come home! She dared not look out the window again. Shivering she switched off the lights and went into the bathroom but he stared at her from the mirror. Her own face, still covered by the mask of the Lone Ranger, seemed small and pathetic compared to his looming over her shoulder. She beat her fist against the glass right where his eyes bore into hers and to her horror it was her image that disappeared while his remained.

Renee ran into her bedroom and hid beneath her covers, pressing her face so deeply into the pillow she thought she would suffocate. It was so quiet that she swore she could still hear his questions and she could hear herself answering sorrowfully. Then she realized she was listening to her own breath in her nostrils, sounding like two people moaning, a gentle wheezing like a fine wind or like snow falling on an already existing blanket. Yes, his voice whispered from her brain down through her nose. His words entered her mouth like some fetid waste. . .

Her mother shook her in the morning. "For pity's sake. Well, really this is too much. A ten year-old girl going to sleep in her cowboy outfit and with a mask around her eyes yet! My Lord, whatever is to become of you?"

The next afternoon Milly had a disturbing phone call and she could not make up her mind about what course of action to take. She sat sewing pensively at the kitchen table, keeping her eye on a loaf of banana bread that was slowly baking in the oven. Sue played nurse to her dolls in the corner.

Milly regarded Renee, propped on the living room couch watching T.V., with a kind of wariness. Milly had long ago accepted her daughter's eccentricity, if running about as a tomboy could be classified as such. But there was something new which she could not accept: her daughter as truant.

She called softly to Sue, "Take your dollies into the bedroom and play. I want to talk to your sister."

"No, Mommy, they like it in here."

Milly stood and removed her apron. She was firm. "They'll

like it in the bedroom just as well. I told you I want to have a talk
with Renee. A serious talk.''

Sue scooped up her dolls and, pouting, skipped nonchalantly
into the bedroom. Milly inched her way into the living room.
She sat as if on tenterhooks on the very edge of the couch. After a
quiet moment she blurted, ''Why weren't you in school today?''

''Who says I wasn't?'' Renee cried out in astonishment.

''Miss Crane, your French teacher, that's who. . . Oh,
Renee,'' she was becoming distraught. ''She called saying she
was worried about you. She claimed that not only weren't you
in class today but that you've missed other days in the last few
weeks. I can only hold my head and ask, 'Why?' . . .''

''But Mother . . . I haven't missed any other day . . . I
couldn't have. . . No, no, it's impossible,'' the girl lied, turning
red.

''But how could she be mistaken?''

''She could! That's all.''

''But why have you missed any day . . . without telling me?
You haven't been sick. Renee . . . is there something that's
making you unhappy?''

''No! No!'' Renee jumped up excitedly and knelt before her
mother. ''I . . . I just hadn't finished my lessons so . . . so I
thought it would be better to wait and go back to class when I
was completely prepared.''

Milly lifted her daughter's chin. ''Is that really the reason?
You didn't have your lessons finished?''

A cold fear was growing inside Renee. Of course, there was a
reason why she had skipped school on those other days but she
had never considered it, she had been so content to while away
the days by the little pond. Now that the weather was becoming
colder she enjoyed it there even more. Today she had stretched
her wool jacket around her, had climbed the stiff, wide branches
and had had some nice fights with the squirrels. Today also she
had had a definite purpose in missing class. And if she really
thought about it, it was the same reason, wasn't it, that she had
missed those other days too: it was Jennings.

Milly bowed her head. ''If you only thought about how much
money it costs to keep you at Green Bough, I'm sure you would
work on your lessons harder so as not to miss class. After all,
darling, the expense takes food away from our table . . . so that
the money you wasted by not going to school could have bought
nice steaks for you, for Sue and your mother. See. Think of it
that way.''

Renee couldn't stand for her mother to start talking like this. She was overcome by an awesome guilt. She would endure any unpleasantness at school, if only for her mother's sake.

"Oh, I'm sorry, Mother! I promise never to miss another day!" She rested her head in Milly's lap.

"Unless, of course, you're sick," she smoothed Renee's hair. "That's something different. But to stay away from school for spite. . . Well. . . But we won't talk about it anymore." She pinched Renee's cheek and smiled. "All right?"

"Yes."

"God has a way of helping us too, you know. God will come into this and help us out. I know He will. We never have to work alone. Remember that. We're never quite alone."

"I know, Mother, I know."

Sue poked her head outside her bedroom door. "Can I come out now?"

"Yes, darling," Milly nodded and Sue sidled over to watch television, throwing resentful glances at Renee.

Renee had hoped that by staying away from school she could avoid the proposed confrontation with Mr. Jennings. She wished upon a star. She wished upon the porcelain statue of Christ that stood bathed in ivy in the hallway. True, as the new week wore on he never mentioned the note. He seemed to have forgotten all about it. But by Friday afternoon he had found a fresh excuse to chastise her.

Renee ran into the gymnasium a few minutes late. She had become entangled in a rambling conversation about Beethoven with her music teacher, Nina Dobas, and she hadn't noticed the time. Now, in the changing room, she regretted it. Oh, she would be in for it now. She attempted to lace her shoes so quickly that her mind was miles ahead of her fingers and the knot was weakly done and fell apart. She threw up her hands in dismay, catching a glimpse of herself in the oblong mirror that crowned the washstand. Her face was harried, red and puffy and she didn't like it. She calmed herself. The screams of the other girls filtered in from the vast gym. Renee slowly laced her shoes.

When she walked into the gym Jennings had not yet appeared but the girls were waiting in the middle of the floor in a large circle. Renee broke the chain, crowding in between Ann and Gloria.

"It's so damn cold down here," Gloria whispered. "Our

fathers shell out all this money and they stick the gym down here in the basement. Worse than a tomb."

"It's true," Renee answered. "We're eight feet under." She glanced at the ceiling which was so high that the teachers joked about invisible giants holding up the beams. There were no windows and the phosphorescent tubes overhead were broken, the only brightness coming from the klieg lights on a crumbling stage at one end of the room. It was from around the corner in front of the stage that Jennings appeared, trim, neat in starched white, walking confidently like an actor coming into the audience from the proscenium to take his bows.

"All right, girls," he tossed a ball into the circle. "Throw and catch for awhile." And so began the afternoon of athletics which included basketball, tumbling, running and exercising. Jennings left the girls to themselves most of the time as he needed to examine the stage to see if it was prepared for the Christmas play. He hoisted himself up between the gray wool curtains which were half open, revealing a crude set, and busied himself by dusting props and shifting the scenery. The stage was supposed to represent heaven. Huge cut-out blue and white clouds turned slowly on strings, white cotton was stuck to everything, to chairs, to the floor and the curtains. Jennings even had to pick some from the soles of his shoes. Golden toy trumpets were scattered here and there and a grand harp rested against the majestic backdrop. Once while Renee was attempting a vault she caught Jennings, who was moving the harp to a more captivating site, watching her anxiously; she had begun her approach to the horse, running swiftly, when she had noticed his stare. She stopped dead. Jennings let the harp slip to the floor and his hand went through the strings causing a mournful twang. There was a murmur from the girls and Jennings turned his back, pasting giant felt stars to the Milky Way ribbon that ran the length of the stage. Renee began her vault again and completed it successfully.

When the bell rang and the girls moved toward the changing room, Jennings called from the stage, "Renee, may I see you please?" Ann, who had been walking with Renee, looked guardedly over her shoulder at her retreating friend, then caught up with Gloria and tugged at her sleeve. "Wonder what he wants with her now?"

"Who cares?" the other replied.

"Step up here please." Jennings blew dust off his hands as Renee climbed onto the stage and stood patiently in front of him. She smelled mildew, chalk and rust.

"Do you think it looks like Christmas up here?" he asked, still rubbing the dust from his fingers.

"Very much so."

"Well, we do our best, don't we?"

"Yes."

He laughed slightly, then paused, as if listening for the last girl's footsteps to die. When there was silence he regarded her with great seriousness. "I don't like to bring this subject up, but I fear that I must. For your own sake." He rubbed his hands together, then pushed his strand of dull blond hair back above his forehead. "You were a rather awkward sight on the gym floor this afternoon. You were ungainly. Very odd looking."

She frowned. Her eyes began to fill with tears but she held them back. She would keep the water from spilling if it killed her, yes, if it meant she had to die on that stage amidst all those stars and clouds and angels' trappings.

"Why do you suppose that is?"

She shrugged.

He shot impatiently, "Well, if *you* don't know, I couldn't possibly, could I?" Then he sighed and his tone became kinder, more patronizing, "Look, child. There is a substance — an attribute — called grace, which you lack completely, but which has been the glory of every great woman who has walked the pages of history. And the other girls here are beginning to — well," he waved his hands dramatically, "gravitate — toward grace. They are beginning to carry themselves like ladies, have you noticed? They like to go to parties, to dress up. To be feminine. They're girls and they like it that way." He dropped his voice, adding softly, "But you don't want to be a girl. That's it, isn't it?"

"Of course I want to be one!"

Jennings studied her defiant eyes. "You must tell me if I'm wrong, but as I was driving home the other day, I happened to catch sight of you in the middle of a fistfight with a couple of boys. Isn't that right?"

Renee looked past him to a cellophane star turning on a piece of twine.

"Renee," he said sternly. "Wasn't that you? It was you whom I saw, wasn't it?" He shook her shoulders. "Wasn't it!"

"Yes!" she stumbled backwards, her eyes guilty, fixed to the stageboards.

"You were pounding away at them hard, swift, just like you

were one of them. How many of those fistfights have you gotten
into with the boys? How many?"

"One. Just that one." She looked up and his face was full of
rage, then suddenly his shoulders sagged and the lines on his
forehead fell away. He smiled evenly. "Good for you — if it's
just that one. . ." He patted her softly on the neck. "Try to be a
good girl. Please try. . ."

"I'll try, Mr. Jennings. I'll try hard."

"All right, Renee," he said tenderly. "Go on, now."

That December the Christmas spirit took everyone by storm.
There was the right amount of snow — not enough to make life
a drudge, but enough to cast a pretty topping to the ugly gray
ground — all this according to Nina Dobas who had the girls
singing carols for three solid weeks, in the music room, the
library, the halls.

Renee linked arms with Jill and Frieda and yodeled *Bring a
Torch, Jeanette, Isabella* all the way from one end of the building to
the other. When they reached the window on the third floor
which looked out over the trees, Renee allowed the girls to skip
downstairs alone, and only vaguely aware of their fading voices
she lost herself in the bleak wilderness that stole away before
her, the landscape melting beneath a sheet of ice which pricked
and stunned the sky and made her heart grow cold. Winter
bluejays battled on the branches of the nearest pine. An airplane passed far away.

"Don't catch your death before the holiday!" came the lilting
voice of Nina behind her. Renee turned and the frail old woman
grasped her hands. "I feel so lucky this year, Renee Cloverman!
I'm going to Kansas City to visit my mother whom I haven't
seen in six years. God bless her soul, she's ninety years-old!"
Nina bit her lip and Renee embraced her. "God help her, she's
all alone in the world," Nina breathed softly in her ear. "God
bless you, darling! And Merry Christmas!"

There had been no problems with Mr. Jennings since their
discussion on the stage. He seemed to be prey to the Christmas
spirit just like the others and the rosiness of his cheeks and his
unfurrowed brow told Renee she had nothing to fear from him.
Once, however, she saw something peculiar. It was late afternoon, already dark, and she was waiting outside school to be
picked up by her mother. She was strolling through the parking
lot when she came upon a dark green Oldsmobile, its motor

running, the inside light on. Jennings was at the wheel turned towards a young woman whom Renee had never seen before. The woman was trying to light a cigarette but her hands were trembling so badly that it was impossible. Finally the woman gave up. Renee shuddered. The woman was the saddest person she had ever seen. Her eyes were hollow and her mouth was turned down in misery, in utter defeat. Renee ran back to the sidewalk in front of the school building and didn't look in the direction of the Oldsmobile again.

Renee, with the stalwart if incompetent help of Sue, had been constructing Christmas ornaments to present as gifts to her friends and family. She was in a rush to finish them so she enlisted Sue to sit at her feet and cut thin strips of colored felt and lay them in neat rows on the table while she glued glitter and clusters of pearls to the ivory balls.

"Come on, don't be so slow!" she admonished Sue who complained that she had broken three of her fingers already, she was working so rapidly. "How would you like your neck broken, instead?"

Milly appeared behind them. "No one is going to do anything of the kind!"

"Oh, Mother, I'll never finish!"

"Yes, you will, darling. You have enough already." She referred to the row of ornaments sitting on the fireplace ledge. They depicted various scenes . . . Santa and his sleigh . . . the elves in the workshop . . . the Three Wise Men . . . the Star of Bethlehem. There were enough for her favorite teachers, for her mother and sister, for Mrs. Montgomery across the street, even one for Mr. Jennings.

"This is my last one," she muttered.

"Well, I should hope! You've been slaving on that one forever. Who's it for?"

Renee whirled to face her mother. Furious tears began to stream down her face. "It's for my father!" she sobbed. "Wherever he is. . ." And dropping the ornament on the table she rushed to her room.

At school her gifts were a considerable success. Nina Dobas promised Renee she would give hers to her mother in Kansas City who would love the little scene of Christ in the manger. Her friends were enthusiastic. But when she put the ornament on Jennings' desk he looked up at her angrily.

"What's it for?"

"For you," she stammered. "For your tree."

A few of the other girls had sauntered into the classroom and were milling around their desks.

"I cannot accept these gifts from my students. It's completely inappropriate." And with a hurried sweep he knocked the ornament into the wastebasket. Renee's breath caught in her throat. She felt her face go red and her ears catch fire. She heard the abrupt cessation of the girls' chatter behind her and she felt terribly ashamed. They had seen. Jennings was absent-mindedly turning the pages of a book. The ornament was in the wastebasket. She wanted to pick it out. But it was too humiliating! It was too horrible! She wandered into the hall which was an immense tunnel at the end of which was a brick wall which she could smash into without even trying. Her feet were taking her there. To that brittle wall of instant oblivion. But as she came closer the end only seemed to hide in shadows. Her wish was to turn invisible and fight the shadows, to become the bride of the wall, to bleed with the nail of her vows.

"Why, she's fallen! She walked right into it like she didn't even know it existed!" And within moments Miss Crane, with the aid of some students, had carried Renee to the nurse's room and was wiping her face with cool cloths, feeling her pulse, and making her sip some grape juice. Renee developed a raging fever and she hardly knew where she was. Milly was summoned and there was a discussion about whether to send the child to the hospital or take her home.

"If she gets worse, Miss Crane, I'll send for an ambulance. But I want to try and take care of my little girl myself," Milly wiped a tear away.

Christmas passed without Renee's knowledge. The child lay in bed all day, flushed, her face filled with agitation, her mind in another realm.

She had no idea she had been ill until she overheard a conversation two afternoons later between her mother and Fay Montgomery who were talking in hushed tones in the hall outside her bedroom door.

"Milly, my bedroom looks right across the street into your girls' room and you don't know what a scare I had to see their light go on and off through all hours of the night. I told Mother that there must be some kind of trouble, but I had no idea it was so serious."

"She was delirious all night. Sue had to come sleep with me."

"But what was it? The fever kept her up?"

"Of course. Poor child. She's so much cooler now. But last night . . . but for the love of God —"

"No!"

"Fay, she was seized with the worst nightmares. They shook her very foundation. Her very foundation."

"Nightmares?"

"Screams through the night. It kept up until I thought we'd both die. . ."

In the spring two large cherry trees bloomed in the Clovermans' back yard. Renee hosted a party for her friends on a mild Saturday morning and Milly gave everybody small baskets and allowed them to fill them to the brim with cherries. Renee and Sue were more than helpful, climbing the trees and shaking the boughs for the girls. Milly brought out three cakes she had made from scratch — a cinnamon orange, a German chocolate, and a toffee buttercream. After the party Renee embraced her mother: "This was surely the nicest day of the year."

Milly flinched slightly at her daughter's sincerity for she had had an ulterior motive in staging this affair. Renee's grades at school had been falling drastically and none of her teachers could explain the cause. She had hoped that this party would lift Renee's spirits and provide her with a stimulus to improve her work, but before she had carried in the last of the punch cups she realized it had had just the opposite effect. "Wouldn't it be wonderful if life was always made up of Saturdays," Renee sighed, "and we never had to do the silly things in life like go to school."

"What's wrong with school now and again?"

But Renee had no answer. She only whistled, polishing off the last piece of chocolate cake while slipping into her newly shined cowboy boots for an afternoon of play.

One stormy day, when the wind was whipping the furious dark clouds and the telephone wires glistened and thin veins of lightning turned the sky into spider's webs, Renee, walking Sue home from school, noticed that a dark green Oldsmobile had been following them at a short distance for some blocks. She had seen that car before. She was a little frightened and she pulled her sister's collar up around her neck. "Walk faster. The storm's going to break any minute."

"I like to get wet," Sue insisted.

"You'll do more than get wet," Renee glanced over her shoulder to find the car still cruising behind them, "you'll catch a terrible case of pneumonia and probably die."

"Oh, you're always trying to scare everybody. Pooh. It doesn't work with me anymore."

Renee, instead of arguing, increased her speed, forcing her sister to run in order to keep pace.

"Slow down, Renee, I can't keep up."

The whole sky burst with ligtning and the trees began to blow and sob against each other. The girls had turned a bend in the road which sloped down a hill bordered on one side by woods and on the other by a field of baby jonquils. They would be alone, vulnerable, until they rounded the next bend at the bottom of the hill to find themselves at the edge of their neighborhood. Renee stepped faster, grabbing Sue by the hand. But suddenly the Oldsmobile was alongside of them and it moved in close, almost brushing against them. Renee would have been less alarmed if a pack of dinosaurs had lumbered from the woods. She froze and pulled her sister to her and sheltered the girl in her arms. She looked hard at Jennings, alone in the car, hands rigidly gripping the wheel. He was staring at them with the ferociousness of someone gone mad from sorrow. He was shouting to them, words spilling hurriedly, but the windows were tightly closed and Renee could hear nothing, only see his lips move. Rapid-fire. A bolt of lightning seemed to bounce onto the trunk of the car, thunder came too, and Jennings tore at his hair, stepped on the accelerator and his car shot around the curve at the bottom of the hill and disappeared. Renee was left, standing quite still, clutching Sue as a torrent of rain beat down on them.

"God damn it!" Renee screamed up at the sky.

In class the next day Renee seethed with fury. She could not look Jennings in the face and every time he spoke or laughed with the girls she cringed, so disgusted was she by the very thought of the man. At the end of the day she rose from her chair, calmly stretched out her arm and, pointing her finger right at him, shouted, "Quit persecuting me!"

His slight cough was the only sound in the room. He paused briefly at his desk, rummaging needlessly through some papers, then turned to the board and breaking open a new box of chalk he wrote the assignment for the next day.

In the weeks that followed he was remarkably pleasant to

Renee, going out of his way to ask if she needed any extra help with her lessons, never singling her out for humiliation in front of the others, always passing her in the hall with the most benign expression. But for Renee it was too late. She was a dog who had been kicked once too often. Her master was beyond redemption, could never be trusted. She would lick the wounds forever.

"I'm going to miss graduation," Nina Dobas confided in Renee, "because poor Mother is ill and I must go to her. But I shall see you next year." Nina placed her hand on Renee's breast. "You'll be in sixth grade, won't you? You're going to get back in the swing of things then. You're a remarkable child with considerable talent and I'm not going to let anybody tell me differently. I *know*, you see. . ."

Renee was jealous of the older girls who were graduating. For them it was over. They paraded gaily down the halls in their special dresses and imaginative permanents discussing all the boys they would be dating in the fall. Renee still had one last French report which she had to turn in to Miss Crane. She had only spent fifteen minutes on it when she should have given it an hour's attention. She guiltily slipped it into Miss Crane's hands. The teacher smiled disappointedly. "Thank you, Renee."

She ran through her last gym class like a machine, participating with a listlessness that felt particularly good to her.

She walked with Jill back to the changing room. "Thank God that's it," Renee muttered.

"A whole summer of freedom. You have to come visit me at the lake this summer. Mom says you can stay as long as you like."

"Of course I'll come. I wouldn't miss it for the world."

Suddenly there was a scream from one of the girls at her locker. It was Gloria. Dazed, she sank to the bench. The others crowded around. First she held up her bra which had been ripped to shreds and then her underpants on the back of which was written in huge red letters *WHORE*. Gloria's face was ashen. Some of the other girls screamed, others began to cry. Renee and Jill just stared.

Jennings burst into the room. "Cover yourselves, girls. Now what is all the fuss about!"

"It's Gloria," cried Frieda. "Look what someone's done to her clothes!"

It was only moments before the other girls discovered similar obscenities scrawled on their undergarments. On Jill's blouse was smeared *YOU ARE A SICK CUNT*. On some of the others, worse words, some the girls had never even heard of. There was total confusion, and hysteria built. Renee felt queasy, especially when she discovered that her clothes were the only ones to have remained unviolated.

"You mean, nothing's written on yours?" Anne Ewing asked incredulously.

"No. Funny, isn't it?" Renee laughed with embarrassment.

"Not so strange, perhaps," Jennings' voice rang out. "You were gone a very long time when I excused you to go to the water fountain. Maybe ten minutes."

"Well, it was the last day. I mean . . . what did it matter?"

"The other girls must know this, Renee Cloverman. It would be wrong of me to keep it from them. Shortly after you left to get a drink, I walked into the hall and you weren't at the fountain. On my way back to the gym, I saw you slip in here — into the changing room. . ."

To Renee it was all as clear and cold as ice. "What a lie," she answered.

The girls eyed her sheepishly.

"It is funny you were gone so long," Anne Ewing snapped. "And how *is* it that you were the only one whose clothes weren't touched?"

"Anne, shut up!" Gloria spoke from the bench. "Renee didn't do this, she's not that kind of person."

The others nodded weakly in agreement but they were very tense and their faces clearly revealed that they were not at all certain. Renee's eyes drifted to Gloria's underpants. The word *WHORE* screamed at her.

An hour later she was carefully hidden at the back of the stage in the shadow of the harp. Sure enough, there soon was some rustling a few yards away and the figure of Jennings appeared. He crept softly across the floor, a flashlight in his hand, its white circle making a path for him in the blackness. He knelt at a spot quite close to where Renee was hiding, holding her breath. Opening a make-up kit he replaced a tube of carmine stage paint in its rightful spot. He then waved his flashlight around the stage and put his ear against the wool curtains to ascertain if anyone was in the gym beyond. Satisfied that it was empty, Jennings walked on, disappearing in the far wing. Renee was left alone in the dark. But she was rather pleased with herself.

She had guessed immediately back in the changing room. After all, people were not exactly full of surprises. Men were who they were. They didn't change — for better or worse. There was something to be learned here in the dark. Where one could think. Where there was peace. *Praying doesn't make a wish come true. . . Nothing does. . . All wishes are invisible. . . You never wake to hear the sounds you dream of. . .*

Next year Renee was sent to the same public school that her sister, Sue, attended as Milly had run completely out of funds. Her grades did not improve, her enthusiasm for her teachers and classmates was nil. She did not write a new list of her favorite friends or potential enemies as everybody seemed draped in gray and they took on very little color, ever. When during the year's first snowstorm a boy dropped all his books in the middle of the intersection and skinned his knee, she neither laughed nor cried but only looked the other way.

Chapter Ten

The summer was on the wane, but the heat kept up so fierce that Perry would finish each day in a sea of sweat, with a headache from the sun. Yet the only thing that bothered him was the increase in gnats and mosquitoes. His lanky white arms looked as if they'd been nibbled away, while his legs were swollen with chigger bites which itched until he wanted to scream out loud for mercy. Ella panicked that Perry would be called for a television commercial and that she would have to refuse the offer. She made Perry promise to avoid striding through the tall grass, burnt brown now and rough to the touch, and to stick to excursions in his boat or bike trips along mowed, clear-cut trails.

Perry's favorite spot was a cool orchard about three miles from his house, where green and yellow apples were already ripening, their blossoms shutting out the power of the sun. The paths were hard dirt and easy to master and Perry sped along in the shade, protected by high clipped hedges which created a maze in which he sometimes lost his direction but never worried as there was no Minotaur blocking the exits, nor any human being to chance upon. It was in this orchard that he sometimes rested on gnarled stumps and considered life. A whole field was going to waste beyond his bedroom window, under his very eyes, a field that should be cultivated with wires to provide the earth with a new pair of ears. If only his father could see it that way. But he was stubborn and resisted new ideas, especially if they came from his children; he was used to running the lives of the entire family from in front of a mirror which reflected his ample prejudices. But convincing him need not be impossible.

Perry just had to keep thinking and never give up. He would win in the end. Half the battle was finding his father in the proper mood.

One afternoon after Perry wearily parked his bike in the garage, he came across his father sunning in the garden, sipping a whiskey sour, reading the *Times* and looking terribly relaxed. The man listlessly raised his hand in greeting. This movement screamed indulgence and Perry zeroed in for the kill.

"Go back there and take a look now?" Scotchsmith balked. "I'm so comfortable here. I was just about to steal a couple of winks."

"It'll only take a minute."

He tousled Perry's hair. "You kids rule the roost here."

Perry led him to the edge of the acres in question which stretched for a mile to where trees bent over to prevent the weedy clearing from rolling on forever.

"Well, who's going to do all the work, clearing out that mess?"

"I am."

"You are and who else? After a day's work, you'll clear a few feet and then be done with it. It will be a project you'll abandon because of the back-breaking work involved."

"No I won't because I'll just keep thinking how exciting it'll be to start building the telescope. We can do that together, Dad. Come on. Think of how much fun that will be."

"I'll help with that, Perry. But I'm not going to pull all those rotten vegetables up, especially with the mosquitoes lying low out there. If I give you permission, your mom will turn right around and say no."

"She won't, Dad. I'll spray myself all over head to toe. I mean I can't get any more bites than I have already. You come to the point when they don't want your rotten flesh anymore. They want new blood."

"You won't stop at anything," Scotchsmith chuckled. "The fact remains that you can't clear out as big a patch as you claim to need all by yourself."

Ron happened to be hanging out the upstairs window, threatening to drop the cat to the pavement unless Martha gave him back some money she supposedly owed him. She was tugging at his sleeve and begging her father to intervene.

"Stop it, Ron. Let the cat go," Scotchsmith ordered at which point Ron dropped the dangling cat and watched enthusiastically as the animal struggled to turn itself upright in time to land on its feet, which it did, unhurt but shaken, and it scampered away into the bushes where it licked its sides fanatically.

"All right, that's it!" Martha cried. "You'll never get that money now. I've washed my hands of the whole affair!"

"Ron, come down here at once," his father's voice was sharp. When the boy appeared, a bit sheepish, Scotchsmith simply said, "Your brother wants to build a radio telescope out here. Will you help him clear the field?"

"What do I get?"

"You'll have to take that up with him. After all," he turned to Perry, "why should Ron help if he doesn't benefit? It'll take two of you to do the job. You boys make some kind of bargain."

Perry shrugged. "Well, what do you want?"

"What do you got?"

Perry racked his brains. "I don't have money. . ."

"If you let me ride your bike —"

"No! You lost my last bike and I had a hard enough time getting a new one."

"Well, I don't want to do a lot of dirty work for nothing."

"Wait a minute — how about if I name something after you — you know, the first thing I discover. . ."

"What, like a star?" Ron cried skeptically. "I don't believe you'll ever find anything. Ever!"

"Ron Scotchsmith, you're so stupid! Your name could be in the almanacs forever. And it might not only be a star I discover but a whole galaxy!"

"I don't care what you say, I won't believe it till it happens."

"Then I don't want your help."

"Good." And Ron was off.

"Why can't you two boys get along?" Peter said angrily. "My brother and I never quarreled. Well, we may have quarreled over one or two important things, but at least we never quibbled!"

"Can't you see it's not my fault!"

"I don't take sides. You two make up and if you want me to buy you this wire and help you set up, you talk your brother into giving you a hand with this. I'm not going to play favorites."

Perry wheeled around and went inside. "Christ," he muttered as he climbed upstairs. "What are brothers for?"

The whole house was on edge. The children, bored by the

long vacation, could only think to spend the last free days fighting and tormenting each other. Ella's youngest sister was combatting severe emotional problems and Ella left suddenly for Pennsylvania to stay with her and try to be of some comfort, hurriedly scribbling the number where she could be reached on the board above the refrigerator and quickly kissing each of the family goodbye. Peter Scotchsmith began to drink heavily, worried by some fanciful investments he'd secretly made. He never got drunk, only pleasantly high, just so he could put himself to bed each night feeling happy.

It was only three days until Renee would meet Jake in New York and she was anxious to leave the house. If she never saw any of the Scotchsmiths again it would be reason to celebrate. That evening as she began to climb the stairs, the door to the den opened and Peter Scotchsmith called to her, "Renee, don't go up to bed yet. Come in here and have a nightcap with me."

She agreed and he made her sit on the leather sofa as he poured her a brandy.

"Since Ella is away and I'll be at work, I hope you'll be able to keep an eye on the kids tomorrow."

"What am I — a glorified babysitter?"

"I know it's no picnic," he laughed.

"Yeah, I'll watch them. You know I'll be leaving for New York in a couple of days."

"Ella should be back by then. By God, she has to be. Her family is here." He sat beside her, sipping his gin and tonic. "We'll be sorry to see you go."

"We'll run into each other again, I'm sure."

"Of course . . . I expect to be invited to the wedding."

"What wedding? . . . Oh . . . Jake . . . We never talked about that."

Scotchsmith grinned and thumped her knee with his fingers. "I imagine it will come about. Listen. Why not have the reception up here? We could set up a nice big tent and have a regular lawn party."

"It's a thought."

"Didn't you say your father passed on when you were a girl?"

"Yes."

"I'd be glad to give the bride away."

She was becoming annoyed. She stood up.

"That is —" he continued, "if you don't have someone else in mind."

"I'm afraid you're putting the cart before the horse."

Scotchsmith wasn't used to such a quick rebuff. He scowled slightly, then crossed to the bar and added ice to his drink. He began talking about going into his office in the morning, about the tremendous work load that was waiting for him. Renee realized that his office was directly across the street from Roger Fourne's penthouse. Some mornings she had wakened before Fourne and after making coffee she had watched the world go by from his picture window. She had studied the men filing up the steps of the office building, all in clean wool suits carrying worn but expensive briefcases. She had probably seen Peter Scotchsmith many mornings. How ironic. Here he was, back turned to her, not knowing she was a spy. What would he think if he knew that she had been watching him from Fourne's apartment? She wondered bitterly what his reaction would be if he knew what she had been up to with Fourne . . . if he knew what her past had been, what she was really like. . . But she was too hard on herself. Scotchsmith must have secrets of his own. He had to. Everyone did. There was a skeleton in everybody's closet, no, not just one, but row upon row of corpses, springing up and multiplying fiercely like dandelions in the wind, commonplace and uneventful as weeds. So what, anyway? The terrible secrets are part of the landscape. If white roses grow in a garden don't forget the dark flowers beneath giving them life.

There was a tap on Renee's door next morning just as the sun was beginning to show. "Who's there?" she called.

"Patricia! I'm hungry!"

Her heart sank as she remembered she was alone with the children and would be expected to perform Ella's duties. "Well, Martha is a better cook than I am . . . go ask her," she turned comfortably on the sheets.

There was giggling outside her door. After a pause, Ron's voice piped up, "She doesn't feel good this morning. You have to fix breakfast."

"All right. Hold on," she pulled open the slits and searched for her robe. She glanced at the clock on the bureau: only 6:30. She located her slippers and stumbled into the hall, wiping the sleep from her eyes. Ron and Patricia had disappeared already. They were probably down in the kitchen making a mess of things. Perry's door was shut tight, he must still be sleeping.

To her surprise, she found Ron and Patricia waiting patiently at the kitchen table.

"Hurry up," Patricia said. "We're starving!"

"Shut up," Renee answered. "I'm not your slave."

"Daddy said you're supposed to take care of us."

"My dear young lady, I don't care what your father told you. I'm in charge here now. Don't forget that."

"You aren't in charge — and you don't scare anybody." Ron challenged her.

Renee sighed, leaning against the refrigerator. "Look. Do you want something to eat or shall I go back upstairs to bed?"

"We're hungry. We told you that a hundred times already!" Patricia whined.

"Then what do you want?"

"Eggs and bacon," Ron said.

"And pancakes would be nice," Patricia added.

Renee began to cook the meal with no enthusiasm. She didn't know where half the ingredients were and the children refused to help her find them. It was a slow process but an hour later she was putting down a hot breakfast before them. They made faces and complained that the eggs were cold, the bacon under-cooked and the pancakes had black specks on them that looked like dirt, but they wolfed it down anyway. When Renee announced she was making some hot tea and toast for their sister they began to snicker. And when she carried it upstairs on a tray they followed her, even though they hadn't finished their breakfast. She soon discovered the reason for their mirth: Martha's bed was empty and there were muffled cries and pounding coming from the closet. When Renee opened the door she found the girl bound and gagged on the floor. She quickly freed her as Ron and Patricia stormed about the room in complete hysterics.

"Oh!" Martha shook her fists. "How could you shut me up in the dark like that!"

It was a rather pathetic sight, this big girl all puffy and red-faced, yet to Renee it was somehow funny too. It was the icing on the cake. She just shook her head exasperatedly at everyone and returned to her room. If Martha was dumb enough to let herself be trussed up like a cow and stuffed in the closet by her little brother and sister, well, maybe she deserved it. Besides, what else did any of them have to do except play tricks on each other? She fell back on the bed, breaking into laughter. It was all so absurd. She closed her eyes and suddenly Jake was looking down at her from the foot of the bed . . . Jake without a shirt, his arms folded. She could almost feel his skin. Soon. . .

The rest of the day was uneventful. She helped the children with lunch and when she tried to make them clean up afterwards they rebelled, which she expected. Martha did manage to come to her aid and dry the dishes, only because the girl wanted someone to talk to. Martha also helped her fix dinner which proved a success, Peter Scotchsmith stating that it tasted as delicious as if his wife had prepared it.

Throughout dinner, and even as he toyed with the banana pudding, his favorite dessert, Perry seemed moody, untalkative.

His father lost patience. "Quit pulling such a long face at the table."

But Perry didn't cheer up.

"It's probably because of that old field in back that nobody'll help him clear away," Patricia said.

"Yes. That's it," Perry looked up defiantly. "That's it exactly."

"You're just spoiled!" she countered.

Renee, not knowing why, but feeling flushed from a few glasses of red wine, spoke angrily, "He's not spoiled at all. Not compared to the rest of you. Why shouldn't he expect some support from his brother and his sisters? Why doesn't somebody offer to pitch in and help?"

Everybody just stared at her. Martha had trouble swallowing a mouthful of pudding.

"Oh, you don't know anything," Ron threw down his fork.

"It seems to me," she said, "that what Perry is asking is next to nothing at all. I, for one, would be glad to help clear the field."

A new silence crushed the old. Perry grinned. "Well, Dad?"

Scotchsmith hesitated, then nodded. "Well, fine. You heard Renee."

"Can we start tonight, after dinner?" he cried.

Scotchsmith traded glances with Renee.

"Why not?" she replied. "It beats working under the boiling sun."

After spraying each other with insect repellant and finding some tools for digging and some workmen's gloves on the basement shelves, they pulled an old wheelbarrow onto the field. They decided the best method would be to fill large plastic bags with the rotten vegetables and stack those in the wheelbarrow, pushing it periodically to the garage where they would leave the bags with the rest of the trash. They surveyed the field which was like a silver sea in the moonlight.

"Gosh, it's bright enough out here for a doctor to perform an operation!" Perry exclaimed. "So we shouldn't have any problems."

"It's just knowing where to begin," she mused.

Perry finally chose an acre to clear and marked its boundaries with croquet wickets. Then he and Renee attacked. They worked hard and silently at first, tearing desperately at the dead plants rooted firmly in the ground, but finally they became amused at their own seriousness and couldn't help laughing.

"You're already a mess," she told the boy, dirt caked on his chin.

"Me? What about you? Shall I bring a mirror out so you can see?"

"Don't bother. I have a good enough idea," and she unfastened her blouse with her soiled gloves to try to shake some of the loose dirt from her breasts.

They soon noticed that the children were watching them from the hall window.

"Isn't that something?" Renee wiped her brow. "They thought this would be such a boring, terrible task and now they can't tear themselves away from spying on us."

"Let's look like we're having a great time," Perry cried, tossing the vegetables high in the air, crossing his fingers that they would land in the barrow.

"Well, we are."

Much later she caught glimpses of small faces in the lighted windows. "Isn't that always the way? People just seem to want what they can't have. . . Well, they made their own beds. . ."

They worked steadily for another hour and at last were making some headway. With Perry running back and forth from the kitchen with punch and cookies and cool washcloths, they were able to keep up their energy and clear an eighth of an acre by midnight.

"I'm not tired at all," Renee paused, downing her glass.

"Me, neither."

They began to dig again, ripping the weeds from the earth. Renee was bent double and her eyes were so close to the ground that she honestly looked as if she were searching for a tiny needle and the moonlight had grown so bright that if one had been there she would have found it.

"Renee?"

"Hmmm?"

"You should be my assistant. You know, Professor Hewish in England who discovered the pulsars — his assistant was a young woman. In fact, she was left in charge of constructing the telescope. She planted the field with thousands of small antennas — all by herself with just a sledgehammer. Did you know that?"

"No, of course not."

"And she was the one who actually made the discovery." He sat back on his heels.

"Perry, I'm not fucking smart enough to be your assistant. So drop it."

"You're impatient, that's all."

"Maybe so," she picked at a fetid, decaying turnip that was resisting her pull.

"You'd like to clear this whole field tonight, if you could."

"Got it!" she screamed, pulling the plant up by its roots and holding it in the air as if it were a prized catch.

"You're beautiful, you know that?" It just came out.

She tossed the turnip into the wheelbarrow. "Thank you."

Blushing, yet feeling safe that she couldn't see it by moonlight, Perry hummed up at the sky. He was always on the lookout for falling stars. It would not be unusual for him to spot half a dozen within a few hours on a clear night.

It wasn't until after three that they called it quits with at least a quarter of the acre weeded.

"Just dirt now," Perry said proudly and together they pulled the wheelbarrow to the garage. They scrubbed their hands in the kitchen and fixed some hot chocolate as a victory drink, then Perry went up to bed while Renee stayed below a moment to lock up.

As she climbed the stairs in the dark, she was frightened to see a tall figure waiting at the top. Her eyes adjusted to the dimness and the moonlight revealed Peter Scotchsmith.

"Sorry if I startled you," he whispered. "I just wondered how everything went?"

"Fine."

"You're all right?"

"Yes . . . I'm filthy . . . sweating, covered with dirt and insect spray. . ."

"I can see," he said softly. He slipped his hands into his robe pockets and stared at her.

"Not very appealing," she continued, her breasts heaving.

"Let me judge that," he said.

She remembered she had unbuttoned her blouse in the field so her chest was exposed. She didn't bother to pretend to be modest but just stood there sweating and mopping her forehead. Scotchsmith studied her thoughtfully. She felt her nipples harden under his gaze. He reached out and squeezed one. His hand was huge and covered her breast, his fingers felt hotter and stickier than her own flesh. The top of his robe slipped open and she saw his chest, strong, milky white and looking like a very young man's. He pulled her against him and held her. She suddenly hoped he would pick her up and carry her to his bed and put his hands all over her body, but at the same moment she was thinking this she found herself pulling away and drifting down the hall, finding her own room and shutting herself inside. She threw herself on the bed, still perspiring, turning the sheets a muddy gray. It was too late for a bath now. It would have to wait till morning.

So he wanted her. She had never guessed. She supposed it was just the idea of a young woman in the house while his wife was away. Or was she making too much of it? Had he really reached for her like she remembered? Or had she fallen against him? No. He had wanted to take her. She laughed. She had never guessed. . .

She was awakened early in the morning by a crash against her door. She assumed it was Ron and Patricia's way of letting her know they expected breakfast. She was exhausted, after only three hours sleep, so she screamed, "Go to Hell, you brats!" and pulled the pillow over her head. But moments later she heard the sound of someone choking and a heavy thumping against the floorboards. Confused, she edged out of bed, threw her Chinese robe around her and opened her door.

Ron and Perry were pounding away at each other with the savageness of two fighting cats which would stop at nothing to claw each other's skin to bits. Ron had pulled himself from under Perry and was now sitting on top of his brother's chest, slugging hard at his face, hoping to give him a black eye. Perry warded off the blows as best he could and when, for an instant, the left side of Ron's face was unprotected, Perry took advantage and gave him an alarming wallop which echoed through the hall. Bewildered, Ron let out a little cry like a bird, then anger overcame him and he began throwing wild punches at Perry's chest.

Martha and Patricia had by this time joined Renee and the three of them managed to lift a struggling Ron into the air and finally pin him against the wall.

"That is enough!" Renee was really disgusted.

Ron broke free and flew down the stairs, taking them two at a time. Perry, meanwhile, staggered to his feet and leaned over the bannister, waving his fist in a rage after his brother, shouting, "I hate you! I hate the sight of you and I never want to see you again! I never want to look at your face again!" Then he shut himself in his room.

"Let's make breakfast," Patricia yawned, nudging her sister and they left Renee standing alone, tired and shaken. She wanted a bath more than anything, but something told her to look in on Perry to make sure he was all right. She tapped at the door. "Perry, may I come in?"

"O.K.," he sighed.

Renee found him lying face down on the bed. He seemed to be having trouble inhaling.

"Did you get the wind knocked out of you?"

"Yeah," his words came painfully. "It's like what happened to me on a rollercoaster once, when the car rounded a curve. Dad had to pound me on the back so I could get my breath."

"Well, do you need me to do that?"

He looked up at her. "I don't think so." She realized by the way he was screwing his face that he was trying to hold back tears.

"What was the fight all about?" she asked softly.

"He came in my room this morning when I was still half asleep and grabbed my star chart off my desk, for no reason. Well, I figured he was up to no good, so I followed him and found he had locked himself in the bathroom. I pounded on the door and asked him what he was doing with my chart and he yelled back, 'I'm burning it.' I threatened him and kicked the door and asked him why, but there wasn't any answer and then I smelled smoke. Finally, he opened the door. True to his words, he had set it on fire in the tub then had put out the flames by turning on the tap. Wet ashes. All that's left of a year of work. I never want to see his face again."

As Renee left the room she decided that Ron's meanness to his brother was somehow directed at her too, though she couldn't say exactly how or why. At least he would be gone for a good part of the afternoon as he had been invited to a neighbor boy's birthday party. Good riddance. She dressed and went downstairs to fix something to eat. She found Ron fastening a holster with two toy pistols around his waist and cramming a paper bag full of chocolate bars to take to the party. The child filled her with revulsion.

"That was a pretty vicious thing to do to your brother."

"Nobody asked you."

"Why do you want to destroy everything?" Her heart beat faster and her lips quivered. "What's wrong with you?"

"Oh, shut up. It was a game."

"You were jealous, weren't you, of Perry clearing out the field last night?"

"So long." And he was off, arms full, a cowboy hat a size too large wobbling on his head.

Renee was in a lethargic mood. She could hardly even summon the energy for a sponge bath. She stared numbly at the garden, the colors of the flowers fading in the August heat. Later she caught a glimpse of herself in the bathroom mirror and realized she looked horrible. Her hair was twisted round and stuck up in strands like a bird's nest, her bright yellow blouse with the white half moons spilling down the front was a bit soiled, and her vinyl skirt was creased and looked like last year's throwaway. There were circles starting under her eyes. Sighing, she wrung her hands through her hair, then pouted in defiance. She squared her shoulders.

It wasn't long before Ron was back with an army of little buddies, all in birthday hats, racing through the garden, trampling the peonies and lilies. Next she found them causing an uproar in the den, smearing cake on the sofa, dragging dirt across the carpet and upsetting Peter Scotchsmith's jigsaw puzzle. She tried to calm them down but couldn't make herself heard through their din. If they thought she would pick up after them they were mistaken. Their screams were finally heard in the kitchen and she walked in to find the boys holding down the dog, Sleepy, on the butcher's block, the animal yelping and squirming as one of the boys raised a long-bladed butcher knife above its heart.

"We're sacrificing Sleepy," Ron proudly informed her.

"The hell you are," she answered and slapped him on the ass. "Tell your friend to put that dog back on its feet."

"We aren't really gonna kill it!" Ron snapped at her.

"You might as well and put it out of its misery."

The boys released Sleepy who jumped from the butcher's block and ran out the back door, the band of boys following. *That little monster is trying his best to irritate me.* Renee searched the cupboards for dinner ingredients. She thought she would make a roast and a salad and if Martha wished she could prepare a fresh fruit cocktail. A little later, when she thought the world was unusually quiet, Renee happened to look up from her cooking to find Ron staring at her quietly from the lawn outside. He was standing stark still and resembled a tiny statue that someone had set in the ground. Five minutes later he was still there. Renee found it odd since he was an undisciplined boy, always in motion like a wind-up toy. His birthday hat and horn were lying at his feet. His hands hung at his sides. She ignored him.

After a short nap she opened the slits and peered outside. Framed between the wood panels was Ron on the grass below, hands in his pockets, casually walking in circles, casting his eyes up at her window.

When she returned to the kitchen to put the final touches to the roast, he was sitting at the table whittling a piece of wood. He pretended not to look at her, but sometimes when she bent down she could see him from the corner of her eye and he, unaware of her gaze, would turn towards her, staring intently, his mouth pursed. Renee set the plates on the counter. She moved an open newspaper to one side to make room. It was then she accidentally sprang the trap.

The mousetrap had been carefully hidden beneath the opened paper. It had come down fast on her little finger. She yelled. Blood gushed and she held her finger downwards under a stream of cold water. Ron continued whittling the wood.

Renee cast furious glances his way. She said, "Get me a band-aid."

"I don't know where Mom keeps them. I don't even think we have any."

"Of course you don't. You probably made certain they found their way to the trash can this afternoon." Renee had stopped the blood but her finger still was stinging. She sucked it.

"That's what you get," Ron stated.

"My punishment?" she laughed. "For telling you off?"

"I didn't set the trap."

"Ron, don't you think I'm smart enough to figure out you did that to me? You're a calculating little bastard, aren't you?"

He jumped up. "I'm telling Daddy you said those words. Yes, I put the trap there. And I wish it had killed you instead of just snipped your finger! You're dirty, that's why. You talk and act dirty!"

Renee grabbed him by the collar and rubbed her little finger against his mouth. "You did this. You've been trying to find a way to get at me for days. But I'll get even with you if it's the last thing I do."

He broke away and as he ran from the room he hurled the piece of wood at her. She ducked and it cracked the window behind her.

Renee was livid. She knew that she couldn't sit at dinner with the family, as upset as she was, so she wrote a note and left it next to the roast explaining that she wasn't well and had gone to bed early.

She paced back and forth in her room. She packed her bags, anxious to leave for New York the next day, then paced some more, unable to rid her thoughts of that little boy, only eight-years-old. Here she was, helpless, more than three times his age, playing his silly, brutal game. She was afraid she would strangle him to death if she came face to face with him again.

By midnight she was asleep.

An hour later she woke with a start. She felt a terrible pain in her foot. She switched on the light. Blood was dripping from a cut on her ankle. She searched the sheets for a sharp object and felt the mattress to see if a spring was sticking through, but she could find nothing. She washed her ankle in the bathroom then returned to bed. When the lights were out she was suddenly afraid. The dark was oppressive. She thought she heard her mother's voice, *Still having those awful nightmares, Renee?* She began to sweat. She had been seized by a nightmare, that was it, wasn't it? She had woken from the depths of some awful struggle. And as her eyes adjusted to the room and she could perceive light, so her mind slipped the other way into darkness until she slowly remembered the black dream she had ripped apart. . .

She was walking through an aluminum corridor, pulling Ron by the hand. She was walking swiftly with an unrelenting

determination. They walked on and on until it seemed there
was no end for them. Finally, Renee reached a door on which a
wreath of pine cones and hazelnuts blazed. She rang the bell.
The door flew back and she stepped inside, dragging a protesting Ron along behind her. They were in Roger Fourne's
penthouse and he waited beside them, smiling, hands on hips.
His living room was dark, the only light trickling in from the
deserted office buildings across the street. Fourne was thanking
her for bringing the boys and she soon realized that she was
holding Perry's hand as well. She suddenly was alarmed and
tried to make Perry go back down the long corridor but he
stared straight ahead, his eyes dead. Fourne led them to the
bathroom. The white tub gleamed beneath the phosphorescent
lights. Renee watched as Fourne dressed the brothers as shep-
herd boys with sweet garlands on their heads and made them
stand very quietly in the tub. Their feet where immersed in
water. Suddenly, he flipped a switch and the boys were electrocuted in a dynamic current of fire. Renee remembered that
she had brought other children here. That was what Fourne
wanted. That was her job. He had dressed a little brother and
sister as angels once and had placed them in the tub, requesting
that they look at the ceiling as if they were imploring Heaven to
take them. Then he pulled the switch. He had clothed two
young girls in the garb of royal princesses, setting golden
crowns in their thick hair and making them hold wands with
snowy ivy twisting up the sides. Renee watched each time yet
the savage jolt always took her by surprise. How many children
had he electrocuted? She had no idea. It seemed she was always
walking down that corridor, holding some little hand. One time
she had come alone and when he had let her in she had said, *So
it's only me you want after all, isn't it? That's what you've wanted all the
time.* . . . And he had scolded her and insisted she was wrong,
slamming the door in her face and instructing her to bring him
more children. . . And now the bodies of Ron and Perry
slumped down into the tub, dead. Fourne took Renee to bed,
and as he was fucking her she saw over his shoulder, in the dark,
coffins stacked against the wall, row upon row in the shadows.
She saw them, each time he moved above her. She was standing
in a low river in the midst of some reeds and above her the sky
was yellow like lemon icing on a cake. She looked around her
and she saw Jake half-hidden in the reeds. They were moving
their mouths at each other and she felt pain somewhere.

Further on she spotted her old music teacher, Nina Dobas, squatting in tall reeds, her shoulders naked and covered with sores. The woman was also talking and watching something and Renee followed the woman's gaze and saw a line of coffins drifting down the river. She felt Fourne turn her over. He was hurting her somehow and his hands were inside her mouth. Then she was walking around his bathtub, dreading to peer inside. The ceiling exploded and the yellow sky poured down upon her and she saw Jake across from her, the reeds blowing. But at her feet something was biting her ankle. It was Ron, half baby, half animal, his teeth piercing her flesh, he was a bloated corpse with a black and blue face, a victim of electrocution. . .

Yes, that had been her dream. And now, with the moon shining through the slits, the room was bright enough to read a book in. It was apparent that she had been tearing her ankle with the toenails of her other foot, no need to search for a dangerous object lost somewhere in the sheets. She closed her eyes now and prayed for a peaceful sleep, resting her face in the light of the moon.

But by morning she was not refreshed. And the first image that came to her mind was of Ron, loose somewhere in the house, forging a new trail of devastation. He would probably have preferred burning her clothes rather than his brother's chart, if he only could have gotten his hands on them. But they were packed in her suitcase, which rested against the door, and she wouldn't take them out again until she reached the hotel.

She took three aspirins, put on a red cotton dress that was too tight, gave her hair a lackluster brush, pinched her cheeks and touched her lips with some invisible gloss. She phoned the cab company, giving them instructions to pick her up between eight and nine that evening so she could catch a train that would get her into the city before midnight. Jake would be back by then so she wouldn't have to shoot the breeze with Bee and the others. She could just shut the door behind her and she and Jake would be alone.

"Gee, if you come back in the fall your room might be taken by a foreign exchange student," Martha warned her. "Mother has accepted a girl from Uruguay."

"She has the room with my blessing," Renee was short-tempered. "And why on earth would you think I'd be coming back here?"

Martha pouted. "Ex*cuse* me."

Renee took Sleepy for a long walk that afternoon since it was the first cool day in a two week hot spell. Sleepy led her to a slender stream in the woods that she had never seen before. She knelt beside the dog as it lapped the water and she scratched its head. "You're a brilliant baby. Lead me anywhere and I'll follow you." They rested an hour there, Renee sitting on a smooth rock, her mind blank, Sleepy stretched on the ground before her, training his eyes on the dragonflies that sipped the water. It was Sleepy who finally rubbed against her legs to let her know it was time to go home. "All right. Come on, then."

It was as they were coming up the front lawn, Renee debating about whether to pop some more aspirins since her headache was back, that she noticed the small figure, waiting by the front door, dwarfed by the bright house yet giving the impression that he was king there for all his smallness.

"Why did you take my dog away!" Ron shouted at her.

"It's not just your dog. It belongs to the whole family."

"It *is* my dog. My father gave it to *me*." And as Sleepy lumbered by him he reached out and gave its neck a shake. "Don't ever go anywere with her again. You hear me?"

"Relax, buster," Renee said. "Nobody touched your precious pet."

The boy's face suddenly reddened and he kicked her leg. "I'm glad you're going!" he shouted.

She slapped him hard across the face and he kicked her again. She whispered, "You touch me one more time and I'll kill you!"

With all his might he butted his head into her stomach and sent her sprawling on the grass. Then he raced inside the house. Renee, enraged, caught her breath and chased him. She saw his shadow disappear into the kitchen so she ran in and cornered him, forcing him back against the butcher's block, all the while fording off the blows aimed at her shoulders and face. Exasperated, Ron began spitting at her, fast globs covering the front of her red dress. She tried to force his head back against the block. He scratched at her, ripping her sleeve. Sleepy ran up to them and began to bark wildly. Finally, Renee had the boy against the block, defenseless, and she grabbed a long knife from the counter and held it to his neck. "God give me the strength to slit your throat!" She only meant to frighten him, she wasn't about to cut him. . . Both of them became perfectly still. Even the dog stopped barking and stared up at them. She watched Ron's eyes but she couldn't find any terror there, only an obstinate kind of hatred.

Renee moved the blade back and Ron pushed himself up. "I'm not afraid of you," he said maliciously. "You know why?"

Renee shook her head, as in a dream.

"Because you aren't one of us. You're different from the rest. You don't fit in and nobody likes you. . . That's why I'm not scared of you." And he marched confidently from the kitchen.

Renee was possessed by one desire only. To cripple him somehow. Nothing else mattered to her, she would follow a burning star of revenge, never taking her eyes off it. Yet to wound him seemed next to impossible because in the final analysis he was just that much more vicious then she, his claws were sharper. In that case, she reasoned, you don't fight fire with fire, but with water.

Evening fell and somehow the heat crept back with the dark, making Renee feel sticky and everything she touched seem wet. After a light dinner the family dispersed, Martha and Patricia going upstairs to redecorate their rooms, Perry out back to work in the field, Ron to visit his best friend who lived next door. His father shouted from the den, "You be back within the hour, young man, because I want you in bed at a decent hour."

"I'll be back by eight, Dad."

"You come and report to me as soon as you're back. I don't want you pretending that you're upstairs asleep when you're over at Billy's."

Ron waved in agreement and darted out the door. Scotchsmith poured himself a drink, turned on the television, keeping the volume very low, loosened his tie and sat down at the table, only now realizing that his jigsaw puzzle had been scattered about the room. "Goddam kids," he muttered.

"I meant to tell you all about it," Renee spoke from the doorway. "The birthday party turned up here yesterday and this is the result."

"I see," he sighed. "If my brother and I had done this when my mother was alive, look out . . . but," he laughed, "times have changed. . ." Scotchsmith avoided her eyes, still embarrassed about the scene on the stairs the other night. He tried to fit the pieces that remained on the table back together.

"What's it of?" Renee still hovered in the doorway.

"This? I don't know. Some covered bridge or something. If I could find the top of the box I'd show you."

Renee walked over to the table and looked down. "I'd never have the patience for this. Mind if I fix myself a drink?"

Scotchsmith was on his feet. "Let me." He turned to her
questioningly at the bar.

"Vodka," she said.

"A toast." He handed her a drink. "To a star boarder."

"Thank you."

He downed his drink and she followed suit. He insisted on
pouring them each another. They sat on the sofa and talked.
Soon they were very loose, laughing at senseless jokes. Renee
became very physical with Scotchsmith, playfully cuffing him
and taking him to task about wasting his important time on an
innocuous jigsaw puzzle. He responded by edging closer to her.
Amidst all the joking there came a quiet moment and Scotchsmith recklessly reached behind Renee and turned off the lamp.
They were bathed in the steady, silent glow of the television.
Scotchsmith began to breathe heavily, staring hard at her.

"You're very intense," she said. "That works on women
though, doesn't it? You're the kind that got lots of girls pregnant
in college, aren't you?" They both laughed. "How many girls
did you get in trouble, Mr. Scotchsmith?"

"I wouldn't know about that now would I?" His voice was
deep and he started to pull her to him. "Your dress makes me
crazy. . ."

"How crazy?" she whispered.

The only answer came from his rough hands which pulled the
red dress down over her shoulders. She slid her hand along his
leg to his crotch and tightened it around his cock. He suddenly
gasped and went pale.

"Jesus," she whispered in his ear. "You're ready to burst.
You're so hard. Oh, Jesus," she whispered again and he leaned
back against the sofa, overcome by weakness, almost to the
point of fainting. "Slide down on the sofa, all the way . . . that's
it . . ." she urged softly. When he was stretched out, his eyes
closed, she moved her hand again to his cock. His expression
was one of pain mixed with shame. He tried to push her hand
away.

"What's the matter?" she asked.

He had wanted her to stop, but now a convulsive sob broke
from his throat and he gave in. "Nothing."

Renee unzipped his fly. "I just want to blow you awhile,
that's all."

A rippling seized his body as she drew his hard cock from his undershorts, then he was still. She licked the head of his cock for a few seconds, then let the whole tool slide down her throat. She had been listening, had heard the front door open, had heard the steps making their way to the den. From the corner of her eyes she saw Ron stop dead in his tracks in the doorway, his eyes widening, his mouth opening, ready to scream, yet she kept sucking his father's cock, going at it noisily and with a passion, for the boy's benefit. Ron was finally able to release a gasp and he ran off. She heard him burst out the back door.

"What happened . . . who was there?" Scotchsmith sat up with a jerk. Renee finished her glass of vodka and without looking back walked upstairs. It was accomplished and it was all over. She would take her suitcase from against her door, leave and wait for the cab under the poplar trees down the road. Her life here had ended.

As she turned down the hall she paused. Perry's door was ajar and the first rays of the moon were seeping in through the window and casting white shadows on his bedroom floor. For some reason she felt called to that room, to that spot. She stood by his empty bed for a moment, then glanced out his window. Ron was running violently through the field, clutching his head in an insane manner. Perry was chasing him, trying to catch him so he wouldn't hurt himself. Soon Ron, sobbing, flung himself on the ground in the middle of the square that she and Perry had cleared only two nights before and Perry dropped quickly beside him, and to Renee's complete astonishment, as she had thought that Perry was never going to even look at Ron again, Perry cradled his brother in his arms, trying to console him, coaxing him to share the cause of his misery.

Chapter Eleven

The view from one eye. Mouse path. The eye the master of the floor, detecting the table legs, bits of moldy newspapers and a bedspread knifed to ribbons. Torch slits. All with a gagging of sleep in the throat. His hand stopped the fierce clenching and released. The fingers unclosed one by one and the suddenly free handgun slipped to the floor with a scratch while the other eye opened. Reggino was awake. For the first time in hours, in days, in nights. He noticed the moon lopsided over the pier warehouses beaming down on him and he seemed to remember waking to the same sight again and again, midnight after midnight, without moving from this spot — whenever he saw the silver slipper he surrendered and slept. But now he was fully conscious and his face was on the floor and a kind of terror throttled his bones. What was he doing lying beneath his window, his head on an improvised pillow of a sport shirt and a jockstrap? Why had a gun fallen from his hand? Why were there little dishes next to him filled with stinking sauerkraut, hamburger and water? How long had he been here like this? It was no illusion, the moon trick. He had seen its face like a somber mirror for too many nights.

His room sunk in natural shadow. The legs of the table seemed so solid, stronger than he. He licked his lips and there was a dryness in the corner as from a stream of vomit that had melted there, then cracked. The only clothing he wore was a pair of tan cotton trousers. Fingering the crotch, he felt the wet and saw that they were stained with urine. Fucking Christ, so he was a baby who pissed his pants now. He slipped them off and dipped his shirt-pillow in the dish of water and rubbed the stains furiously. He wanted to find the toilet. He had to shit. Oh, God, he felt sick. He stood up but he was all wobbly like he hadn't used his legs in days and he had to grab a chair back for support. He found the switch over the sink and a dull light streamed. Reggino lit a cigarette. He took a deep drag, it felt really good. He sat on the toilet, blowing smoke. Now it tasted peculiar though and the smoke clouds seemed funny, pink and blue and cold, coming from the bowels of a spring. He saw his old crib, an ugly affair, with that floral pattern that looked like the smoke. The crib was pushed against the wall as far as it could go and the traffic noise from the outside was unholy. Stop screaming. Remember those cars all night and Daddy coming in and you didn't want him to? Blue and pink clouds drifting towards Candyland. He dropped the cigarette in the toilet and stood up. Maybe when he wiped he would find the blue and pink clouds too. He started to laugh. Where the fuck had he been these last few days? Not at work, obviously. He'd been recovering from a giant hangover without ever having been loaded. He stared at the dishes beneath the window. He guessed he'd just been lying there for four or five days.

Christ, they'd have his balls at work. His watch on the table said 8:30. Still plenty of time to get to the plant tonight and he'd sure as hell better show up. Daddy, don't you come looking. . . What? Get this crib nonsense out of your head. Why did that ever come to you?

He sank to a chair in front of the long mirror and began to dress himself, lethargically pulling on his thick white wool socks and lacing the strings to his boots. He soon caught a glimpse of himself in the mirror and cursed. He'd forgotten to put his pants on — he'd have to try to ease them up over his boots. He'd like to walk in stark naked. His body was in fantastic shape. He stood and, smiling, knowing already what he would see, confronted his image. Six feet of power, of smooth muscle and chiseled chest, of hard brown thighs. On the table lay his arsenal. He grasped his hunting knife, the fat blade shaped into a death tool. There. Image complete. Deflower. Deflowerer. Prince among men. Decapitate. Naked blond decapitator. The fat blade longed for the touch of flesh and he moaned.

Enough. Turn away. Put your eyes back on the floor track, the mouse path again where there are only table legs and newspaper shreds.

He wanted to throw himself on the bed but he shrank back

from the mattress, bleeding in the dark. There was something there. Something in that corner to fear. Sweat poured from his temple and the hell-bent beat of his heart bothered him. Something to be afraid of. Something to run from. The moonlight whitened the sheets. The knife dropped from his hand. There it was in his bed. That thing. The bones of dogs, of animals, placed just so, with the skull of a terrier resting on the pillow, the flesh neatly cleaned away, all shiny teeth and vacant big sockets and its body, its body put together of clean bones resting — oh, God, yes . . . he had found the bodies along the highway . . . the night drives were never barren, they always birthed the dogs, the bitches . . . the ones that had been crucified by the speeding cars and were splattered immediately, before you could whistle . . . or crept away to die in the space between the tar and the grass . . . he would shoot those dogs between the temples and end their misery, then throw their carcasses in the trunk . . . he knew the dark grove behind the rest stop, the last one before the lights of Manhattan and the World Trade Center stole the horizon . . . there he would pick the bones free of flesh, tidily, more delicately than if he had rubbed along the marrow with a cloth of poison or yellow acid . . . then he carried the bones home . . . upstairs . . . and put them to bed. This sleeping creature here was made of the best parts of many dogs, it was a corpse of seven breeds at least, a sorcerer's brew. But it was a monster — one whole terror — that drove him to despair, that stared from his pillow — that scared him so badly that he dared not approach it and stayed on guard beneath the window, a gun in his hand, alternately sleeping if he dared, and keeping a fearful vigil against the dog through the brightness of the day and the murderous black of morning. Oh, God. His hands covered his eyes. The creature's bones ballooned. Untouchable. Unendurable. Reggino sobbed and his cries echoed, a lonely sound.

He stumbled across the room and flung the dishes against the wall in a fit of rage. Glass shattered and showered out the open window and he heard voices cursing below, complaining of some crazy party that must be going on upstairs. He sank against the window. The moon curled his hair. That crib against the wall, pushed so ludicrously close to the traffic was still there all those days his father beat him, with a bag of sand that his uncle had collected at Iwo Jima. The sand cut him every night and his screams must have stopped the traffic for awhile. Mommy used to melt into tears, standing between his bed and the cradle... "I'll protect you, darling, protect you. . ." And Stewart believed her. But she left, he guessed to die somewhere off with her family in Tennessee. And the day she walked out the door Daddy dumped the sand down the toilet, it trickled down into the basin like something important going forever, something that had to do with time. Oh, God. The night was airless. Stewart thought of Daddy's kisses later on, directionless, sour. Oh, he had been strong and had never wanted them again. And he had been courageous and was a better boy than he ever prayed to be. Silly to remember. He never thought of them or about his past life in general. Nothing ever came to him like this. If his father had shined his hide once or twice, he had never really hurt him, showed no more mean-ness than any other boy's father, in fact, less than most, and often he was very kind and his mother always smothered him with love. So, what was wrong? No use making a melodrama out of childhood when it didn't stick. And no use saying that you didn't have a ball as a teen-ager when every other guy was your slave. And now you didn't have it so bad, a fucked up job maybe, but it's what you wanted . . . after trying it as a cop which you didn't like . . . no major problems are on your shoulder, buddy, shake yourself clean . . . so what's wrong? Nothing.

Nothing but a sweetness, a lightness in his head and he slumped back down on his shirt. His eyes closed. He tightened his hand around his cock and started tugging gently, trying to work it up. He wasn't the naked one now, he was in an un-spotted uniform, starchy, smelling of peach blossoms, khaki-colored. His boots were black. His SMG was trained on the row of men who worked at the plant . . . they had suffered the indignity of having to strip to nothing in front of him and were embarrassed about going from one foot to the other with their less than perfect bodies and their scared eyes. But Reggino threw out commands and they marched single file around the plant, Reggino sometimes sticking the muzzle of the SMG against their skin to humiliate them, prodding them, moving the cold steel against their asses and watching them squirm. He made them kneel before the cycles and he executed them, cleanly, swiftly. One boy didn't die. He was wounded in the legs only, but badly enough that he fluttered like a moth and was unable to stand. Stewart approached him with a machete. He

bent his head back so that it pillowed the cycle seat, then he
pressed the weapon to his throat, straddled the boy's shoulders
with his legs so that he couldn't squirm away, looked down at
him and said, "Come on, baby, come to Daddy. . ." Then
decapitated him. Stewart came, a steady flow of thick white
cum, no, silver, silver, but it caused his body to arch only a
ripple, and his face was creased with annoyance, not pleasure.
You're a jerk-off fuck, he wiped his hands and stomach clean, a
jerk-off fuck. He lit a cigarette and smoked, staring at the moon,
half buried beneath the pier. He had murder in his heart and he
felt calm. Stop fucking jerk-off, man. Get up. Get up off your ass
and kill those fucking guys. And he found himself sweeping his
arsenal into his suitcase, the .357 Magnum, the daggers, the
sawed-off shotgun, the Colt .45s. He'd just walk in, cooler than
shade, and start shooting. That's all. No use pretending it all
hadn't come to this. No more lying. What happened after —
well, it didn't matter. He didn't give a shit. He saw the naked
killer in the mirror again and it was just like before. It was as if
he hadn't spilled his seed, he felt more potent than ever, harder,
with plenty of hate swelling to the surface that longed for
release. He struggled, fighting his tan cotton trousers, hiking
them up over his boots. He pulled a dark T shirt over his chest.

On his way out the door he nearly died of fright. The dog lay
in the bed, watching him. He arched carefully against the wall
and tiptoed to the door, opening it quietly, keeping as great a
distance from the bed as possible.

He sprinted down the stairs. He was surprised to be forced to
a halt on the landing by one of the two guys who lived in the
apartment below him.

The young man glared at Stewart. "I just want to let you
know I saw you last night. You didn't manage to keep yourself
hidden in the shadows!"

"What do you mean?"

"Don't pull that innocent face. I saw you beating that dog,
between those two buildings across the street. Beat the poor
beast to death with your fists."

Stewart was shocked. He couldn't remember. He didn't
believe him. "It wasn't me," he murmured.

"The hell it wasn't. And I'd have called the cops if I thought
it would have done any good, but seeing that they don't even
come around when a man's been murdered, I didn't expect
they'd come for a dog. You never know though. Dogs sometimes

mean more to people than men do. You wouldn't know about that."

"It wasn't me, it wasn't me," Stewart repeated slowly, over and over.

"And later I saw you carry what looked like its skeleton upstairs."

"Liar!" Reggino cried, choking, shoving the man out of his way and hurrying downstairs to his car, where he threw his suitcase in the trunk and started driving. The sky kept cracking like eggs. Dark blue and vinyl now. Black nothing in return. Taxis hissed around him like serpents. The Empire Diner was full. He laughed. It was one of his favorite spots. They had the best chili in the world and he remembered he had wanted to take Jake there when he got back to town. Jake would really love it. But maybe he knew about it already. The diner windows were like panes of pure gold, they were utterly staggering. The diners behind were on the other side. Yes, the other side.

As he bore ahead on the too familiar road he enjoyed the hate within him; he gave himself up to it, the most pungent opiate he had ever known. To take those men by surprise. To see their miserable faces just before he cut them down. That would be the true beauty of it. He wanted them to see his hate that he had kept secret for too long. Whether he chopped down one person or fifty, it didn't matter. Al Blane, Ed Ubal, George Koppfler . . . random targets with familiar faces, all of them.

He pulled into the mud lot behind the plant. It was so still that he could hear a goddam frog as soon as he cut the motor. He emptied the bag on the ground. He would casually stroll in with an SMG in his hands, pistols and daggers in his belt. When the first guy questioned him or looked startled Stewart would butcher him. That's the way he suddenly saw it. So he dressed himself with the weapons. The walk to the door was too quick, he wanted to go in slow motion, like in movies when desperate lovers run across wheat fields towards each other, arms outstretched.

Too late. He pulled the doors back. Drip of water from a sink. His heart stopped cold. The plant was empty.

Fucking Christ. Sunday night. He had never thought about what day it was. It wouldn't open up again until his own shift came on Monday night. . .

The weapons around his belt were unexpectedly heavy. Lights flickered at one-sixth of their power. The machines seemed to rise like dough before him. There was a breath of mystery.

So he was cheated.

Yet there was no way to turn back. There was no home to return to, no sanity to find comfort in. A giant press, used to fabricate the side panels, shot up in the middle of the draughty hall like a knife. Reggino walked closer, timidly, like a child inspecting an insect he had discovered beneath a cold, smooth stone in the back yard, an insect he had never seen before, perhaps one with a hundred legs all moving at once, or one with two heads, or one that breathed through its feet with gills like fishes, or one that made a high-pitched cry. He grabbed it in his palm and inspected it more carefully. The insect was all of those things, rolled into one, and Stewart bent over the press and pushed the button and the steel began to lower towards his head.

It was then he felt that numbing hostility leave his body, felt it fade like a stain on a clean white wall. He embraced himself and forgave himself for the first moment in his life.

He felt the weight of the press touch his head. He stopped the machine. A moment later and his brain would have been crushed. It was comfortable this way. There was something resting there like a crown. Only a crown. Though it was growing heavier and heavier all the time. Was he killing himself? Was he? He tried to move his head away but it was impossible. He noticed his blood beginning to run down the machine and flow beneath the legs of the cycles. He could try to pull the switch. No, it wasn't worth it. The steady stream of blood told him that his skull was already smashed. Too late. Death would come a little slower than he expected perhaps, since he didn't feel anything.

Suddenly, he began to cry out, "Mama, Mama . . . there's something in my bed! Go look, upstairs, in my apartment. Mama, Mama, there's something there . . . oh, no, something's lying in my bed!" Then he died.

It was almost twenty-four hours later when Al Blane arrived, the first on his shift. He was appalled to find Stewart bent under the press, his feet still glued to the floor, his blood dried and dull. Blane prayed to God to make him see a ghost instead of his pal, Reggino, crushed there. But it wasn't the will of the Lord, Blane guessed, and there was nothing he could do about that. But Dorothy Pulley and the rest of the girls would be on soon, making coffee and puttering about as usual, and there was something he could do for them. They mustn't see Reggino like this. He had to save them the horror. He carefully released the press and picked Reggino's body up in his arms. He carried him into the men's room. He laid him gently on the floor between the toilet stalls and the sink. This would be the best place for him, to keep his hammered body out of sight for the women's sake at least, until the ambulance could come and get him out of there.

Jake and Renee drove to the funeral in a rented VW and afterwards followed the hearse and a few limousines to the Long Island burial ground, a rose-hedged cemetery, triangular and green, home to stray cats and gulls. There they stood, somberly, shoulder to shoulder with the other mourners as the priest offered the last rites and the Latin words hung heavy in the sunlight. The coffin was lowered and the hole filled with sweet smelling dirt and it was over except for the scattered whispers of "Amen".

Jake slipped his arm around Renee's waist as he guided her back to the car. He recognized Stewart's father, hunched, with faltering steps, blowing his nose intermittently into a hand-kerchief which Mrs. Clark held for him. She was cloaked in her heavy wool even in the smoky heat of the first of September and reminded Jake of a lumbering polar bear out of her element, forced to a strange desert habitat. He nodded respectfully and they acknowledged him, somewhat curtly, he felt.

As he pulled onto the main road Jake spoke for the first time since the funeral had begun. "I won't pretend that this whole thing didn't tear me up. But the most horrible part was having to face his father just now. I was afraid to look at him too closely because I thought he might be blaming me somehow."

Renee squeezed his arm. "When something like this happens, there's nobody to blame."

"Yeah, but with Reggino . . . well, it's different. You should have known him. . ."

"You were very close?"

"Like brothers . . . the last couple years though, we didn't see that much of each other. That was probably my fault. . ." He added slowly, "Well, he took a little bit of me with him when he went."

Renee stared at the trees and the pastures. You died each

day, didn't you? The past was a corpse that you remembered well, each limb waiting to swell with another day. But Renee wasn't anxious to feed the corpse her day yet. She felt very much alive, her skin prickled with excitement, she smiled all the time.

"Jake," she leaned back in her seat. "Jake. . ."

"What is it?"

"Nothing."

She had wanted to say that she was terribly content. In the week they had been back together they had never left each other for a minute. And Jake didn't have to report to his job until after Labor Day.

They kept their days simple. They talked, slept, held each other in bed or on the chair in front of the bureau or on the window sill where they would watch the cars crawling angrily down 42nd Street. They liked the view best on black mornings full of rain when the traffic came to a standstill and they pretended the trucks were hollow tin robots that had captured the street and were beginning to rule with an iron autonomy. At night Jake would work in the darkroom he had built in the attic space over the bed, developing and pasting on the wall the photographs he'd taken in the last few weeks. Renee would sit below at her bureau, rearranging her perfumes, emptying the last drops of one scent into an almost full bottle of another variety so she could throw the container away and keep the space in front of the mirror uncluttered, all the while listening to Jake pacing back and forth upstairs, loving the sound. When he came down the room would smell magical, the heat of the perfume rising, scents blending, suggesting a garden of women, dark and potent.

"I know you," Jake would scold, "you're trying to keep me under your spell. . ."

"Stop here!" Renee commanded.

"What for?" Jake balked.

"I need to stretch."

Jake pulled to the side of the road against a thick drop of trees stuck together by glue, the sunlight shivering erratically from one spot to the next, turning the scene a deep black and white, the light pulling back like a curtain someone keeps opening and closing.

They wandered through the narrow jungle of elms, spruce and fir. At a spot where two trees broke apart and allowed the blue of the sun to find the ground, Renee turned to him and seizing him by the shoulders said, "Make love to me."

Jake smiled, not moving.

She had never said those words before to anyone, yet they

sounded very right. A chill wrapped around her. She softly repeated, "Make love to me."

"I'll make love to you, baby," he answered easily.

Their lips brushed and when they pulled apart Jake was so hot he would never have let her off the hook even if she had begged with her life. "Tell me you love me," he tortured her sweetly with the words. "I've got to hear it from you."

"I do. Oh, I do," she sobbed.

He undressed her slowly and laid her gently on her back against the warm earth. Then he stripped. They clung to each other, moaning, until the sun passed from overhead and it was the yellow time before the twilight and they were through and feeling again, the dirt staining them, the gnats and mosquitoes quivering around their ears and eyes.

Jake sat up. "Eaten alive. That's gonna be our end. What the hell are we doing lying here as bait?"

"I don't care," she answered.

He waved a small army of flying ants from her back. "And these kids sting. The Winged Menace."

He pulled his pants on and stared down at her naked figure. "Get up."

"No," she covered her head with her arm.

"Come on," he kicked her lightly. "Get up, crazy."

"No, it's too nice."

"Want me to leave you here?" he buttoned his shirt.

"You wouldn't do that."

"Oh, wouldn't I?"

"Yes, you probably would. And on the way back you'd spot some fifteen-year-old hitchhiker in blue jeans with long blonde hair and give her a nice ride."

"And what about you? When a couple of hunters pass along this way and find you lying here, your legs spread. Huh, how about that?"

She grabbed hold of his legs. "Oh, let's don't tease each other. I'm not in the mood for it today. Why don't you lie back down here with me just for a little while?"

"Because," he tucked his shirt in his pants, "I want to get back."

But Jake turned moody as soon as he reached the hotel. He gave up working in the darkroom after about fifteen minutes and leafed through the musty old magazines on the bookshelf, his eyes wide and far off.

He didn't fool Renee. "You aren't interested in those old things. Are you still thinking about Stewart?"

"I guess so. You don't brush something like that away with the snap of your fingers, you know." He was more bothered by Reggino's death than he wanted to admit. He saw no reason for the suicide and was afraid to look under the surface to find one. Sometimes a flash lit his brain and he saw his friend still as eternity in his coffin and he frantically banished the image from his mind. "I don't like to dwell on it though," Jake continued. "It's morbid. Damn morbid, that's what it is."

Through the evening he was very edgy and chewed Renee out about every little thing. Once he glared up at her after a long lull in a conversation and said, "You know, we can't go on living here. It's too depressing. We're going to move into my place."

"I thought you said that was —"

"Forget what I said," he interrupted. "We all say a lot of things, most of it's bullshit . . . you know, you should get a job or something. You have too much time on your hands. You aren't occupied by anything. That's no good. Just gives you time to dwell on morbid things."

"And what do you recommend?"

"Anything, goddamit, anything, but find something to do, that's all."

"Look. Your friend's death has got you down. I don't blame you —"

He jumped up and paced. "That's not it, damn it. Can't you see anything?"

After dinner Jake refused to go to a movie or take a walk. Renee wanted to keep his mind off the funeral and so she talked him into joining Bee for a game of hearts in Pandora's room. Jake couldn't concentrate and lost almost every hand. He was annoyed at Pandora who was reading some cop's fortune with her pack of tarot cards at her little table across the room.

"You're coming into money this year," Pandora said slyly, her dimples widening.

"By honest means or otherwise?" he asked.

"Oh, otherwise, I can assure you," they both laughed as Pandora turned the card towards him. "See these swords, five of them, you've stolen them and you're running away."

"I think you know about a certain something," he beamed at her.

"Perhaps. At any rate, be careful when you're dealing with

goods that aren't yours. Don't be over-confident. There may be some betrayal at your heels. Watch out for those around you."

"I don't need no divine power to tell me that."

"Jake, you're just eating those cards like some carnivorous plant!" Bee exclaimed, downing her glass of wine.

"Can't help it. I'm bushed. C'mon, Renee, let's go to bed."

Pandora turned towards them as they made their way to the door. "Stay. Stay and finish the wine at least."

"Another time," he was firm. The cop eyed them warily, wondering if they might be the ones Pandora warned him to look out for.

Jake slipped immediately into bed, Renee snuggled close, feeling warm with wine. It was early so the traffic outside had not yet subsided and there was a rush of horns and wheels. She inched her hands along his briefs, trying to slide them down. He roughly shoved her hand away. "Hey, come on, haven't we done enough of that today?"

"It's never enough."

"That's what I've been saying. You're hard on me. I'm gonna be coming home from my job and you're gonna be here all intense, every night just waiting for me, having done nothing all day except wait. See what I'm saying? You've got to get onto something else, for both our sakes."

"But Jake, it's just that I've missed you. You don't know. You don't understand how it's been. Living up there with them and missing you."

"Yeah, but I've been back now for a week. You act like you're still missing me and I'm lying right in the fucking bed next to you."

"But Jake," she dared to rub her hand through his hair. He groaned a little. "Jake, don't make it so I'm afraid to even reach out and touch you for fear you'll pull away."

"Come on," he cried. "Go to sleep."

She pulled herself together the next day, agreeing that she should look for work of some kind and admitting that it would be preferable to live in his studio on Gramercy Park than remain at the Hotel Dove.

"Don't you think it just might give us both a brighter out-look?" he asked as he opened the door for her and she drifted into his sunshiny room, the walls luminous with the chalk white paint.

"We won't have much to bring in," she smiled. "Nothing to

take away from your photographs certainly."

"Oh, knock it off, Renee," he sighed.

"I'm being serious."

Jake was still in a slump. He spent the afternoon cleaning his kitchen and clearing out a corner of his loft, practically ignoring her as she sat dusting dishes on the floor by the window, sometimes stopping to watch the children dancing in the park or an elderly couple helping each other up the steps of the church. She felt as if she were in a completely strange place where she had arrived after being blindfolded and carried a long distance. Yet the unfamiliarity of everything put her at ease. Nothing at all was real. She called out questions to Jake from time to time and he would mumble a quick reply and begin hammering away at something up there. The floor? The wall? She didn't know. She began to talk aimlessly as she looked for specks on the glasses and soon found herself telling him again how she had missed him. She spoke in a matter-of-fact tone, but underneath she knew she was unburdening herself, saying things she wanted him to know. Though she hedged and never quite revealed every detail, she confessed to her night of desperation when she could not reach him at his hotel and her terrified flight to the city where she had let herself be brutalized by Donny. And suddenly Jake spoke from the loft, calmly, "Well, as long as we're being honest, I might as well tell you I was seeing someone in Colorado. A very nice girl who was out there on a summer vacation. She lives in Washington, D.C., procures art or something for the Smithsonian Institute. She's got the smarts, don't ask why she liked to fool around with me. Anyway, we did see each other. It bothered me at the time and I was ashamed to tell you about it but since you're breaking the ice I can go ahead and get it off my chest."

"Breaking the ice?" she stood the glasses in a little row.

"Since you started telling me about some of your activities, I can talk about mine."

"But . . . that had nothing to do with you and me."

"Well, neither did this." He leaned over from the loft. "This is something separate and doesn't change anything. She asked me to come down and see her from time to time in the fall. And, well, Jesus," his voice cracked, "I've thought about it, I can't deny that."

"Yes," she murmured. "I guess you've been thinking it over these last few days, haven't you?"

"I guess I have. And maybe I will see her from time to time."

"I guess I don't have any choice in the matter, do I?"

"What choice did I have when you let that guy get you?"

"But Jake, Jake," she reasoned, "I was never unfaithful to you. I may have done these things, but. . . It was like you were there with me. There was never any feeling on my part. . . I was never unfaithful to you. I was never." She stood up and looked at him desperately. "I did it because I was *crying* for you." Her mouth gaped and he finally jumped down.

"You're crazy," he said. "Come on, let's not jeopardize this move in here." He grabbed her around the waist. "I start work tomorrow. When I get back we'll bring your things over from the hotel and never spend another night in that pit. It'll work out. Just don't push. That's all I'm asking." He messed her hair. "Don't push."

She never said another word that day. At night she went to bed early and never looked at his face on the pillow or touched his body. In the middle of the night she thought she was having a heart attack. She opened her eyes wide and at the window she saw herself floating there in the air, screaming. Then the ghost burst and she fell back on the pillow.

She knocked on Bee's door in the morning. "What is it!" cried the sleepy voice inside.

"It's Renee. Are you going shopping today?"

"Oh, who knows!" she called angrily. "It ain't even noon yet."

"Well, I need some clothes and if you want to go we could keep each other company."

Bee let her in. She moaned all the while she was dressing, complaining about the trick she fucked last night. "He must have been filled with syph, he stunk worse than dirt!" She shook her head sadly as she pinned up her hair and sprayed herself with orange and ginger mist. "Forgive the room, sweetie, it's like a pigsty, I know."

But Renee laughed just like a little girl.

All afternoon they traipsed from one shop to the other and Bee was stunned to find Renee in such a good mood. "You're cheerier than I've seen you in months. May I inquire why?" Bee twisted her hair in front of a mirror at a deli where they had stopped for lunch.

"I found some heart-shaped undies — red velvet — and a nice white leather skirt and a white silk blouse with squash or pumpkin colored stripes. It's just what I was looking for."

"Well, I wish some of your good spirits would rub off on me. I think I could find the Queen's mink today and it wouldn't even wake me up."

Renee had a nice long shower and put on her new clothes, adding some old coral colored fishnet stockings. She fluffed her hair and started to put on her make up, then chucked the whole box into the wastebasket. She sat in the window filing her nails.

Jake came in hot and sweaty from work. He had brightened considerably from the last day or two. He kissed her, then bent in front of the mirror and gave his fine hair a comb through.

"You're dressed up," he said.

"Really?" she was patronizing.

"Yeah, really." He threw down the comb and faced her, hands on hips. "Ready to go?"

"Jake," she continued smoothing her nails. "I've decided not to go. I'm going to stay right here in my own room."

"Come on, don't give me a hard time. I've had a fucking tiring day and I don't feel like playing. Get your things."

"I'm not going."

"Get your clothes."

"So long, Jake." She looked up.

He knew she was serious. A red fury fought to the surface but he controlled it. Goddamit, she wouldn't get the best of him. He shrugged. "O.K. If that's how you want it."

"Yeah, it's how I want it."

"O.K. Call me there in a couple of days." He moved toward the door. He'd call her bluff. He put his hand on the knob, then turned around. "Come on, this is your last chance."

"Sorry, I have other plans tonight."

"What plans?"

"Can't you tell? I'm gong whoring."

"Lucky you. See you —" And he opened the door, still calling her bluff.

She bit. "And to think," she said, her voice breaking, "to think I almost let you kill me."

He shut the door and approached her casually. "How is that?"

"To think that I put you before anything else in the world. How is it that someone can be so blind as to care more about one small body than the whole wide world? And be more intimidated by it than by all the catastrophes the earth throws up at you. To think I let you bleed me like a vampire bleeds a poor dog, fastening the teeth wherever he likes and when he's sated he goes on to the next victim."

"Not used to being the victim, are you, Renee?"

"Damn right."

"You want to be bloodsucker, don't you? Well, you've been doing a great job of it yourself."

"Go on. Get out. Go to your new whore." And she sank quietly on the bed. It gave Jake a start to see her like that — the same way he had seen her sitting there with her bags of fruit and nuts that first night he had been in her room. His shoulders suddenly sagged. He wanted peace.

"Come on," he came towards her. "Leave with me. Leave this place."

"I wouldn't set foot in your fucking ugly little room for anything. That place is like a tomb. You belong there."

"Don't . . ." he reached for her.

"Yeah, sure," she spit angrily and moved away toward the window. "Don't think you can come toward me anymore and fuck me when you like. Then when I want to touch you you get all holy, don't you? You fuck me when you want and how you want just like every other fucking man I've every known. You're no different. Know what you are?" she cried angrily, waving her pointed finger at him. "Know what you are standing there? A dick, that's all, you're just a fucking dick to me. A bleeding dick, no more no less."

"Don't let yourself go all ugly like this."

"Don't come near me. Just get the hell out of here and never come back! You're a fucking —"

He grabbed her by the shoulders and shook her. "Cut it out. You can't tell me you didn't love me and you can't tell me you don't love me now —"

"You never loved me — you only half-loved me and tried to make me grateful for that."

"Bullshit. You know much better than that."

"Oh, these lies. It's all I've ever heard. People making me believe I'm a monster. If I am one, then I am, there are no apologies. . . What I need is a good fuck tonight and I'm going to get it. I'm going downstairs where I was when you first came in, remember? You didn't get me that night and you won't get me tonight! And whoever it is, I'm going to give him the ride of his fucking ugly life."

Jake raised his hand to slap her, then stopped.

"Yes, I'm a foul-mouthed bitch. But that's what you liked about me, wasn't it? That's what made you horny for me."

"No!" he gasped, raising his hand again.

"You'd like to slap my tongue out of my head because it reminds you of what you've made me do to you. It tells how you've used me. It tells how disgusting you are."

His hands fell to his sides. He choked back a sob. "You want me to hit you. That's what it is. You want me to beat you to a pulp. It's only then you'll feel better, isn't it? It's only then you'll get all right again. Well, I'm the wrong guy for the job."

He moved slowly toward the door, leaving her panting in the middle of the room, then reconsidered and sat in front of the bureau, fiddling with his money clip and wiping a little sweat from his cheeks. She began to re-arrange things in the room with a solemn air, never looking his way. He kept sending her hopeful glances but they were ignored. Christ. He hoped she'd come over to him and make up. That's what he was sitting there for, wasn't it? Once he caught her eye in the mirror. It wasn't clear if she had been watching him or not but at least she had been forced to meet his stare — but the expression she sent him was one of such unrelenting contempt that he sighed, grabbed his suitcase from under the bed and was gone.

Nobody heard from Renee for several days. When Bee knocked there was never a response. But one day one of the girls came to Bee and told her she had heard Renee making strange threats from behind her door about burning the whole place to the ground. Bee walked down the hall. She tried Renee's door. It was locked.

"Renee, it's Bee. Open up now."

There was a little laugh as if from a doll that talks in nightmares.

"She's *off* —" the girl nodded gravely to Bee.

"It'll pass." Bee moved back to her room. "She never behaves quite like you'd expect."

But one night the girls on Renee's floor smelled smoke. Then they saw a thin grey cloud flowing under her door.

Bee pounded, "Let me in, Renee! For God's sake, let me in!"

There was no sound. Bee sent for Donny who ran up and broke the door down with an ax. The room was dark. Coughing, they located the fire, which was contained in a wastebasket in the closet, and they were able to put it out.

Then Renee leaped at them from the shadows, screaming and swinging at them with her fists. She was half naked and her hair was caked with dirt. She attacked like a maniac, an incredible destructive storm pouring from a body so weak and small and directed at any person in her path. Still she screamed and wouldn't stop until Donny drew back and struck her across the face with his fist, throwing her against the bed, and she was out like a light.

In the end it was Roger Fourne who saved her. Bee had told him that Renee was in sad shape, so one day he came for her, scooping all her possessions into his limousine and making her understand that she could stay with him forever if she wanted to.

Renee adjusted rapidly and felt as if the summer had never even come. Her life found the slow routine of the winter months, the period she had met Fourne and had first moved into the hotel. She soon was amazed at how she had let herself go limp like something left in a rainstorm. Why hadn't she gone to find shelter? She had not been herself.

"How's my baby doing?" Fourne asked her one night.

"I'm fine, Roger. Really."

"You don't go out much anymore. Miss the hotel? Your friends there?"

"Oh, sometimes, not much."

As a surprise Fourne invited Pandora and Bee over for dinner. Renee was delighted. The catch to the evening was that the three girls had agreed to prepare an Italian meal from scratch. They were knee-deep in pasta and had practically destroyed the kitchen by the time midnight rolled around. Fourne complained of severe hunger but when he tried to set foot in their sacred kitchen they pelted him with food.

Finally they set some edible green noodles on the dining room table with hot loaves of French bread and began to devour that. They had already had plenty of the best red wine and were feeling giddy.

Fourne soon turned the talk to the girls' latest conquests, demanding to be filled in on their activities.

"Roger," Pandora warned. "You don't know what you're asking."

"Well, I'm thinking of having a special party here and I want to know if you girls are hot enough to join in. You know I don't want to ask a couple of wet rags."

"Do I look like a wet rag?" Bee protested. "Do I?" And when no one answered she nearly fell off her chair she was laughing so hard.

"More wine," Fourne refilled their glasses. "And come on, I'm still waiting to hear. You tell me and then I might give you some details about what Renee and I have been up to."

"Well, in that case. . ." Pandora snickered, wiping her brow. "I did see one thing of interest a couple of weeks ago."

"Oh, please tell us," Fourne implored.

"You know," she giggled. "I sometimes think that that elevator accident was the luckiest thing that ever happened to me. I get more business now than ever. Seems people always are looking for a kink and it seems some of the best looking guys like cripples. I had one that was as nice looking as Jake."

"Jake Adams?" Renee asked.

Pandora lowered her eyes tactfully, then her lip curved up into her funny, coy smile. "Who else?"

"You can have him, Pandora. He's all yours — if you can find him."

Pandora looked at her questioningly.

"Yeah," Renee laughed. "You can have him. You can go eat his ass out."

"*Thanks*. Anyway, to return to my story, I had this trick the other night. This sailor. Talk about tall, dark and handsome, with a body that didn't stop. He really had it all. He was drooling when he unscrewed my leg. You know, I don't flatter myself. I'm a mousy little thing he'd have passed by if it hadn't been for that. If I close my eyes, I can feel those amazing muscles right now and on his left arm he had this big red heart with the words *The Human Revenge* tattooed across it."

Chapter Twelve

Hayden Planetarium, under the wing of The Museum of Natural History which crushed it like a pompous older brother, tried to rise above an October mist that completely clouded its base, while across the street in Central Park the purple dying leaves quivered in fear of the creeping fog.

The Scotchsmiths drove up Central Park West. Perry sat white-faced in the back seat hedged between his sister Martha and Andrea Gomez, the pretty red-haired exchange student from Uruguay who was exactly one year to the day older then Martha. He clutched his prize-winning paper to his chest. Having been selected as one of the five most promising astronomers of tomorrow alternately thrilled and petrified him. He tugged at his light lamb's wool suit.

The family was in high spirits, probably because they sensed a kind of reward coming to them, but they preferred to think it was because of the grand apartment buildings lining the drive, sleeping in the autumn morning, firing their imaginations — especially the children's. There was quite a game of which one do you want, no you can't have that one, it's the one I want, until Peter put a wet blanket on it all, making them pipe down, saying they would never be moving into any of them as it was far too expensive these days to keep an apartment and the city was no longer a pleasant environment in which to raise children.

The room used for the reception was an echoey square chamber with grey pillars protruding from the wall and pots of cheery chrysanthemums beneath the windows. There were chairs for a small audience facing a long wooden table where the presiding professors sat, behind them was a podium, a clean

blackboard and a dark map of the universe. It was in this room
that the five young winners and their families became
acquainted with one another and with the three professors of
astronomy who sponsored the contest. Perry became a special
favorite of Dr. Ramsey from Columbia University who had a
stubby white beard and balding head but whose hands were
very young looking.

The presentation of the orders of merit and sterling silver star
pins was dispensed with immediately and the shaking of hands
and flashing smiles were caught by the reporters who streamed
into the room, clicking their cameras hundreds of times. Then
they were allowed to ask the five youngsters questions, after
which there was a break for lunch. The cafeteria downstairs was
remarkably agreeable and the food better than expected. The
families and the professors sat at two long tables in the back,
slightly removed from the museumgoers, so the meal was not
harried or conditions claustrophobic. Even Ron behaved.

Afterwards they went back upstairs to hear the reports.
When the Scotchsmith children learned that the winners were
to speak in alphabetical order and then each was to be
questioned by a professor, they groaned and then rebelled.

"That means Perry will be last!" Martha scanned the program. "Oh, boy, he won't be up for hours!"

"Come on, let's go play!" Ron cried and he and Patricia,
Martha and Andrea fled from the room just as the first young
astronomer stepped to the podium.

The children ran into the lofty hall at the end of which was a
long marble staircase that led into distant recesses of the
museum. They were about to follow it when Andrea called out,
"Ven acqui! Ven acqui!" She called them to a blank wall at the
end of the corridor where their shadows loomed up black and
sharp. Andrea at once began to shape shadow puppets with her
hands, pursing her lips and making sounds of the creatures she
was creating.

"Oh, a rabbit is easy!" Patricia imitated her. "Anybody with
half a brain can do that!"

"I can do others!" she insisted. "How about a wolf?" They
had to admit it was rather marvellous, as was her dog and her
ostrich.

"Teach us how to make those!" Martha begged.

"No, let's go, we don't have time," Ron shouted and he
hurried them down the stairs.

When Perry was called to the podium it was late in the afternoon and when he peered out the window he was startled to see a lilac mist enclosing Central Park. He studied the faces of the audience for a moment, exchanged a smile with his nervous parents, nodded to the professors, then began.

The life of a star. . .

First, to set things in perspective, he described the vast size of the universe, pinpointing the earth as part of our galaxy, The Milky Way, which contains over two hundred billion stars alone. He discussed Edwin Hubble's discovery of a vaster universe — the existence of countless other galaxies stretching sixteen billion light years away, seen and heard through the stars in our own Milky Way. And each galaxy composed of billions of its own stars . . . the galaxies racing away in our expanding universe at thousands of miles each second . . . the infinite universe peopled by fleeing galaxies . . . fleeing where? . . . to a point beyond existence? . . . or to a fixed point, only to come crashing back, turning on themselves in fury, preparing to explode again?

A star is born by chance, by an accidental collision of gas and dust particles in interstellar space which over millions of years accumulates into a giant cloud which then becomes a star as matter crashes to the center and heats up. Hydrogen atoms unite to form helium. Millions of years later there is stabilization, a balancing by the internal pull of gravity.

Perry described the birthplace of stars — the nebulae — and how stars are formed in these swirling cloud masses. He pointed to The Orion Nebula and The Lagoon Nebula on the map behind him as examples of the most active nurseries in the sky and he also located The Carina Nebula where the bluest, most ponderous stars in our galaxy are found.

Next he mentioned the supernovae — the exploding stars that have been chronicled by star watchers from all corners of the world ever since man learned to draw and write. The death throes of a dying star result in the supernova when, at a billion degrees, all oxygen near the star's surface is consumed in a cataclysmic explosion. The supernova can outshine an entire galaxy and can shed more light in several weeks than hundreds of millions of suns. Perry pointed out that a supernova in The Crab Nebula was spotted in China in 1054 A.D. and that a supernova explosion possibly occurred in The Gum Nebula in the not too distant past of space.

Perry outlined the fate of other stars, taking them to their cold deaths as dwarfed black embers. He told them how a star's color provides clues to its age and temperature and distance from earth. He enthusiastically ended his report with a detailed scientific description of earth's own star, the sun. During the last sentence he looked up bleary-eyed and took a deep breath as the audience applauded.

Dr. Ramsey patted the boy on the back and thanked him. "I'm very appreciative of your thoughtful analysis of the life of a star from its birth pangs in the gas nebulae to its final gasps as a white or black dwarf and I have some questions for you." He smiled at the families assembled before him. "One thing we have learned from these young people this afternoon is that our universe is not peaceful, though it would seem so as we gaze up at the Heavens, but a violently active place. And as to its origin we have few clues. As to its destiny, fewer still. Perry?"

"Yes, sir." Perry had begun to sweat even though the room was cool and damp and his eyes strayed to Andrea and Martha who had just snuck noiselessly into the room. He wished that Dr. Ramsey would finish with him so he could leave the podium. He wouldn't have minded a talk between the two of them, but with an audience it was just a little bit uncomfortable.

"One last thing," Dr. Ramsey cleared his throat. "To be an astronomer is a very serious and rewarding undertaking. One must be prepared to face the monumental challenges of the universe and sometimes to see concepts we considered unchanging in a new and frightening way. For example, what is a black hole, Perry?"

"It's when a massive star shrinks drastically — oh, to about ten miles across in diameter — so that its gravity becomes so powerful that nothing can escape its surface — not even light."

"So, then, how does your concept of time change, Perry?"

Perry turned pink. "Time?" he stuttered. "I'm not certain."

Ramsey laughed. "In the environment of a black hole, space becomes curved. So light rays as they pass it are bent from their normal path, and the nearer to the hole they go the more their path is curved, so that once the ray of light goes within the hole it enters into a circular orbit." He stared gravely at Perry. "So, looking straight ahead you would see the back of your own head."

Ella squeezed her husband's hand and she winked at her son.

"Thus," Ramsey continued, "gravity affects matter. It

affects light. It also affects time, the fourth dimension. Say that Perry here stood on the surface of the black hole. He wouldn't notice the slowing down of time because his heartbeat and wristwatch would slow down in synchronization. But if we were far away watching Perry with a telescope we would notice that his watch would slow down with the shrinking of the star until by the time the star had reached the event horizon, measuring about ten miles across, the watch would stop. In other words, time would stand still." He turned Perry towards him, his hands on the boy's shoulders. "The mysteries before you are amazing . . . you've studied the sinkhole — the space warp that encloses a black hole and cuts it off from the rest of the universe — but have you heard of the wormhole? . . . it suggests that whatever is pulled into a black hole will burst out of another hole, a white hole, somewhere else in our universe . . . or perhaps in a different universe. . ."

In April Perry received a phone call from Renee. She asked to see him and suggested that he take a train into the city on the first Sunday with mild weather and she would treat him to a ride on one of the Circle Line's sightseeing boats that cruise around the island of Manhattan. Perry, quite surprised to hear from her, but curious, agreed to meet her at noon on the 44th Street pier. But on Sunday it rained steadily so he stayed home and the next Sunday was cold and windy and he had to go on a drive with his family anyway. It wasn't until the first Sunday in May that the sun glowed and the air was green with spring. Perry debated about travelling to New York City as he wondered if she still wanted to see him. After all, she had phoned a few weeks ago and he hadn't heard from her since. *Well*, he sighed, *an agreement is an agreement. What if I didn't show up and she waited there all day or something? The weather is good. I'd better go.*

The pier was crowded with tourists fidgeting, anxious to board the boat. It took several minutes of earnest searching before Perry spotted her waiting on the plank. She seemed very much the same. She was dressed in a navy blue suit and wore white gloves with mother of pearl clasps. In her hands she held a black sweater. He approached her.

"Oh," she was shocked. "You've changed. I was looking for a much shorter boy. You're taller than I am now, aren't you?"

He smiled timidly. "I don't think quite as tall."

"Of course it doesn't matter, does it?"

There was an awkward pause.

"How are you?" he asked.

"Oh, fine. You?"

"Fine."

"You look really well . . . have you been on the Circle Line before?"

"No, but Dad always threatens to take us every summer."

"Well, we beat him to it. Come on, we'd better get on board."

Perry offered to search for seats. Renee preferred to sit on the deck outside and if it got chilly she would put on her sweater. He found two wooden chairs near the front of the boat and Renee insisted he sit next to the rail so he would have a good view. The boat pulled into the Hudson and began to turn south. Grey, weather-beaten gulls flapped tiredly overhead as a group of schoolboys tried to take their pictures.

"Oh, no, they got away!" one cried.

"It wouldn't have come out anyway," his friend shoved him. "Sun's too bright."

"Silly, aren't they?" Renee said.

Perry smiled.

"That's New Jersey over there. And on this side behind all those piers and warehouses is the Village."

He nodded silently but his eyes were cloudy.

"Are you uncomfortable?" Renee asked.

"Maybe. A little. Why did you want to see me?"

"I saw your picture in the paper months ago when you were honored at the planetarium. It gave me a start to see it, actually. But I was very proud of you. I wanted to congratulate you . . . it meant something to me to see your picture and know you'd won that contest."

"Well, thanks."

"So I just wanted to tell you, that's all."

"Dad says you wanted to destroy our family," the boy suddenly blurted.

"Destroy your family?" She was incredulous. Then she became thoughtful. "I don't know . . . maybe I did want to destroy your family. Do you hate me for that?"

"I don't think so."

The boat moved past Battery Park, the southern tip of the island, and the skyscrapers lapped the oxygen and the water was white and dull. There was a murmur of excitement as the guide inside with his megaphone announced that they were approaching the Statue of Liberty. Even when he stopped speaking, static from the amplifier stabbed the air like little gunshots and when be began to give the statue's measurements he turned the volume up to ear-splitting level. His voice was scratchy, shrill. The crowd pressed to the edge of the boat and began to take snapshots as the captain weaved familiarly, intimately near the statue. There were several newlywed couples who took turns clicking each other's picture in front of the giant. The sun fell behind a cloud and the boat curved abruptly and charged for the East River and the heights of the Brooklyn Promenade where solid, elegant old townhouses faced the west.

Renee turned to Perry. Her voice quavered. "Have you heard from Jake?"

"We don't hear from him often. He moved down to Virginia or something. Bought a car. Has a nice place — I think he converted a 19th century barn into a country house. And his photographs have been in a few magazines."

"Jake always was able to take care of himself."

"Yeah. Hey, remember that day when we all went out rowing and the weird fog came out of nowhere?"

"Oh, yes, I remember very clearly. . ." Her voice drifted. "You, me and Jake. . ." A little smile came to her. "You know, for a moment it was just like we were the only three people left in the world. The only three people who existed. We were surrounded by the dark. And with you in between us, it seemed like you were our child."

"I had that feeling too."

Renee became very still and she blocked out the guide's thunder voice.

"What have you been doing lately?" Perry asked finally.

"I can't say my life is very thrilling. I'm going to try to find an apartment of my own. I'm staying with a man now whom I don't like much. We're kind of tired of each other, really. My mother in New Jersey wants me to come live with her. I may have to for awhile since I don't have any money. It wouldn't be so bad. My mother's easy to get along with. She makes few demands on me, and the ones she does make I can ignore."

"Well, that sounds good."

The sun was hiding behind cloud after cloud and Renee began to shiver. She slipped her sweater on. "Perry, go get yourself some ice cream or candy. Here, take this dollar."

"No, I've got it. What can I bring back for you?"

"Nothing. I'm fine."

While she waited for Perry she watched the spray lashing the boat. A foreign man was staring at her from the other side. Probably a student from India. She didn't encourage his stare. She was not in the mood. When Perry returned with his ice cream sandwich she put her arm around his shoulder and the man turned away. To their left the United Nations loomed while behind it rose the dramatic spire of the Empire State Building.

Renee took her arm from his shoulder and began to nervously twist her gloves. "Perry, sometimes I miss Jake so badly. It's so awful. The day he left I didn't care if I saw him ever again. But the next day I wanted him. And I honestly expected he'd be back, that he'd walk in, tired from work, sweating in his white shirt, pulling at his tie, flopping on the bed, teasing me until I couldn't see straight. But he didn't come back. Sometimes the pain of his absence crushes me. Like today. Why can't he be here with us like that other time when we were in your little boat? Why is this so different?"

The sun stopped hiding. Now the world was flooded with light. Gracie Mansion. The Harlem River. Yankee Stadium and The Bronx. Turning down into the Hudson.

"You know, I fell in love for the first time when I was your age. With the lifeguard at our swimming pool. The boy with the yellow trunks.

"One summer day, Mother took Sue and me to the board-walk in Atlantic City. I remember that long wooden expanse and how friendly the sea seemed that afternoon. Mother wore a white straw hat and she walked between Sue and me, holding our hands. It was exciting for us as we never got to go anywhere and the shops with their postcards and souvenirs looked regal and the broken shells on the dirty sand looked like clean pink conches from the South Pacific. Suddenly at the end of the walk, I saw him. The boy in the yellow swimming trunks. He had come up for the day as well and he was sleeping in the sand, arms outstretched like a yellow Christ. He seemed so peaceful. His sandy hair stirred in the breeze and his chin was round and covered with gold. I thought he was the most beautiful person I had ever seen and I stopped caring about anything else. Though my mother held my hand, she wasn't there at all. The world slowly ebbed away and died. . .

"We had a special dinner that night in a sea palace strung with colored lights that shone like Christmas. Sue and I got to try lobster and crab and have pink fizz cocktails and the waiter was so good to us and we watched the sunset turn our hands red and mother's hair a wild purple. For dessert we had a flaming crepe of caramel that was so sweet I almost passed out. And then I begged Mother to let me walk a moment along the boardwalk before we left for home. It was hard convincing her as Sue was tired and whining and Mother wanted to get her home and put her to bed, but my obstinacy won out. As soon as I was free from the sea palace I ran, holding my breath, along the boardwalk, bumping into people like a stubborn goat, until my feet brought me to the spot where the boy had slept. I hadn't expected to find him lying there still, but in the light of the new moon his perfect imprint shone in the sand . . . like a gingerbread ghost that comes out of the oven all perfect and light brown. I knelt and touched the outline . . . I embraced the air above it. *Come back, come back, come back.* And then I saw the sky and I felt as if a photograph, a polaroid had been taken of the boy from somewhere up there and that they were sending this imprint back down to me . . . some photograph taken by a mystical force. A Heaven image. You know, I think when we go to the skies for exploration, we're only returning to the womb. We're only finding the polaroid. . .

"And so we left Atlantic City that night, but I had fallen in love. But then that feeling left me. How? And with Jake? . . . I hardly dared let myself love him, but I think I did for a moment. How is it that we care so much, then it all just drifts away? We lose our feeling and become numb. That's how I know this is not our real life. This is some other life. It's just a trick. We're supposed to think it's the real thing. Everyone's fooled. But not me. I've got another life coming, I promise you."

Grant's Tomb to the left. The New Jersey Palisades — cliffs of brown dust to the right. The gulls returning.

By the time the boat eased onto the pier Renee and Perry had become a little giddy. They were joking with each other like in times past.

"I have more of that field cleared out, Renee. I'm going to get that telescope built this summer if it kills me!"

"I know you will. Perry, we'll see each other again, won't we? Let's keep in touch."

"Sure we will."

The boat docked, closing the circle, and there was a stampede to the exit. Renee felt the Indian press up against her and she laughed. Perry understood and grabbed her hand, pulling her through the wedding couples, tourists and school-boys to the safety of land.

Within two weeks Renee packed her bags and left Roger Fourne's penthouse. He wasn't sorry to see her go. He was so bored with her that he couldn't even get an erection when he took her to bed.

Renee went by bus to the Toms River station. From there she walked the familiar road to her mother's house.

Twilight was falling.

Her mother had just sat down to dinner and she leaped to her feet when her daughter came through the door.

"Honey, I didn't expect you this early. I would have waited to eat."

They kissed each other.

"I got an early bus."

"Well, let me put something on the stove for you," Milly pushed her hair back from her face, trying to look refreshed, but she looked old and tired and there was no hiding the fact. "And let me turn on some lights in here. No use sitting around in the dark."

"Don't turn on the lights on my account."

"When you live alone you can do what you like, but when somebody else is with you you have to take them into account. I've been on my own too long now and have got set in my ways—"

"For God's sake, Mother, sit down and finish your dinner. Calm down."

"Well, I'm too excited. Honey, you'll be happy here. I'm going to make it real nice for you. Summer's coming and we'll sit out on the porch like we used to, in the evenings. We can play cards and talk."

"Yes. . ."

Renee walked to her room. Her mother followed.

"What's that?" Renee spotted a dark object by the bed.

"Oh, that old trunk from the attic," she flipped on the light. "When I knew you were coming I brought it down 'cause it has some of your old clothes in it. Dusty old thing and weighs a ton."

"All right, Mother. Let me get cleaned up and I'll come out

and we can eat together," her voice was weary and hollow. Milly nodded and left the room. Renee shut the door behind her. She sighed. She opened the chest to find a pile of old dresses and scarves packed clear to the top. She shook her head in annoyance. Suddenly her eyes spotted something shiny and black and she fished it from the trunk. It was her Lone Ranger's mask and below it her guns and boots wrapped neatly in cellophane. She uttered a fierce cry and fell to her knees in front of the trunk, clutching the mask to her heart and rocking from side to side. Tears streamed down her face and she sobbed, sobbed as if her heart would break. She clutched the mask tighter to her bosom and continued heaving, the tears spilling onto her chest. She slowly pressed the mask against her cheek, then laid it gently on top of the clothes. Then covering her mouth with her hands she sobbed harder than ever.

A knock on the door. "Renee?"

Renee tried to stop herself from shaking. She didn't want her mother to discover her in such a state. She took deep gasps. Only when she had enough control did she whisper, "Yes, Mother, what is it?"

Milly's voice was soft. "Renee, you've come home."

***